PRAISE FOR *THE*

"A delightful read from cover to c[over] [...] ry of Pandora Carmichael, a woman of modest means thrust into a world of privilege and opportunity. When she finally finds her happily ever after, a devastating secret shatters Pandora's world, forcing her to rethink her dreams. Abriel weaves a stunning tale of love and friendship while taking the reader on a masterful journey of self-discovery, where at the very heart is a woman of courage, loyalty, and ambition."

—Rochelle B. Weinstein, author of *When We Let Go*

"*The Life She Wanted* is a vividly crafted story of self-discovery and resilience set in one of the most transformational periods in America's history: the Roaring 1920s, a time of radical social, artistic, and cultural change, especially for women. Abriel did such a masterful job painting the brilliant backdrop of this heartfelt novel, I found myself dreaming about it long after the last page was turned."

—Suzanne Redfearn, bestselling author of *In an Instant*

"A compulsively readable coming-of-age story set against a dazzling Roaring Twenties backdrop, *The Life She Wanted* had me flipping pages late into the night. Full of intricately researched history and characters you'll root for, Anita Abriel's latest proves it might be a long and winding road, but true love always finds a way. Fans of *The Gilded Age* will devour this treat of a novel!"

—Kristy Woodson Harvey, *New York Times* bestselling author of *The Wedding Veil*

"Anita Abriel's *The Life She Wanted* is the captivating story of Pandora Carmichael, a young woman growing up among the elite upper class of 1920s New York, though she is merely a spectator to the extraordinary privilege that money provides. But with dreams of both romance and a career of her own as a fashion designer, Pandora blends into New York society and ultimately finds herself on a path in life that is both heartbreaking and illuminating. With meticulous historical detail and a protagonist you root for from the very first page, *The Life She Wanted* is a charming tale of one woman's quest to shape a future for herself that is authentically her own."

—Jane Healey, bestselling author of *The Secret Stealers*

"*The Life She Wanted* radiates with realistic, lovable characters; stunning plot twists; and the glorious description of the opulent life of the elite class in New York. Told with care and tenderness, the novel is a mesmerizing and triumphant tale of love, loyalty, and how a talented woman discovers herself, desire, marriage, and success in a world full of prestige and prejudice. Spellbinding, joyful, and timeless, *The Life She Wanted* is a gemstone of a novel. I couldn't put the book down!"

—Weina Dai Randel, author of *The Last Rose of Shanghai*

"The glamorous cast of characters in Anita Abriel's *The Life She Wanted* captivated me from the start, while the unforgettable setting had me dreaming about stepping inside every mansion in wealthy 1920s New York. But I adored Pandora most, the novel's plucky heroine whose single father works at one of the region's grand estates, giving Pandora entrée into a world of glittery formal balls and suitors with deep pockets. And while Pandora seems like she's on a path to good fortune, her story shows us it's rare that life turns out as planned—no matter how much money you have. For anyone who loves a sweeping rags-to-riches tale, Anita Abriel's novel delights!"

—Brooke Lea Foster, author of *On Gin Lane*

"From the shimmering tennis courts of Hyde Park to the glamorous townhouses of 1920s Fifth Avenue in Manhattan, Anita Abriel perfectly captures the romance of the Gilded Age through the prism of one ambitious woman's lofty dreams. Lovely and engaging storytelling on every page."

—Sophfronia Scott, author of *Wild, Beautiful, and Free* and *Unforgivable Love*

The
LIFE
SHE
WANTED

ALSO BY ANITA ABRIEL

A Girl During the War
Lana's War
The Light After the War

The
LIFE
SHE
WANTED

a novel

ANITA ABRIEL

LAKE UNION
PUBLISHING

Text copyright © 2023 by Anita Hughes
All rights reserved.

Published by Lake Union Publishing, Seattle

www.apub.com

Amazon, the Amazon logo, and Lake Union Publishing are trademarks of Amazon.com, Inc., or its affiliates.

ISBN-13: 9781662509827 (paperback)
ISBN-13: 9781662509810 (digital)

Cover design by Faceout Studio, Lindy Martin
Cover image: ©Sophia Molek / ArcAngel; ©ERSP / Shutterstock

Printed in the United States of America

To my mother

Chapter One

Tonight was the night that twenty-year-old Pandora Carmichael would be asked to become the future Mrs. Owen Winthrop, she was sure of it.

Pandora couldn't recall a time when she didn't have a crush on Owen. Owen had been coming to Riverview, the Van Luyens' estate, where Pandora's father was the private tennis instructor, every summer for ages. Pandora always loved sneaking glances at Owen on the court when he played tennis with Archie, the Van Luyens' son and her close friend. How could Pandora not develop feelings for Owen? He was good looking and charming and had always been so kind to her.

This weekend, Owen's parents were hosting their annual July Fourth weekend party at Rosecliff, and Pandora was thrilled to be invited.

Archie, sitting in the driver's seat, glanced over his shoulder and smiled. "If Pandora's jaw drops any lower, she'll swallow a butterfly," he joked.

As the car inched closer to Rosecliff, Pandora allowed herself to be swept up by its grandeur. The house was built in the neoclassical style with arched French windows and pink marble pilasters. The forecourt was adorned with a bronze statue and manicured hedges. Gardeners must have had to prune them every day. Flowers bloomed everywhere, and to the side of the house there was a greenhouse, a tennis court, and a swimming pool.

~

"Don't make fun of Pandora," Archie's sister, Virginia, chided from the front passenger seat. "The first time I saw Rosecliff, even I was impressed. At least the Winthrops were smart enough to invite Pandora to the party. She's more interesting than any of the other young women who'll be there. All they care about is finishing their season with a diamond ring on their left hand and an appointment to view the bridal suite at the Plaza."

"Most girls aren't like you; they want to get married," Archie reminded her. "Even Pandora. Why shouldn't she? There's nothing wrong with wanting to have a husband and family."

"That's easy for you to say; you're a man. No one's going to stop you from doing anything," Virginia replied darkly. "You weren't thrown out of Princeton simply for hosting a literary discussion."

Virginia had been asked to leave Smith College last April for using the dormitory as a literary salon. If she had asked permission, the college president, William Neilson, explained to Virginia's parents, it might have been different. Instead, Virginia bought up all the copies of *The Awakening* by Kate Chopin at the bookstore and distributed them to the girls on her floor. Her roommate was so upset by the novel's themes of female sexual awakening and women's discontent with becoming only wives and mothers, that she called her mother and insisted she pick her up and take her home.

After Virginia was expelled, she spent the next month applying to other colleges. Vassar in Poughkeepsie agreed to let her take a few classes in the fall, as did Barnard in New York. But neither school would let her attend full time or live in a dormitory.

"I envy Pandora," Virginia continued, resting her elbow on the car window. "She gets to live in New York by herself in the fall. I'll be cooped up at Riverview or under Mother's strict supervision at the townhouse on Fifth Avenue."

Pandora listened quietly from the back seat. She was supposed to attend secretarial school in New York in the fall, although it was the last thing she wanted. She couldn't imagine spending her life taking dictation and fending off unwanted advances. Instead, she dreamed of being a fashion designer—of opening a dress boutique in Hyde Park and one day having a larger boutique on Fifth Avenue in Manhattan. Being married to Owen would not only mean marrying the love of her life, it would also give her the status and resources to pursue her goals. The doors that had never been open to her, the life she had merely caught glimpses of in the years that her father worked for the Van Luyens, would be hers.

Their conversation was interrupted by a flock of chickens coming close to the car.

"Don't tell me the Winthrops have become chicken farmers like the Vanderbilts and Roosevelts," Archie said, slamming on the brakes to avoid running over a chicken. "As long as the chickens don't wander onto the tennis courts. I'm only here for the tennis. I can do without the dinner that will drag on for hours or the obligatory games of poker."

Archie pulled up behind a royal-blue roadster and turned off the ignition.

"Will I be sent away because my car's a Model T Ford instead of a Winthrop GT?" Archie joked. He jumped out and lifted his overnight bag from the back seat.

"Explain it was a birthday present from a great-aunt." Virginia climbed out after him. "As long as you praise Clarence Winthrop's whiskey, you'll be fine."

Prohibition had hardly affected people like the Winthrops. They could find every kind of liquor on the black market, and rumor had it Clarence Winthrop had bought out the inventory of two liquor stores and housed the whole in his wine cellar.

Pandora followed Archie and Virginia up the steps. This was her first house party, besides the ones that the Van Luyens held at Riverview. At those parties, Pandora usually helped Esther, the cook, in the kitchen. When Archie and Virginia invited her to play croquet on the lawn or go boating on the river, Pandora knew it was because they felt so close to her. But she was the daughter of one of their staff; she didn't really belong with the Van Luyens' friends. Even though Pandora was used to the house parties at Riverview, she was still nervous. At Rosecliff, she couldn't slip into the kitchen and watch the festivities on the lawn from the window. She wondered if the Winthrops' other guests would welcome her or if they would question who she was and why she was invited.

But Archie and Virginia were her best friends, and she was thrilled to be joining them. If it weren't for them, she would never have met Owen. They had always been so caring and accepting. One day, she hoped to return the favor when her dreams had come true and she had her own family and parties to throw.

A butler stood at the front door, escorting guests into the reception rooms.

The ceilings were painted with a fresco as rich and detailed as the Persian rugs that covered the parquet floors. Gilt mirrors graced the walls, and silk sofas were upholstered in a color that was new to Pandora: not quite pink and not quite white, like the pale lipstick Virginia hid from her mother in her dressing table. Chandeliers hung so low Pandora could see the glass prisms, and white columns topped with plaster rosettes reached the ceiling.

The French doors to the garden opened, and Owen entered the reception room, trailed by a few of the younger guests. Owen wasn't classically handsome like Archie. Archie had blue eyes that were so light they were almost violet. His hair was blond, and he had a strong physique that made girls stop and stare, even when he left the house without brushing his hair, wearing his father's gardening clothes. But Owen had his own unique appeal. His light brown hair was styled by the best barber, and his clothes came from his father's tailor in London.

4

Today Owen wore tennis whites set off by a Piaget watch that made the light hair on his wrist stand out.

"Pandora, there you are," Owen said as he greeted her. His smile widened, and he looked delighted to see her. "I was afraid you weren't coming." He turned to Archie and Virginia. "I should have known these two made you late. Archie probably only got up an hour ago. At Princeton, I have to drag him out of bed on the weekends."

"That doesn't mean I'm lazy," Archie replied. "I like to read in bed, not that you'd know about reading. I've never seen you actually crack a book."

"I get enough of this guy at Princeton. I'm glad you're here." Owen leaned forward to Pandora conspiratorially. He had the same warm look in his eyes as when he had invited Pandora to walk by the river after a tennis lesson last month. "I hope you're staying for the whole weekend."

Pandora could hardly keep the elation from her expression. But she didn't want to appear too obvious in front of the other guests.

"It's lovely that your mother invited me," she replied, searching for Mabel Winthrop. "I'd love to thank her in person . . ."

It was important that Pandora make a good impression on Owen's mother. Owen would never be able to marry her if she didn't. And now, wearing her loveliest dress and feeling like she almost fit in, was the perfect moment for Pandora to meet Mabel for the first time.

"There'll be time for that this evening," Owen cut in. "Where's your bag? You should get changed."

"Changed?" Pandora repeated, puzzled.

She was dressed as appropriately as any of the young women who had started spilling from the balcony into the drawing room. They milled around in small groups, gossiping and finishing each other's sentences the way girls did when they'd known each other since nursery school.

"For our tennis match," Owen said, prompting her. "You're my mixed doubles partner. We're playing Gordon Mott and his date, Susan. Gordon is on the tennis team at Harvard."

Pandora tried to keep the disappointment out of her eyes. She should be happy that Owen wanted to play doubles with her. They'd be together on the tennis court for hours. But she'd imagined strolling around the grounds on Owen's arm, Owen introducing her to his parents and friends.

A girl about her age appeared beside Owen. She was very pretty. She wore her brunette hair in long curls, and her brown eyes peered out from underneath a broad-brimmed hat.

"Owen, I couldn't find you," she said, making a little pout. "You deserted me before you finished showing me the boathouse."

"There's time to see the rowboats later," Owen replied. "I've got an important tennis match."

The girl stood directly opposite Pandora.

"You haven't introduced me to the new arrivals." The pout formed on the girl's lips again.

"Archie, Virginia, Pandora." Owen waved at the group. "This is Lillian Clarkson; we met in Europe last summer. The Clarksons have a townhouse near ours in Sutton Place, and her father's steel company does business with Winthrop Motors."

"Why do men always mention what our fathers do?" Lillian rolled her eyes at Virginia while smiling flirtatiously at Archie. She completely ignored Pandora.

"Your tennis match better be over, and you better be showered and shaved, by the start of cocktails." Lillian turned back to Owen. She moved closer and touched his arm.

Virginia waited until Owen and Lillian wandered off. Pandora tried to shake the fear that gripped her. Owen hadn't mentioned Lillian before. What if he didn't have feelings for Pandora? What if he liked Lillian instead?

"Don't worry about Lillian Clarkson," Virginia whispered to Pandora under her breath. "She's pretty, but she has no brains. She's as thick as her ankles."

Virginia was the only person who knew about Pandora's romantic interest in Owen.

"I didn't notice Lillian's ankles," Pandora said dully. She was still smarting from Owen only talking to her about tennis and then walking off with Lillian.

Virginia took Pandora's arm and guided her to the staircase.

"That's because you were busy wondering how to poke her eyes out." Virginia grinned. "Forget about Lillian, go and change into your tennis clothes. Once you get onto the tennis court, he'll forget all about Lillian Clarkson and her daddy's millions."

Pandora was about to protest that she wasn't going to use tennis to win Owen; instead, she'd charm him with her wit and intelligence. But she changed her mind. Pandora didn't have the advantages of Lillian or the other girls. She'd use anything she could to make sure no one stole him away.

~

The tennis match had started well enough.

Pandora and Owen won the first three games, and Pandora basked in Owen's praise. Then he played poorly three games in a row and blamed Pandora for distracting him. Pandora was so upset she was tempted to claim a headache and run upstairs. But at that moment, Lillian Clarkson appeared, and Pandora wasn't about to leave Lillian alone with Owen.

Pandora gritted her teeth through the next two sets, and they ended up winning the match on the strength of her serves. Owen apologized for his behavior, and Pandora convinced herself she didn't mind. She liked competitive men, and it meant Owen had ambition and drive.

Just as Owen suggested they take a dip in the swimming pool, Lillian brought out a pitcher of orange juice and a bottle of champagne. She told a story about visiting the champagne growers in France the previous summer, and the others told similar vignettes about vineyards in Tuscany and Spain. Even Virginia told a short anecdote about visiting London last July. Pandora had never traveled outside the state of New York; she had nothing to add to the conversation. She drank one glass of champagne, and her imaginary headache became a pounding in her temples that forced her to excuse herself and escape to her room.

The guest room was as magnificent as the public rooms downstairs, and Pandora couldn't believe she was going to sleep there. The walls were painted sky blue and decorated with a gold leaf motif. A gold-framed mirror took up one wall, and two armchairs faced each other in front of the marble fireplace.

An hour before dinner and dancing would start, Pandora lay on the bed in her guest room, a damp washcloth pressed to her forehead. She had been dreaming about this night for weeks: Owen claiming her and introducing her to the other guests, dancing the first dance together, the stars twinkling down as if they were giving them their blessing. Now she couldn't muster up the enthusiasm to take a bath and get dressed.

There was a knock followed by Virginia flinging open the door. "There you are." Virginia flopped into an armchair.

She wore a white pleated skirt and a yellow blouse with Mary Janes and white socks, her dark hair tucked under a straw hat.

"You can't let Lillian Clarkson upset you because she's been to Europe. She certainly didn't soak up any culture. She didn't mention a single painting at the Louvre." Virginia took off her hat.

"At least Lillian has been to Europe." Pandora sat up. "She has something interesting to talk about."

"Your father was in the semifinals at Wimbledon," Virginia reminded her. "There's nothing more interesting than that." She waved at the books Pandora had placed on the bedside table. "And you've read every book on fashion design. Lillian probably hasn't picked up a book since her nanny read her the Pollyanna books as a child."

"I was practically a baby when my father played Wimbledon; I don't know much about it." Pandora sighed. "And men don't care about women's fashion." She removed the washcloth from her forehead. "All these months, I thought Owen and I were growing close. That by the end of the weekend he might . . ." She couldn't even admit to her closest friend that she hoped Owen would propose—she might jinx it. "Declare his feelings for me," she said instead. "Now I'm afraid he only likes me for my serve."

"You mustn't believe that." Virginia squeezed her hand. "Think of when you first fell in love with Owen. You wouldn't have fallen for him if there hadn't been something special between you."

Pandora let her mind wander to the summer four years ago when she was sixteen. It was the first week of June, and the Van Luyens were hosting a picnic.

Pandora's mother left when she was ten, and Pandora and her father, Willie, lived in a cottage on the grounds of Riverview. Pandora really never got over her mother's leaving. It colored everything she did. But she was fairly happy living at Riverview. Willie became the Van Luyens' private tennis instructor, and after school and during the summers, Pandora helped Esther, the cook. The afternoon she met Owen, she had chopped the potatoes for the potato salad and cut the watermelon into wedges.

She had planned to go back to her room to read the copy of *Vogue* that Virginia had loaned her. It had an article about one of her idols, the French fashion designer Jean Patou. Instead, she found herself gazing out the window at the young people gathered on the lawn. They were playing croquet, and someone had set up a badminton net.

The back door opened, and Owen entered. He seemed to be around Archie's age, a year older than Pandora. He looked debonair in striped suspenders and a panama hat.

"Pandora," he said in greeting. "I was sent in to get lemonade and more of that potato salad."

Pandora quickly turned from the window, hoping Owen hadn't noticed that she had been staring. She walked to the icebox and took out a large bowl.

"I helped Esther with the potato salad; she makes the mayonnaise herself," Pandora said. "She uses double the amount of egg yolks as in the recipe."

She didn't know why she was discussing potato salad; she had no interest in cooking. For some reason, she didn't want Owen to leave. She had seen him at Riverview before, but he was always with Archie. There was something about his smile and the easy way he carried himself that made her want to talk to him.

"Tell Esther it's delicious," Owen said companionably. He gathered the bowl. "Perhaps you can carry the lemonade. It's too much to carry by myself."

"Of course," Pandora said, chiding herself for not offering.

Owen waited while she took the pitcher of lemonade from the icebox.

"Why don't you join us," he suggested. "I could use a badminton partner."

"I wasn't invited to the picnic," Pandora answered.

If Virginia were there, Pandora might have joined them. But Virginia was at a friend's sweet-sixteen party. And Archie was too busy fending off the advances of a group of girls to notice that Pandora wasn't there.

"I'm sure the Van Luyens wouldn't mind," Owen said encouragingly. "Archie always tells me they treat you as part of the family."

Pandora's face flushed with pleasure. Archie and Owen had been talking about her.

"I've never played badminton, but I could try," she said, hugging the lemonade pitcher a little too tightly.

"Excellent!" Owen beamed. "Afterward you can tell me more about Esther's potato salad recipe. I'm always hungry."

At that moment, with the sun making diamond shapes on Owen's hatband and his smile pointed directly at her, she felt as if something special had passed between them. No one had ever paid much attention to her before, and Owen was so handsome and assured. Yet it went deeper than that: she felt it in her heart. She had to be falling in love; there was no other explanation for how she felt.

The image dissolved, and Pandora brought her mind back to the present. She flopped back on the bed.

"It's no use. The Winthrops want Lillian Clarkson, with her knowledge of French champagne, as their daughter-in-law. They don't want the daughter of their neighbors' tennis instructor."

"Don't worry about that. What are you going to wear tonight?" Virginia asked. "It has to be something stunning so Owen can't take his eyes off you."

Pandora took a dress from the hanger. She had been working on it for weeks.

The dress was white lace with butterfly sleeves. The floor-length skirt was threaded with silver beads, and it had an appliqué bodice, which she had topped with a lace wrap decorated with pink and yellow flowers.

Pandora had used the fabric from a dress that Virginia had given her from her season. Pandora's allowance paid for the beads, and she found the flowers for the wrap in a chest of dress-up clothes in the Van Luyens' nursery.

Virginia held it up to the light and made a low whistle.

"It's breathtaking. It deserves to be on the runway in Paris."

"Do you really think so?" Pandora inquired.

"Who needs Owen Winthrop," Virginia declared. "You're so talented."

"I can be a fashion designer and raise a family too," Pandora replied. "Women have more options now."

"I agree about love, especially sex. It's the marriage part I'm not sure about," Virginia said naughtily.

Pandora smiled to herself. She and Virginia were different in so many ways, but they adored each other and were as close as sisters.

"Anyway, this isn't the time to discuss it," Virginia said. "You get dressed and I'll do your makeup. Dark kohl under your eyes and red lipstick."

"I've never worn lipstick before," Pandora objected.

"Well, it's time you started. All the young women in New York use lipstick," Virginia commented. "I wish we were the same shoe size; you could wear the pumps Mother bought for me in London. Hand-painted satin from Stead and Simpson."

"If I did, what would you wear?" Pandora frowned.

Virginia twirled the straw hat. Her expression changed and she looked slightly guilty.

"That's what I wanted to talk to you about. I won't be at dinner. I hoped you could cover for me."

Pandora's eyes opened wide.

"Don't look at me like that. I'm not doing anything wrong." Virginia fiddled with the hatband. "But you're right, my parents wouldn't approve. I'm going to borrow Archie's car and drive to Woodstock. I'll be back before midnight."

"What's in Woodstock?"

"A writers' colony called Byrdcliffe. I learned about it from an English professor at Smith. I'm going to have dinner with the couple that founded it. They're considering hosting literary salons and opening them to the public."

Pandora had heard about writers' colonies in the Hudson Valley. They were more like communes. The residents grew their own food and dined together in one large dining room.

Pandora still thought Virginia wasn't telling her something.

"Wouldn't it be safer to do that during the day? You're not an experienced driver."

Virginia stood up. She put on her hat.

"I know how to steer and brake, what else is there to know? Don't worry about me," she said. "We need to focus on getting you ready. I'll be right back."

She returned a few minutes later with a black velvet jewelry case. Inside was a diamond-and-sapphire choker necklace. She fastened it around Pandora's neck and stepped back to admire it.

"That will keep Owen's attention," Virginia said approvingly. "Your hair is lovely—anything in it would distract from the necklace. But Mother has sapphire earrings that would go perfectly. I'll get them from her guest room."

"I can't wear your mother's earrings, and I can't wear this necklace," Pandora insisted, while thinking it would be a shame not to. The sapphires made her eyes look even bluer. "Owen knows I can't afford anything like it."

Virginia snapped the jewelry case shut.

"You might not be able to afford it, but an admirer might have given it to you as a present." She smiled her most wicked smile. "Sometimes I can't believe how clever I am. You'll be the most beautiful woman at the dance and make Owen jealous at the same time."

~

Pandora forced herself to wait until the party was in full swing before making her appearance. When she paused to stand on the balcony, she was glad she had. All heads turned in her direction, and she could tell she was making an impression.

Virginia had decided Pandora should go for a virginal look, so instead of kohl and dark lipstick, she wore powder and pale pink blush. Even her hair was understated compared to that of the other girls, who all wore silk headbands and jeweled hair clips.

"Whose heart do you plan to break in that dress?" Archie asked.

Pandora had to admit the finished effect was stunning. The lace dress made her feel as if she were floating, and the necklace and earrings twinkled in the candlelight that flickered around the lawn. Her hair was scooped up to reveal her neck, and her eyes looked large and luminous under a touch of mascara.

"You're the heartbreaker." Pandora turned to Archie. "I saw two girls practically having a catfight to come talk to you."

"They just like me for my new car," Archie said, grinning. He studied Pandora. "Let's get down to the important thing. Where's Owen, and what's he going to say when he sees you resembling a blond Clara Bow."

"I do not look like Clara Bow," Pandora said, pleased despite herself. How she'd love to have the beauty and charm of America's hottest new film star. Every woman under thirty dreamed of being like her. "What makes you think I have any interest in Owen. If Virginia . . ."

"My sister would never reveal secrets to me," Archie replied easily. "Hers or anyone else's. I've known you for too long. It was all over your face at the tennis match this afternoon. Owen's a decent guy, but you're special, Pandora. He doesn't deserve you."

Pandora caught sight of Owen across the lawn. Her heart lifted and she gave a little wave.

Owen climbed the steps to greet them.

"Owen, we were just talking about you," Archie said. "You'll be captain of the tennis team this year with more matches like that. You put Harvard's Gordon Mott in his place."

"It was because of Pandora," Owen said gallantly. "Gordon couldn't touch one of Pandora's serves."

Pandora fiddled with her evening bag.

"You were wonderful; you could have won it by yourself," she said, looking up at Owen.

"I worried that I upset you when I got angry and that you weren't coming tonight," Owen admitted. His eyes moved down her dress. "I'm glad you did. You look lovely in that dress."

Pandora was speechless. Owen rarely complimented her looks.

"She does look stunning, doesn't she," Archie affirmed. He turned cheekily to Owen. "If I was you, I'd claim the first dance with Pandora now. I heard a couple of the guys planning a duel for the honor."

Pandora was about to jab Archie in the back to let him know that he had gone too far when Owen took her arm.

"That's a good idea, and I have to introduce you to my mother," Owen said to Pandora. "I've been telling her all about you."

Owen handed her a glass of champagne and led her into the garden. He told her about the new convertible he'd ordered. It would arrive by the time he returned to Princeton, and he said he thought Pandora would love it. That was a good sign, she thought, that he was including Pandora in his future.

But she found it difficult to concentrate. All she could think about was that she was making her entrance on Owen's arm.

"Could you make it down to Princeton in the fall?" Owen was saying. "The tennis season isn't until spring, but there are football games every weekend, and we could . . ."

A woman in her midforties approached them. Pandora recognized Mabel Winthrop from the society pages. She wore a beaded gold lamé dress with a fringed hem. Gold cuff bracelets with an Egyptian cat motif snaked up her arm, and she carried a gold fan.

"Owen, there you are," Mabel said. "The Buckleys are looking for you. Alice Buckley's son is starting Princeton and I said you'd give him some tips."

"Mother, this is Pandora. We were talking about Pandora coming to Princeton. She can take the train from Penn Station, and I'll pick her up."

Mabel studied Pandora curiously.

"What a stunning gown," Mabel commented. "Do your parents keep a townhouse in New York? Sometimes I wish my husband didn't love Rosecliff as much as he does. New York is much more exciting."

Pandora was about to reply but stopped. She could hardly say she'd soon be living in New York to attend secretarial school, and she wasn't going to admit she made her own dress. She didn't want Mabel to know that she couldn't afford to buy one.

"Pandora is Willie Carmichael's daughter," Owen said to his mother. "I was telling you about her earlier."

Recognition crossed Mabel's features.

"Of course, that's why Owen wanted us to meet," Mabel exclaimed. "I've taken up tennis. Imagine, we've owned Rosecliff for ten years, and I've never been on the tennis court. Owen said you could give me lessons."

"Pandora would be happy to." Pandora was surprised Owen answered for her. "She's going to help me work on my serve when she comes to Princeton. I'll be the strongest player on the team."

Pandora's cheeks flushed, and she gripped her champagne flute. Was that the only reason Owen invited her to Princeton? Although, she thought to herself, it was good that he wanted to play tennis with her. Couples needed to have things in common.

"I'd be delighted," Pandora said, willing herself to smile.

Pandora heard a rustling sound and smelled a distinct perfume.

"Owen, where have you been hiding?" Lillian Clarkson approached them. "I had to drink my first glass of champagne by myself."

Pandora had to admit Lillian looked beautiful. She'd replaced the sporty clothes she wore to the tennis match with a tiered chiffon dress and long white gloves. A jeweled hairpin held her curls, and she carried a beaded evening bag.

"Hardly hiding," Owen said cheerfully. Pandora watched him take in Lillian. His eyes stayed on her décolletage longer than Pandora preferred. "I found Pandora," he continued. "She's going to give Mother tennis lessons. Maybe you can have lessons too."

"I can't play tennis. I burn too easily without a hat." Lillian addressed the group. "I discovered that last summer when we were in Portofino." Her brow furrowed. "I hope the lessons don't start next weekend. My parents want to invite your family to a house party at Beechtree Cottage. It will be the first house party we've given since we moved to Hyde Park."

"We'd love to come." Mabel turned to Lillian. "I can't wait to see what your mother did with the interior."

"It's not as big as our place in Palm Beach, but it's sweet," Lillian said airily.

Pandora had heard Maude Van Luyen talking about Beechtree Cottage. It sat on twenty acres bordering the Hudson and had forty rooms plus an equestrian facility.

"Perhaps you can help Mother with the invitation list." Lillian turned to Mabel. "It will be quite intimate, and she wants to invite the right people."

"Why don't we find your parents now?" Mabel suggested.

Lillian put her arm through Owen's. "You must come and meet Daddy. He's arranging a hunting trip to Georgia, and he wants you to come."

Pandora waited for Owen to say something —that he couldn't meet Leland Clarkson now; he was talking to Pandora. Or that Pandora must come to Beechtree Cottage as his guest.

Instead, Owen tucked Lillian's arm under his.

"Do you mind if we finish our conversation later?" he asked Pandora. "Archie can show you around; he knows everyone here."

Pandora gulped the last of her champagne.

"I don't mind at all, in fact, I'm quite thirsty." She tried to keep the hurt out of her voice. "I'm going to get another glass of champagne."

She waited until they drifted off. Then she gathered the lace wrap around her shoulders and hurried past the gazebo, all the way down to the river.

Until the sounds of the party were a distant murmur, and she was completely alone.

Chapter Two

July 1926, Hyde Park, New York

It was colder next to the river than Pandora expected. The warmth of the party, the little plates of pig pastries, the candles flickering on tabletops were gone, and a cold breeze drifted onto the banks.

Pandora huddled on a bench. She was furious with herself for running away, but staying would have been worse. She couldn't bear to see Lillian flouncing around with Owen as if they were already a couple. She needed time to refocus.

Had she been mistaken about Owen's intentions? Over the last month, she had gotten her hopes up, imagining the moment when Owen would propose so often that it became as real to her as the moon shimmering on the river. She first got the notion a few weeks ago when Owen invited her to walk in the Van Luyens' garden after a tennis lesson. Owen had needed a tennis partner, so Pandora's father asked her to complete the foursome.

Owen and Pandora won every set, and afterward Archie brought out a pitcher of lemonade. Pandora was about to clean up the glasses and change her clothes before she helped Esther prepare dinner when Owen pulled her aside.

"Don't go yet," Owen suggested. "It's the first warm day. Why don't we walk by the river?"

Owen had always been friendly, but he had never asked to spend time with her alone. It was at moments like this that she missed having a mother to guide her. Pandora didn't want to do anything improper. But it was the middle of the day, and anyone could see them from the house. It wasn't as if they were doing anything wrong.

They strolled through Maude Van Luyen's rose garden down to the dock. The sky was a pale blue, and the sun reflected off the grand mansions that lined the riverbank.

"You're wonderful on the tennis court," Owen said when they reached the shore.

"I got in a few lucky serves," Pandora said with a shrug.

"I wasn't talking about your tennis game exactly." Owen turned to her. "It's more about how you carry yourself. You have so much confidence."

It was true, she was a confident player. She had practically grown up on a tennis court. But that wasn't the way she wanted Owen to see her. She wanted him to think of her as someone special, a girl he wanted to spend more time with.

"I don't want to be a tennis player; my dream is to be a fashion designer," she replied. "I've always loved beautiful clothes."

"I'm sure you'll be good at that too." Owen studied her appreciatively. "Archie said you were special. Now I see that he was right. I hope we get to know each other better this summer. Perhaps you can visit me at Princeton in the fall."

Pandora was so taken aback she found it hard to swallow. She didn't know much about men or dating, but Owen wouldn't say something like this if he didn't mean it.

"Yes, I'd like that," she replied.

Owen smiled, and he had never looked so handsome. The sun caught the golden glints in his light brown hair, and his eyes radiated warmth.

"I'm glad that's settled." He nodded. "Perhaps we can do this again after our lesson next week."

The tennis lesson the following week was canceled because Archie had an engagement, and Owen and Pandora didn't meet up again. But she felt as if everything changed between them, and she had been sure Owen felt the same. But had Owen said those things only because he wanted help with his serve?

She couldn't let herself believe that. Pandora was as pretty as the other girls at the party and just as intelligent. Even if she didn't have Lillian's father's millions and hadn't traveled to Italy and France, she had enough good qualities for Owen to be interested in her. Is this what her mother had felt before she left? That without a certain pedigree, she would never amount to anything?

If only Pandora could offer Owen something other than tennis lessons: a sailboat they could take on the river, a ride in a sporty car. Even if she could ask him to be her date at a dinner party, she might have a chance. But Pandora didn't receive social invitations of her own. Pandora was only invited this weekend because Owen knew her through Archie and Virginia.

The lace wrap didn't keep her warm, and she regretted spending so much time on it. No one cared that she had sewn the flowers with silver thread to make them twinkle under the lights. The women in the Winthrops' social circle purchased their wardrobes in Paris and London. They weren't interested in what the Van Luyens' tennis instructor's daughter wore.

Pandora had made her first dress when she was fifteen. She'd been clearing out a closet in her father's bedroom and discovered a rack of her mother's dresses. She and her father rarely talked about her mother, Laura, who had left when she was ten. Pandora's memories of her were unclear, but she still missed her very much. She missed the way her mother had smelled when she gave Pandora a bath when she was small, and she missed the way her blond hair bounced at her shoulders. Once,

Pandora heard a man on a bus comment that Pandora's mother was very pretty. Pandora had only been nine, but she privately agreed. Her mother was the loveliest woman she knew.

Laura hadn't been the kind of mother who spent time with Pandora when she was young. Her father did most of the parenting. Laura preferred working as a saleswoman at a department store, being surrounded by pretty clothes and makeup, instead of staying at home with Pandora. In the evenings, she often ate with other women in the store's cafeteria, and Willie made soup or stew for him and Pandora.

Pandora blamed herself for her mother's departure. She knew from the limited conversations she had with her father on the matter that Laura had thought Willie was going to be a famous tennis star. She thought all the things she craved—social standing, a beautiful home, enough money to give parties and travel to Europe—would be hers after they were married. When Willie was injured and stopped competing, Laura lost interest in Pandora and her father.

Surely that wouldn't have been the case if Pandora had been worth staying for—if Pandora was a beautiful singer or was a talented dancer. But Pandora wasn't either of those things. It must have been something lacking in Pandora herself that made her mother leave.

After Laura left, Pandora made up scenes in her head. Pandora and her mother going to the movies, spending rainy afternoons creating new recipes. Visiting fashion boutiques together and trying on pretty dresses. She berated herself for not paying more attention to her mother. She could have tried to engage her in conversation. She could have complimented her hairstyle or her choice in lipstick and asked about her customers.

Pandora would never have another mother. She wanted to talk to her father about it, but she could tell it was difficult for him to discuss, and Pandora couldn't bring herself to cause him more pain. So for the first five years after Laura left, Pandora had kept her questions and doubts to herself and tried not to think about her. But the day she stood in front of the rack of her mother's dresses, she had found a reminder of her, and she couldn't resist trying the dresses on. Most of them were a little wide in the waist and not the right length. But the fabrics were lovely, and there were some nice designs. She was twirling in front of the mirror when her father appeared at the door.

"What are you doing?" he asked sharply.

Willie had sandy-colored hair and leathery skin from years spent on the tennis court. He was very tall, almost six foot three. But he was so gentle, it was unusual for him to raise his voice.

"I found some of Mother's clothes." Pandora turned around. "We're almost the same size."

Willie sat on the bed and studied Pandora.

"Laura wore that dress to my first national competition at the US National Championships in 1903. Back then it was held at the Newport Casino in Rhode Island. The Astors and the Goelets owned mansions in Newport and attended the tournament. Your mother loved it; we were treated like celebrities. Caroline Astor even invited us to a cocktail party."

"I'm sure she looked beautiful," Pandora said, imagining her mother holding a martini glass and floating from room to room.

Her father nodded. "She was the prettiest woman there. All the men wanted to dance with her."

He waved at the dresses heaped on the bed.

"Those dresses are gathering dust; you should take them to a thrift shop. You can keep whatever you get for them."

"If you don't mind, I'd like to keep them."

"Keep them?"

Pandora noticed her father's pained expression. She couldn't walk around in her mother's dresses; it would bring back too many memories.

"To use the fabric to sew my own clothes," she said hastily. "Esther said I could use her sewing machine. It would save money, and I've always been interested in fashion."

Willie stood up and kissed her on the cheek.

"I'll leave that between you and Esther. I don't know a thing about clothes, except that I'm thankful you offered to do the ironing."

~

Pandora started making her own dresses the same afternoon. At first it was so she could imagine herself like her mother when she was young. Attending dances and dinner parties, instead of serving the bowls of Jell-O to the Van Luyens' guests between courses. But gradually, Pandora's desire for a more glamorous life merged with a love of fashion itself. She pored over Maude Van Luyen's copies of *Vogue* and *Harper's Bazaar*.

Pandora often asked herself why she wanted to be a fashion designer. Was it because it made her feel closer to her mother and the pretty dresses she'd discovered in her father's closet? Or was it because she wanted something of her own, so people didn't look at her and say, "That's Willie Carmichael's daughter, he played at Wimbledon."

Or was it because she hoped that someday wearing a beautiful gown would allow her proper entry into the world she loved: the drawing rooms of families like the Winthrops and Vanderbilts.

It was all of those things, but it was also more than that. When Pandora sat at the sewing machine, her sketches propped on the windowsill and yards of fabric fanned out on the table, her whole being came alive. She longed to see her gowns in the pages of fashion magazines, to have them worn by wives of senators and congressmen. She had a talent that would benefit other women, if only she had the time and resources to work on her designs.

Pandora's inspiration came from the female designers taking the fashion world by storm: Coco Chanel, who opened her first boutique in Deauville in 1912 and a second boutique on the most elegant street in Paris, rue Cambon, six years later; the Italian designer, Elsa Schiaparelli, who like Pandora had no formal training but was making a name for herself in Paris; and Madeleine Vionnet whose quote "When a woman smiles, her dress must smile with her" Pandora kept taped to the wall in front of her sewing machine. And male designers too: Paul Poiret for his brilliantly colored turbans and harem pants. Jean Patou for his bold, geometric designs.

When Virginia was home from boarding school, she was happy to be Pandora's model. Pandora never felt more confident than when she was kneeling in front of Virginia with her mouth full of pins. She loved transforming an idea in her head into a finished dress, embellished with appliqués and buttons and perhaps a matching cape.

A puff of wind blew in from the river and brought Pandora back to the present. She tightened her wrap around herself. She couldn't let Lillian spoil her evening. Tonight, Pandora was an invited guest, just like the Van Luyens and the Clarksons.

The band was playing a Cole Porter song as she walked back toward the house. She admired the scene. This was a world Pandora was familiar with: the delicious smell of baked ham, well-dressed men and women talking about their boats and horses, young people laughing, and the air thick with perfume and cigar smoke. Although usually at parties she was helping in the kitchen or serving in the dining room at the Van Luyens'.

She couldn't help but wonder if the cooks and maids who worked at Rosecliff felt the same as she did. Perhaps the dark-haired girl in the black uniform serving hors d'oeuvres on the balcony dreamed of being invited to house parties. And perhaps the redheaded maid who turned down Pandora's bed in the guest bedroom imagined filling the closet with her own dresses. Like Pandora, perhaps they longed for the heady buzz of slipping on an evening gown and a pair of satin heels for a party.

Her thoughts were interrupted by Archie waving to her from across the lawn.

"Pandora, come join us." Archie stood up and pointed to the chair opposite him.

Dinner was being served on the terrace in front of a stage with gleaming instruments. Guests sat at round tables covered with white tablecloths set with silver candelabras and china with a gold-and-blue flower motif.

Pandora was glad to see that Archie sat at the same table as Owen. Archie wore the traditional top hat and tails, but the formal wear looked rakish on him thanks to the yellow pocket square that peeked out of the breast pocket. Owen also wore a top hat and tails. He was the epitome of elegance with his gold cuff links and a stiff-bosom shirt with a wing collar.

"I was wondering where you went," Archie said to Pandora. "I can't find Virginia anywhere, and Lillian's gone off with a headache. I was afraid I'd have to talk to this guy all night." He motioned to Owen.

"Lillian isn't feeling well?" Pandora asked.

"She came down with a migraine," Owen replied. "Poor thing, she really does suffer from being too long in the sun."

"More like hung over from drinking half a bottle of champagne in the afternoon." Archie grinned.

Pandora stifled a laugh. Archie's playful digs always improved her spirits. He was like a large, gentle dog, pushing at you with his nose.

"I hope she's better in time for the dancing," Pandora said, resisting the urge to kick Archie under the table.

The waiter set down bowls of clam chowder, and Pandora suddenly felt better. She was sitting across from Owen on the terrace at Rosecliff. Perhaps Owen had only been being polite to Lillian earlier. The Clarksons were new to Hyde Park, and they were the Winthrops' guests. Pandora assured herself that he loved her and everything would be all right.

"Pandora is a great dancer," Archie said. "A few years ago, my mother hired a dance teacher to come to Riverview. Pandora could waltz perfectly after two lessons; it took Virginia and me weeks to master the steps."

The dance lessons were conducted in the Van Luyens' ballroom. Pandora was only included because Virginia was paired with the dance instructor and Archie needed a partner. Virginia hated waltzes, she preferred the foxtrot and Charleston. Once Archie learned the steps, he was a wonderful dancer. It came as naturally to him as walking.

"I've rarely known a girl with so many talents," Archie went on, toying with his soup. "Besides tennis, Pandora is good at croquet, and we're always fighting over who gets to be her partner in board games. I've never lost a game of Pegity with Pandora as my partner."

Pandora knew what Archie was doing. He was trying to make her look good in front of Owen. It was sweet of him, but Pandora worried that he might go too far. It was better if she turned the conversation to Owen. She had to get back the sense of intimacy they had shared by the river last month.

"Archie told me you're going to join Winthrop Motors after graduation."

Owen's eyes lit up. He put down his napkin.

"Wait until you see next year's Winthrop GT40. Its top speed is sixty-five miles per hour, and we're introducing our first sport coupe."

"You should take an engineering class at Princeton," Archie said cheekily. "It would be more valuable than that course you took last semester on the Ming dynasty."

Owen adjusted his gold cuff links so they didn't touch his soup.

"The art history professor gave As to everyone who attended the exhibit at the Met. And engineering classes have too much homework." Owen dipped a bread roll into the soup. "I'd rather spend my evenings playing billiards at the eating clubs."

After dinner, Pandora danced with two men she didn't know, and took a break to watch other couples on the dance floor. It reminded her of the big top at the circus when the performers and animals came together for the final encore.

The female guests wore all styles of gowns. Dresses with dropped waistlines and large sashes, beaded gowns with elaborate bows, and dresses with shockingly low-cut backs. Their hair was held back by rhinestone combs, and Pandora noticed a few tiaras. One woman carried a feather boa that kept getting in her partner's face as they danced.

The men were all dashingly handsome in topcoats and trousers with satin stripes. Some of the young set wore the new style of tuxedo dinner jacket and white waistcoats. A few even wore soft collared shirts instead of the more traditional winged variety that Owen wore.

Pandora loved all of it. She kept touching the diamond-and-sapphire choker as if to remind herself she really was part of the party.

The song ended, and Owen crossed the dance floor. His hair was damp, and his cheeks were flushed from either dancing or more champagne.

"We haven't danced yet. I don't want to miss out," he said, standing beside her.

"No, we haven't," Pandora replied. She glanced around to see if Lillian was anywhere on the dance floor.

Owen held out his hand. "We better dance now. They'll play a fast number next, and that won't be half as enjoyable."

The band played "The Man I Love" by Gershwin, and Owen placed his hand on her back. Pandora had never experienced such happiness. Owen was tall enough that her head fit under his chin, but not so tall that she had to crane her neck to look up at him. And he held her so close, she was certain they were dancing closer than other couples.

When the song ended, she hoped he would ask her for the next dance. Instead, he led her to the side. He wiped his brow with his handkerchief and took two champagne flutes from a passing waiter.

"You do look lovely this evening. I can't get over how pretty you are," Owen said, handing her a glass of champagne. "I've rarely seen you in anything but a white tennis skirt and long cardigan."

Pandora basked in Owen's praise. She had to make him see that she fit in with his social set. Not just on the tennis court but anywhere.

"I'm like any girl, I love nice clothes," she said lightly. "It's a wonderful party. I can't wait until tomorrow. Virginia said there would be fireworks and a treasure hunt."

"Mother loves her treasure hunts; she misses the Easter egg hunts we had when we were children," Owen said. "At least our party is early in the season. By the time school starts in September, I've drunk so much champagne, I can't stand the taste." He smiled. "Though hardly anyone drinks champagne at Princeton; the bartender at my eating club makes the best sidecars."

Pandora had read about Princeton's Eating Clubs in F. Scott Fitzgerald's novel, *This Side of Paradise*. There were seventeen clubs, all lined up in a row on Prospect Avenue. They had names like Ivy Club and Cap and Gown Club, and only men of a certain social pedigree were invited to be members. The houses had their own ballrooms and held parties called "Boxers and Blazers" and "Butts, Butts, Butts."

"The Enrights are having a house party at the end of the month," Owen said. "You should come."

"I'd love to, but I don't know the Enrights," Pandora replied.

She had heard of them, though. Their summer estate, Blythdale, was supposed to be one of the loveliest in Hyde Park. It sat high on the Hudson surrounded by woodlands and a pond.

"I'll have Mother get you an invitation," Owen responded. He pointed across the dance floor. "I should go. I promised Mother I'd dance with Lucy Vanderbilt."

Owen drifted off and Pandora returned to their table. The waiters had removed the entrée plates and replaced them with silver dessert bowls. Each bowl was filled with cut-up pieces of tropical fruit and topped with a maraschino cherry.

Pandora dipped her dessert fork into the fruit, going over her exchange with Owen. He had complimented her looks, and he obviously enjoyed dancing with her. He had invited her to another house party. All of that boded well.

"There you are," Archie said as he approached the table. He pushed his hair from his forehead. "You have to dance with me. The last two girls stepped on my toes, and my feet hurt. I need to dance with someone I trust."

Pandora stifled a laugh. He was exaggerating, of course. All the girls were in love with Archie and wanted to be held close by him. But Archie didn't want a serious girlfriend. He was happiest reading by the swimming pool or chasing the Van Luyens' two English setters around the lawn.

"I'd love to dance, but first let me finish my fruit cocktail," Pandora said. "I know what you were doing at dinner, praising me in front of Owen. It was very kind, but you didn't have to."

"I didn't say anything that wasn't true." Archie sat opposite her. He speared his cherry with a fork. "You've grown quite lovely, Pandora, and you don't even notice it. You should have seen Owen's face when you walked down that staircase. He couldn't take his eyes off you."

"You do say nice things sometimes." She smiled at Archie. "I've had enough fruit cocktail. I'm ready to dance."

The band struck up "Swanee," and Archie took Pandora's hand. Archie was a very good dancer, and he spun her effortlessly around the floor. Other couples watched them approvingly, and she felt a surge of happiness. She felt so at ease with Archie, it was a relief to be in his arms.

The outdoor lights twinkled on the lawn, and candles flickered in the candelabras. Tonight, she belonged on the dance floor at Rosecliff. She was going to enjoy every minute of it.

Chapter Three

The next morning, Pandora came down to breakfast before any of the other guests. She was used to getting up early to help Esther in the kitchen. Maude Van Luyen insisted on a large, formal breakfast even if it was just the immediate family. While Esther prepared the cod fish and bacon, Pandora would make the porridge that Archie ate by the bowlful and lay out the silver coffee and tea set.

She loved arranging the coffee and tea set in the Van Luyens' dining room. The sun streamed onto the long maple table, and the bird's-egg-blue china from Tiffany's looked lovely on the embroidered lace table-cloth. Pandora dreamed of presiding over her own dining room table. She'd serve warm muffins with English marmalade. There would be a pitcher of orange juice, as well as newspapers so she and her husband could read about current events. After breakfast, she'd retreat to her study to sketch a new dress or drive into her boutique in Hyde Park.

The breakfast laid out in the Winthrops' dining room on Saturday morning was even grander than breakfast at Riverview. There were three different kinds of eggs and a platter of broiled chops and creamed potatoes. The coffee was strong and fragrant, and the maid said Mabel Winthrop brought the jam back from London.

Pandora had hoped she would see Owen, but he didn't appear. She ate eggs, a slice of toast, and some bacon and went back upstairs to her room.

The door opened and Virginia poked her head in.

"You're all dressed and it's not even ten a.m." Virginia flopped on the bed. She wore crepe de chine knickers and a camisole top with a pink silk robe tied at the waist and satin slippers.

"You can't go around dressed like that," Pandora said, horrified. "What if someone sees you?"

"None of the guests are up this early." Virginia yawned. "They're all nursing their hangovers."

"I was wondering why no one was at breakfast." Pandora sighed. "I thought I was the only one with an appetite."

"When you attend enough house parties, you'll discover the only thing that sounds good before noon is tomato juice mixed with vodka," Virginia commented. "You look much too fresh faced. Didn't Owen keep you up, plying you with champagne and boasting about his billiards prowess until the small hours of the morning?"

"You and Archie are too hard on Owen." Pandora turned to the mirror on the dressing table. She knew she was lucky; she had inherited her mother's classic looks: straight blond hair, a small nose, and high, angular cheekbones. But sometimes she wished she had more unconventional features such as Lillian's curls or a wide, sensuous mouth.

"Owen said I looked lovely in my dress." Pandora tugged at her hair with a hairbrush. "And he's going to get me an invitation to the Enrights' house party."

"I didn't know the Enrights have a tennis court," Virginia remarked.

Pandora's cheeks flushed.

"Owen didn't say a word about tennis," she retorted. "This afternoon is the treasure hunt, I bet he'll ask me to be his partner."

Owen hadn't said anything about being partners. But Pandora was almost certain he would.

"Tell me about your night." Pandora changed the subject. "Your light was off when I came upstairs. Did you get home early?"

"Not exactly." Virginia's face took on a noncommittal expression.

"Don't tell me you were out after midnight." Pandora gasped. "You're a woman, alone at night. What if you had a flat tire or got stopped by the police?"

"I'm perfectly capable of changing a tire, and I drove too fast for anyone to stop me," Virginia said, the smile creeping back into her voice. "You should see Byrdcliffe: a dozen wooden cottages built in a clearing and the Catskill Mountains right behind them. There were poets and playwrights. I attended a poetry reading and got this." She jumped up and stepped out of the room.

She returned a few moments later with a thin book.

"Did the poet give it to you?" Pandora asked.

"I borrowed it from him," Virginia replied. "We did eat dinner together. Wolfgang read more of his poetry while we ate."

"Wolfgang?" Pandora repeated.

"Wolfgang Bryant. He's named for his German grandfather," Virginia said excitedly. "Wolfgang attended Fordham, he's twenty-four. He grew up in a house of strong women." The color in her cheeks heightened. "His mother is a lawyer, she's one of the first women to argue a case in front of the state supreme court. And his sister is in law school in Chicago, she wants to be a judge. We talked about women wanting careers rather than husbands and children. He agrees there's nothing wrong with wanting a family, but he also agrees that women should know they have choices."

Virginia jumped up. She marched back and forth as if she were delivering a lesson in a lecture hall.

"Women can do anything. Edith Wharton won the Pulitzer Prize in the Novel, and Helena Rubinstein and Elizabeth Arden own their own cosmetics companies." Her forehead knotted together. "But most colleges put more emphasis on finding a husband. There's a tradition at

Smith that the first girl in a class to get engaged runs around the dining table while everyone congratulates her. Getting married is considered more important than graduating."

Virginia looked so radiant, as if a light had been switched on and refused to be dimmed.

Pandora wondered if Virginia was falling in love.

"What does Wolfgang look like?"

"I hardly noticed," Virginia said with a shrug. "He has longish dark hair, and when he reads his poetry, he rubs the stubble on his chin. I'm not interested in his appearance; we have so much in common. We've read all the same authors. He loves T.S. Eliot and thinks *Ulysses* is overrated, and when he was a child, he read *Peter Pan* so many times, he almost memorized it."

Virginia and Pandora had spent hours reading *Peter Pan*, even once they became teenagers. It had been Virginia's favorite book, and her favorite character was Wendy.

"Wendy wanted to be a mother and have children," Pandora reminded her.

"Yes, but that's not all she wanted. She also wanted to leave home and have grand adventures." Virginia glanced at the silver watch on her wrist. "I have to get dressed. I'm going back to Byrdcliffe tonight. I'm going to have dinner with Wolfgang again."

"You can't go, you'll miss the fireworks."

Virginia tied her robe more tightly around her waist.

"I've seen the Winthrops' fireworks a dozen times. Besides, Wolfgang is going to tell me about the literary salons in New York. Once, he heard Anita Loos read some of her short stories." Her eyes were as playful as a cat's. "The stories are so risqué they make *The Awakening* seem tame in comparison."

～

That afternoon, Lillian was the first person Pandora saw when she stepped onto the terrace. She was lying on a chaise lounge near the swimming pool.

A large floppy hat covered her hair, and a magazine lay open in her lap. All traces of the party—the elegant candelabras, the bar overflowing with cocktail glasses, the dance floor where Pandora had danced with Owen—were gone, and the lawn was set up for croquet. She thought of all the parties at the Van Luyens', where it was her job to take the tablecloths from the tables and stack them in the laundry room for the laundress.

"Pandora, come join me." Lillian waved to her. "Owen and a few others went boating. I couldn't face being on the water. I was afraid I'd get another migraine."

Pandora was disappointed; she would have loved to go out on a boat. The river was a brilliant blue, and the air was thick with summer scents. But she had been in her room with Virginia when they left. Owen wouldn't have known where to find her.

"I hope you're feeling better," Pandora said, sitting on a chaise lounge next to her.

"Much better, I should have been more careful." Lillian nodded. "The same thing happened last summer when we were on the Lido of Venice. We were at the Excelsior of course, it's the only place to stay. I got so sunburned I had to lie in my room with a cold cloth on my forehead. From Venice we drove to Portofino, and the road was so winding, I got a migraine all over again." She lifted the brim of her hat. "I adored Portofino. It was nothing more than a fishing village until a few years ago. It became popular because some British author wrote a novel set there. My mother read it; it's called *Enchanted April*. I tried, but I couldn't get past the first chapter." She opened her mouth in a yawn. "Portofino is much less touristy than Naples or Capri. Have you been?"

Pandora shook her head. "I've never been out of New York."

Lillian studied Pandora as if she were some kind of foreign species. Pandora wondered if that's how the animals felt at the zoo.

"That's right, your father is the Van Luyens' tennis instructor. Owen said he went all the way to Wimbledon."

"That was a long time ago," Pandora said uncomfortably. "He's been an instructor for as long as I can remember."

"It must be strange for you," Lillian went on. "Always being dependent on others for everything."

"We're all dependent on other people," Pandora said, working to keep her voice pleasant. "Archie's parents gave him a car, and Virginia's mother buys Virginia's clothes in London. The breakfast I ate this morning was made by the Winthrops' cook. I didn't go out to the henhouse and collect the eggs myself." She had to be courteous, but Lillian was making it difficult.

"Parents are supposed to give their children things," Lillian said airily. "I meant it must be difficult for you. Being part of all this but not really." She waved at the house. "You were only invited to the house party because of Archie and Virginia. It's like that story, *The Prince and the Pauper*, by Mark Twain."

"I don't know what you mean," Pandora replied, even though she knew exactly what Lillian meant.

"We performed the play in school. Spence is a girl's school, so I played the lead," Lillian continued. "The prince and the pauper change places because the prince wants to know what it's like to be a regular boy. It doesn't work out." She looked at Pandora archly. "We're born to be who we are. There's nothing we can do about it."

Pandora had read *The Prince and the Pauper*, and that's not what she took away from the story. Prince Edward learns what it's like to live in a London slum, and Tom sees the drawbacks and responsibilities that come with being a prince. When they switch places at the end, they're both kinder and more understanding of others.

But Pandora had already said enough. She couldn't afford to get in an argument with Lillian.

Lillian stretched out on the chaise lounge. She did have a lovely figure. A belt encircled her small waist, and she had full breasts and shapely legs.

"My father wanted me to go to finishing school in Switzerland to learn how to be a good society wife." Lillian set aside her magazine. "I told him I didn't need to. I was born knowing the right people to invite to dinner parties and how to serve afternoon tea." She gave Pandora a small smile. "And I already know what kind of man I'm going to marry, so why waste my time on European men?"

~

Later that afternoon, guests mingled on the lawn and waited for the treasure hunt to begin. A buzz of excitement ran through the crowd, increased by the cocktails being served. Pandora had already drunk two sidecars. She knew she shouldn't drink in the afternoon, but her conversation with Lillian caused a pain behind her eyes, and she had to do something to make it go away.

"There you are." Archie approached her. He wore knickerbockers and a white V-neck sweater. Though he had a straw hat jammed on his head, his face looked tan from boating. For a moment, Pandora envied him. Archie didn't have to spend hours choosing the right outfit. No matter what he wore, he fit in.

"I'll need one of those," Archie said, pointing to Pandora's cocktail. "You haven't been to one of Mabel Winthrop's treasure hunts. The items are impossible to find, and she gives extra clues to the people she likes best. It's as if we're in grade school and have to compete with the teacher's pet."

"Or you're lazy and can't be bothered to look." Pandora laughed.

"The whole purpose of a house party is to be lazy," Archie grumbled. "Instead, I spent hours rowing on the Hudson. My arms are tired."

"I'm sure you'll find a partner who'll do the work for you," Pandora said sweetly. Already girls were looking with interest in their direction.

"I thought you'd be my partner," Archie objected. He glanced at the terrace, where Owen had appeared. "Is that the way it's going to be from now on? You're going to wait on Owen hand and foot while Virginia and I get shuffled to the background?" He sighed theatrically. "If I had known that ten years ago, I wouldn't have risked a broken arm to get your cat down from that tree."

"Whiskers wasn't my cat, I was taking care of him for the stable boy." Pandora smiled at the memory. "And you're the one who put him in the tree."

"I was eleven. I thought cats liked trees," Archie said in his defense. "Owen doesn't deserve you as a partner, but at least you'll get the best clues." He glanced around for a waiter. "I'm going to find a cocktail. I need something to get me through the next hour."

Pandora spotted Owen. He was dressed similarly to Archie, but he wore a vest instead of a sweater. She took one more gulp of her cocktail for courage and raised her hand in a small wave.

"Pandora, it's wonderful to see you. Mother's gone all out with the treasure hunt," Owen said. "I hope you have your thinking cap on."

"I've never been to a treasure hunt before," Pandora admitted.

"It's great fun; she hides things all over the house and grounds. At Christmas, she hid six live partridges in the pantry, and last July she hid a lion cub in the boathouse."

"I'll let someone else search the boathouse," Pandora said with a smile.

"I talked to her about the Enrights' party," Owen continued. "The Enrights are away, but you're as good as invited."

A sparkling feeling formed in Pandora's chest. Owen hadn't forgotten about the party! And he hadn't mentioned tennis. Pandora was right. Owen must be in love with her.

"Owen, I found you." Lillian approached them. "I just finished helping your mother with the final clue. Are you ready?"

"I better go." Owen turned to Pandora. "Have you chosen a partner?"

Pandora faltered. Her drink spilled on the ground.

"He's around here somewhere," she said offhandedly.

She hated not telling the truth. But she couldn't let Lillian believe Owen chose her over Pandora.

"My parents and I attended a treasure hunt at the Ritz in Paris last year. That's where treasure hunts started," Lillian said knowledgeably. "One guest found a diamond bracelet in the chandelier and was allowed to keep it." She put her arm through Owen's. "The trick is to start early. While everyone else is fighting over the clues, you and your partner start looking."

Pandora glanced around for Archie, but he was talking to a pretty girl wearing a lilac tea dress. Virginia had taken the car to Byrdcliffe, and Pandora didn't know anyone else at the party. She was going to have to hunt for treasures by herself.

"He must be inside," she said. "I'll go find him."

Even without a partner, the treasure hunt was more fun than Pandora expected. For a while, she forgot about Owen's promises, about Lillian's jarring comments, and concentrated on the clues. Archie and Owen were right, Mabel hid things in the most unlikely places. Pandora found a live lobster in the swimming pool. The gardener fished it out and gave it to the cook to boil for dinner. She found an American flag rolled up in the piano in the music room and a pistol that Mabel's ancestor used in the Revolutionary War inside a head of lettuce in the greenhouse.

Archie and his partner found the most outrageous treasure: a six-foot Statue of Liberty wearing a diamond tiara. It stood in the statuary in the garden, but only Archie noticed that it was different from the others.

As the hunt wound down, the guests gathered on the lawn. "There's one more treasure," Owen announced, standing on the stone steps.

The guests each glanced at their sheet of clues, puzzled. All the items had been found.

"Please follow me to the front of the house," Owen instructed.

Pandora's feet hurt, and her head throbbed from the alcohol. She longed for something cold and sweet to drink.

The latest model Winthrop GT stood on the gravel. Pandora didn't know much about cars, but she could tell it was expensive. It was lime green, with a white canvas top and leather seats. It had a spare wheel displayed on the side and a jump seat in the back.

"No, I didn't drag everyone here to admire the newest car from Winthrop Motors," Owen said when the guests gathered in a half circle. "Though she's a beauty. She's the 1926 touring sedan with the Winthrop-patented engine."

Everyone laughed, and a few guests clapped.

"This treasure is a little different. I hid it myself, and it's only for one person." Owen took a piece of paper from his trouser pocket. "One might say it's the Winthrop way of welcoming the Clarksons to Hyde Park."

Pandora wondered what Owen was talking about. Owen's mother had hidden the treasures and written out the clues.

Owen addressed Lillian, who stood in the front row.

"To find this treasure, think back to our drive from Nice to Monte Carlo," he read from the paper. "Don't be afraid to look thoroughly. Whatever oil or grease you encounter will be worth it."

Pandora felt a small stab, as if she'd pricked her finger on one of the rosebushes. She knew that Owen met Lillian in Europe last summer, but she hadn't realized they'd spent time together.

Lillian smiled prettily at the crowd. She ventured close to the car and opened the glove compartment. She looked beneath the seats and in between the spokes of the wheels and finally under the hood. Suddenly Lillian squealed and emerged, holding a small velvet box.

"Well done." Owen joined her. "Your hands might be greasy. Let me open it for you."

He took off his straw hat and dropped to one knee.

"Lillian Grace Clarkson," he began. "I knew from the first time I saw you on the beach in Cannes, that you were right for me. You'll be the perfect mother to our children and the best wife I could ask for. I can't imagine a better way to celebrate America's birthday than asking you to marry me."

Lillian stuck out her hand. "Yes, yes!"

Owen took out the ring and slipped it on her finger. The yellow topaz looked huge, even from a distance. It was a rectangular cut, surrounded by a burst of small diamonds.

"My mother insisted I use her ring, which is yellow topaz and diamond, that my father brought back from Brazil," Owen said, addressing the guests. He turned back to Lillian. "I promise to add to it with the latest trinkets from Tiffany's."

Lillian kissed Owen and ran straight to her mother. A champagne bottle popped, and everyone started cheering.

Pandora's stomach dropped, and she was afraid she might faint. She glanced up and saw the other young women crowding around Lillian to get a closer look at the ring. That ring should have been Pandora's. She should have been standing in the center of the group, the diamond made even more sparkling by the joy in Pandora's heart.

Archie was nowhere in sight; he had probably grown bored with Owen's lengthy speech and gone inside before Owen proposed. If only Virginia were there, she would have made some kind of dry comment that would force Pandora to keep breathing.

She ducked into the house and walked through the kitchen to the pantry. The pantry at Riverview was often her refuge. She found something soothing about hiding away in the neat rows of jars and spices.

But here, seeing the English marmalade that only this morning she had imagined serving at her own dining table with Owen, the pain became unbearable.

The full force of Owen's betrayal washed over her. Owen's words by the river had meant nothing. In the fall she'd have to start secretarial school. She and Owen would never live on a grand estate together, with children and dogs romping on the lawn.

More important than anything, she loved Owen and had been confident that he felt the same. Last Christmas he gave Pandora a bottle of No. 4711 eau de cologne. He had brought gifts for Virginia and Archie too, but Pandora's gift was special: No. 4711 eau de cologne was her favorite scent in the world. She always stopped to smell the sample bottle at the pharmacy in Hyde Park.

At Easter, Owen had sat with his family in the church pew in front of her. He glanced back so many times, Pandora became embarrassed. Six weeks ago, when Princeton let out for the summer, he greeted her by picking her up and twirling her around. Archie laughed that Owen greeted the Winthrops' poodle in the same way, but Pandora ignored him. Then there had been the walk to the river, when Owen said he wanted to get to know her better. Pandora had been so sure of his intentions. She had believed he was in love with her.

She had been wrong. Owen didn't have feelings for her. He thought of her as his tennis partner, and as part of the household staff at Riverview. Not as someone who could fit into his world, someone he might marry. The worst part was that she'd let herself fall in love with him. How could she have developed feelings for someone when he didn't feel the same?

Owen was the first person besides the Van Luyens and her father who had paid attention to her. Pandora had mistaken that for love.

A few tears spilled onto her blouse. Pandora brushed them away.

She couldn't go back to the party and watch Lillian fawning all over Owen. Celebrating the fireworks with the other guests was out of the question. She needed to find a chauffeur who would take her back to Riverview. Virginia could make Pandora's excuses when she returned from Byrdcliffe and bring her suitcase home in the morning.

Pandora ducked out the kitchen door and ran out to the driveway. Daniel, the Van Luyens' chauffeur, lounged against a late-model black sedan. Maude and Robert Van Luyen were spending the night at Rosecliff, the car wouldn't be missed if it was gone for an hour.

She explained to Daniel that she had a terrible headache, and he offered to drive her to Riverview. She had never ridden in the Van Luyens' car. Despite her distress, she couldn't help but marvel at the supple red leather upholstery on the seats and the bird's-eye maple dashboard.

Pandora sighed in relief when the car pulled into the gates of Riverview. They passed the paddock where Robert Van Luyen kept his horses, the pond where Archie liked to fish, and the greenhouse where Esther grew vegetables.

Riverview was built in a different style from Rosecliff, but it was just as imposing. It was Georgian style with a red brick colonial facade and lush ivy climbing the walls. When they were young, Pandora and Virginia and Archie used to play hide-and-go-seek in the forecourt. Once, Archie had climbed up the ivy and slipped in through an upstairs window, and it had taken Pandora and Virginia ages to find him.

Pandora thanked Daniel and stepped out of the car. The lights were off in the main house. Esther had the night off, and Pandora's father was probably relaxing in the cottage.

She wasn't ready to face him. Willie would be shocked to see Pandora. He wasn't expecting her to come home until tomorrow morning.

Pandora sat on a stone bench near the garage. The dress she had picked out for the treasure hunt, yellow tulle with a sheer overlay and tiered skirt, bunched at her waist.

She remembered when she arrived at Riverview as a child and felt so happy and accepted. She and Archie started a tradition of collecting leaves in the fall. Archie found an old shoe box, and every year they'd write a wish on the best leaves and deposit them in the box. The first year, Pandora wished that her mother would return, and Archie wished for a new puppy so his dog, Speckles, had a friend. Another year, Pandora wished that her father's shoulder would stop hurting, and that she'd get a new hairbrush for Christmas. Archie wished not to have to wear suspenders to church and to be the fastest runner in his class. They only stopped collecting leaves when Archie turned eighteen and Virginia teased him about their childish fun.

She often thought she'd pass the tradition on to her children—children she'd hoped to have with Owen. But that wouldn't happen now.

And there would be no more house parties, no more festive tea dresses sewn on Esther's sewing machine, no more discussions with Virginia about what colors best suited Pandora's fair hair and blue eyes. On Monday, she would have to go to the bank and withdraw the money her father set aside for secretarial school.

The Van Luyens' striped tabby cat, Thomas, jumped into her lap. She stroked his fur meditatively. She thought about what Lillian had said about people being born to be who they are and that there was nothing anyone could do about it. But what if Pandora had been born to live in a grand estate, to have a family she cherished and a career she was passionate about?

First, she had lost her mother, and now she had lost Owen. She couldn't keep losing the things she loved. Somehow she had to find a way to achieve everything she dreamed of.

Chapter Four

Pandora spent Sunday afternoon helping Esther in the kitchen. She was almost grateful to have work to do. It kept her from going over the previous days' events in her mind.

Everything about the Winthrops' house party had been humiliating. She was ashamed she'd left without thanking her hostess. But the thought of facing Mabel Winthrop while she twittered on about Owen and Lillian being the perfect couple had been too painful to contemplate.

Pandora told everyone at Riverview that she'd had a wonderful time. Her father wanted to hear about the tennis matches, and Esther was interested in the fruit compote they served with dinner, and Mary, the maid, wanted to know if the Winthrops' maids really had to change the guest room sheets twice a day.

But when she was alone in her room, she couldn't contain her disappointment. Everything that she had looked forward to—a glorious summer of parties and dances with Owen, the anticipation of their first kiss, Owen declaring his love for her—had disappeared before her eyes.

She had been so sure Owen would propose before he returned to Princeton. Instead of moving to New York to start secretarial school, she'd hoped she'd spend the fall at Riverview, planning their wedding and creating designs for her boutique. She had dreamed of a ceremony at the church in Hyde Park followed by a grand reception at Rosecliff. Her father would walk her down the aisle, looking dashing in a top hat and tails. At the reception he would give a speech. Pandora would sit at the head table, dazzling in a white gown, surrounded by the people she loved, and bursting with happiness.

On Sunday evening, Pandora cleared the dessert plates from Riverview's dining room while Maude and Virginia chatted at the table. Archie had gone upstairs to his room, and Robert Van Luyen was in his study, smoking a cigar. Earlier that day, Pandora had described to Virginia Owen's proposal to Lillian. It still hurt: Lillian's glee when she discovered the jewelry box under the hood. The way the other girls clustered around her. What hurt more than anything, though, was knowing that Owen had never loved Pandora.

"Vivian Clarkson is holding a bridal tea at Beechtree for Lillian next Sunday," Maude said, sipping her glass of port. Maude was a stout woman with thin lips and dyed brown hair. She wore a floral ankle-length dress with full sleeves, a rope of pearls hung around her neck.

"Lillian got engaged yesterday, isn't it a bit soon for a bridal tea?" Virginia asked. She flashed a cheeky smile. "Or had Vivian and Lillian been planning the tea for weeks, betting on when Owen would propose as if it were a horse race at Saratoga Springs?"

"Vivian was going to hold a welcome tea for Lillian anyway, it's a perfect excuse," Maude commented.

"Well, I can't go," Virginia declared. "The New School is holding a lecture on the literary legacy of Fanny Fern. Did you know that besides being a successful children's author, Fanny was the highest paid columnist of her day? In 1855, she was paid one hundred dollars a week for her column in the *New York Ledger*."

"I won't allow it. You don't know what kind of people attend those things." Maude pursed her lips. "The Clarksons are important people, I already said you'll go."

Virginia set her sherry glass on the table. She knew when her mother wouldn't change her mind.

"All right, I'll go," she relented. She glanced at Pandora. "But Pandora is coming with me. If I have to spend an afternoon with young women who've only heard of Romeo and Juliet because wearing a Juliet cap headpiece on your wedding day is all the rage, I need Pandora beside me."

At first, Pandora thought the last thing she wanted was to attend Lillian's bridal tea. And what would she wear? But just then, she had an idea. She realized what she could do with a roomful of Hyde Park society women. She may not be able to afford to open a boutique, but perhaps she could start by selling her dresses to Hyde Park women by word of mouth.

She could take the money her father had set aside for secretarial school and use it to buy fabric instead. Then she would sew gorgeous dresses for Virginia and herself to wear to the tea. Dresses unlike anything the women of Hyde Park had seen before. The older women in the Van Luyens' circle might stick to fashion designers they knew, but girls Pandora's age were more open to trying new things. And they admired Virginia. They would clamor to buy a gown similar to what she was wearing.

The more she considered her plan, the more excited she became. She was certain Virginia would help her, and she wanted to let her in on her plan immediately, but after dinner Maude whisked Virginia away to evening services at church.

The next morning, Pandora set aside her heartache over Owen and went straight to the bank. The teller handed her an envelope containing $186.29. She had never held so much money in her life.

Her father would be furious if he knew what she was doing. But this was her only option. She couldn't bear the idea of going to secretarial school and toiling away for years until she saved enough to open a boutique. This would give her the head start she needed.

At the fabric store on Main Street, Pandora sifted through bolts of muslins and ratinés, a new blend of silk and cotton that resembled linen. The muslins were pretty, and the ratinés came in forty-two colors, but neither of them would do. The girls at Lillian's tea were used to their mothers buying their dresses abroad. The fabric Pandora chose had to be special.

"I have just the thing," the saleslady said when Pandora explained what she wanted.

She brought out a catalog and placed it on the counter.

"We don't keep the fabrics on the showroom floor; we can't risk getting handprints on them," the saleslady said. "You can look through the catalog."

Pandora flipped through pages of the most beautiful fabrics she had ever seen: crepe de chine and crepe georgette, a chiffon that appeared light as air, a hand-embroidered lace, and a silk where the hue changed from pink to blue. The colors had names Pandora had never heard of: dusty pink and leaf green and old rose.

"How much is the crepe de chine?" Pandora inquired.

The saleslady named a price per yard that made Pandora gulp. The dresses would need embellishments too: pearl buttons, lace trim, glass beads to give them weight so they didn't flutter around when one moved.

"I'll take six yards in thirty-two-inch width," Pandora counted out the money in the envelope.

"You won't be sorry," the saleslady rung up her purchase. "Any dress in that fabric will look like it was made in Paris."

When Pandora arrived at Riverview, she found Virginia curled up on the sofa in the morning room. The sun made patterns on the Persian rug, and vases were filled with lilies of the valley.

"I met the most wonderful female poet at Byrdcliffe." Virginia put down the book she was reading. "Her name is Hilda Doolittle, she goes under the penname H.D. Since Mother won't let me go to the lecture at the New School on Sunday, I'm going to her reading on Saturday instead."

Pandora wondered if part of Virginia's interest in Byrdcliffe was Wolfgang, the poet she had mentioned. This wasn't the time to discuss it, though. Pandora had to tell Virginia about her idea.

"I'm sorry that I suggested you attend Lillian's bridal tea," Virginia continued on. "It's probably the last place you want to be." She smiled wickedly. "Though we could put molasses in the bottom of Lillian's teacup. That always worked with Archie when I was angry at him."

"It's not your fault that Owen proposed to Lillian," Pandora offered. "Anyway, I have an idea and I need your help."

Virginia listened while Pandora described her plan.

"I'll have to sew both dresses in five days, but I think I can do it," Pandora finished. She looked at Virginia anxiously.

Virginia sprang up and strode over to the telephone.

"What are you doing?"

"I'm calling Beechtree to make sure you're invited," Virginia announced, a smile curling around her mouth. "We're going to upstage Lillian at her own bridal tea. I can't imagine anything more fun."

～

Pandora spent hours at the sewing machine every night after everyone went to bed. She couldn't let her father find out what she was doing, and she still had to help Esther in the kitchen during the day.

Finally, on Sunday, the dresses were finished. Virginia's dress was bottle-green crepe de chine. The bell sleeves and tiered skirt would swish when she walked, and Pandora sewed glass beads to the hem. Her own dress was dusty-pink crepe de georgette. The skirt was shorter than what she usually wore. It was streaked with gold thread and terribly full. It would look striking on her slender figure.

The Van Luyens' chauffeur, Daniel, drove Pandora and Virginia to Beechtree. Virginia muttered that her mother only offered the chauffeur because she was afraid that if Virginia drove herself, they wouldn't actually make it to the party. Pandora didn't care why Daniel took them. When they arrived, it felt wonderful to be helped out of the car by Daniel in his smart chauffeur uniform with gold buttons and black cap.

Pandora stood for a moment taking in the estate. Lillian's father, Leland Clarkson, had made part of his money from the railroads that stretched from New York to Colorado. After that, he invested in coal mines to fuel the engines and founded a steel company to build the trains.

Inside, Lillian stood in the middle of a group of girls, showing off her diamond ring. Pandora hadn't expected how much it would hurt to see Lillian, in a turquoise silk dress and looking even more radiant than last weekend.

As the girls moved into the living room, Pandora stayed a few paces behind. The room had a timbered ceiling and paneled walls decorated with hunting trophies. A stone fireplace took up one wall, and round tables with pedestal legs and glass tops were arranged throughout.

Lillian's mother, Vivian, walked toward her. Vivian was quite young, with Lillian's brunette curls and brown eyes behind dark lashes.

"I'm Vivian Clarkson. You must be Pandora," said Vivian. "I saw you playing tennis at the Winthrops' party last week at Rosecliff."

Pandora wasn't here to talk about tennis. She had to get the guests to notice her dress.

"I've played since I was a child." Pandora nodded, eyeing Vivian's dress. "What a lovely dress. Is it a Molyneux?"

Vivian glanced at Pandora in surprise.

"I bought it last year in Monte Carlo. How did you know?"

Edward Molyneux was one of Pandora's favorite British designers. He was opposed to any kind of adornments, and his dresses were known for their simplicity.

"Molyneux has one of the most popular salons in Paris," Pandora said offhandedly. She didn't reveal that she'd never been to Paris, that she'd only read about Molyneux. "Greta Garbo is a big fan."

"Lillian and I hadn't packed enough dresses for all the parties and dances Owen and his family invited us to while we were in Monte Carlo," Vivian recalled, gazing fondly across the room at Lillian. "I knew right away that something was growing between Owen and Lillian. They really are perfect for each other."

Pandora expected to feel upset, but she found Vivian warm and friendly. Pandora couldn't help but like her.

"I'm sure it will be a beautiful wedding," Pandora said.

"The bride makes a wedding beautiful," Vivian said wisely. "And being surrounded by her friends. Lillian didn't have many friends growing up. She missed more than a year of school."

Pandora remembered that Lillian attended the exclusive all-girls' Spence School in New York. She had assumed that Lillian was popular.

"Lillian doesn't talk about it, but it isn't a secret." Vivian noticed Pandora's surprised expression. "She contracted polio when she was ten, during the New York epidemic of 1916. It's not so bad for smaller children, but Lillian nearly died. She could hardly breathe, and we worried that she'd be paralyzed. I didn't leave her sick room for months.

"When she improved, the doctor insisted we move to the mountains for her lungs. By the time we returned to New York, the girls at school had formed new cliques, and Lillian was left out," Vivian said. "In a way, it brought us closer, but young women need girls their own age to confide in."

Pandora knew she should feel sorry for Lillian, but it didn't excuse Lillian's bad behavior. And in a way, Pandora was envious. Vivian had changed her whole life to care for her daughter. Meanwhile, Pandora's mother hadn't loved Pandora enough to stay.

As Vivian led Pandora into the dining room, Pandora wondered if Vivian and Lillian had a deep mother-daughter connection that Pandora had never known. Pandora longed for something like that.

The bridal tea was held in the glass atrium. Old-fashioneds were served in glass jars, and there was champagne and fruit punch. Maids passed around plates of deviled eggs and oysters on the half shell. Pandora had never tried oysters before. They were prepared in a cream sauce and baked with bread crumbs and a squeeze of lemon. Pandora couldn't wait to tell Esther about them.

After they finished eating, the conversation moved from where Lillian and Owen would spend their honeymoon to what style wedding dress Lillian should wear.

"When I get married, I'm going to ask Pandora to sew my trousseau," Virginia announced.

Pandora smiled inwardly. Virginia had vowed she would never get married. She was only trying to help.

"I didn't know Pandora designed dresses," Lucy Vanderbilt commented.

"Pandora works for the Van Luyens." Lillian smiled sweetly at Lucy. "Our housekeeper, Alice, does our sewing. It's wonderful to have someone available to sew on a button or fix a zipper."

The heat rose in Pandora, and it took all her willpower to hold her tongue.

"Pandora is much too talented to do that kind of sewing." Virginia smoothed her skirt. "She made my dress, and the one she's wearing." She sipped her cocktail. "Pandora's father is Willie Carmichael; he played at Wimbledon. A while ago, he was asked to play at Madison Square Garden. His photo was in the newspapers. Pandora was wearing one of her dresses and she was in the photo too. Afterward, the phone didn't stop ringing with women who wanted to know where Pandora got her dress."

Pandora chuckled to herself. Archie often said Virginia should be an actress. She had no problem telling little white lies.

It was true that Willie was asked to play at Madison Square Garden, but only because his former pupil, the French tennis star Suzanne Lenglen, was competing. The newspaper did carry a photo, but Pandora was in the back, and no one could see her dress. The only phone call she received was from a reporter wanting to know if Suzanne was retiring after her win at the French national championships in Auteuil.

Lucy Vanderbilt and the other girls studied Pandora's and Virginia's dresses with new interest.

"It is difficult to buy one's whole wardrobe in Paris," Lucy Vanderbilt reflected. She turned to Virginia. "That is the prettiest fabric. It reminds me of Chanel's latest collection."

Pandora couldn't help but be pleased with Lillian's tight-lipped smile. She was sure the other girls at the bridal tea would ask her to design dresses for them.

~

For the next week, Pandora jumped every time the phone rang. She was certain one of Lillian's guests would order a dress. But the calls were never for her. Her stomach was tied in knots, and she had to force herself to eat.

She dreaded what would happen if her father found out what she had done. She could tell him the truth, but he might get so angry, he'd stop speaking to her. And she'd feel so ashamed. It was better to wait and hope that her plan worked.

On Saturday, Pandora was sitting in her bedroom reading a book on Madeleine Vionnet when her father burst through the door. She had never seen him look so angry.

"I came across this in the drawer," he blurted as he waved an envelope. "You were supposed to mail it last week."

Pandora gulped. It was the registration paperwork for secretarial school. And it was late.

"I went to the bank to withdraw the money and send it myself." Willie kept talking. "The teller said you already took out the money. What did you do with it?"

Pandora hung her head. She twisted her hands nervously. She had hoped to have something to show for her plan by the time he found out, but it was too late. "I bought fabric to sew some dresses."

Pandora explained her plan and how it hadn't worked. When she finished, she could see a vein pulsing in her father's forehead.

"That money was for secretarial school, so you'll have some way to support yourself. I'm getting older, the arthritis in my shoulder is worse. Last week, I had to cancel one of my tennis lessons because it hurt too much to move my arm." He glared at her. "What will you do when I can't teach tennis and the Van Luyens let me go?"

"That's why I want to open a boutique," Pandora said urgently. "So I can take care of both of us."

"Do you really think that's possible? We have no means, and you have no clientele. You're only invited places because of the Van Luyens," he scoffed. "This is my fault. I shouldn't have raised you this way."

"I don't understand," Pandora said, perplexed.

"When your mother left, I took this job because I wanted to protect you from living in poor circumstances in New York. But living at Riverview has only filled you with fanciful notions. Secretarial school might not get you a prestigious degree, but you'd learn skills that are worth something. Now you'll end up working at a factory or married to someone you don't love."

"It's not your fault, and I want to be a designer because I love creating dresses."

"Your mother loved dresses, and look what happened," he snapped. "You'll end up like her. You'll get a job in a department store. You'll grow tired of being on your feet all day and being talked down to by women who used to be your friends." His eyes flashed. "Then what will you do?"

"I'll find a way to pay you back," Pandora said determinedly. "I promise. Then I'll figure out how to open a boutique in Hyde Park and a bigger one in New York." She waved at the book she was reading.

"Madeleine Vionnet has a salon in Paris, and last year she opened one on Fifth Avenue. If she could do it, why can't I?"

Willie's expression was filled with rage and something new. It took a moment for Pandora to realize what it was. It was the look he had whenever he talked about her mother. Pain mixed with defeat.

"Because you're Pandora Carmichael, and your father is a tennis instructor." He stood up. "The only life I could offer you isn't good enough. Now you've wasted your only shot at a decent future. And you've put my future in jeopardy too. That money was going to benefit both of us. It's gone, and there's no way to get it back. Esther is waiting for you in the kitchen. She needs help with the meatballs."

After he left, Pandora put away the book and tied on her apron. She loved her father; she could live with his anger but not his disappointment. She had squandered everything he had saved for their future. She had to get the money back and make him believe in her again. If only she knew how.

Chapter Five

On Monday, Pandora sat in the reception area of Thomas Maisel Dresses on Broadway in New York. She wore a V-necked blouse with a pleated skirt and short white gloves. Four girls sat on the chairs beside her, all wearing cloche hats and clutching the same folded-up newspaper in their hands.

The moment that Pandora had seen the advertisement, she began planning how to get to New York for the interview. The opportunity was too good to pass up. Pandora hadn't told Virginia about the fight with her father. She didn't want to ask for Virginia's help again. She got a ride with the Van Luyens' chauffeur into New York, and now she waited alongside the other girls for the receptionist to call her name.

Thomas Maisel wasn't a well-known designer like Paul Poiret or Norman Hartnell, but Pandora had seen his dresses in the window of a boutique in Hyde Park. He had a showroom in New York, and he was looking for a girl Friday. Pandora hadn't heard the term before. She looked it up and found that it meant a woman who did many different jobs in an office. Pandora thought she'd be perfect for the position. She might not have had secretarial training, but she was well organized, and she knew everything about dress design.

"Miss Carmichael," the receptionist put down the telephone. "You can go inside. Miss Patterson will see you now."

Pandora tried to hide her disappointment. She had hoped Thomas Maisel would interview her so she could impress him with her knowledge and passion for design. Instead, she was greeted by an older woman wearing a navy dress.

"Please have a seat." Miss Patterson pointed to a wooden chair. She flipped through the papers on her desk. "I didn't receive your résumé."

"I didn't bring one." Pandora gulped.

"You can tell me about your experience instead." Miss Patterson took out a long notepad. "Where did you attend secretarial school?"

"Well, I didn't," Pandora began nervously.

"That's all right, not all girls have," Miss Patterson cut in. "How fast can you type?"

"I've used a typewriter before, but I've never timed myself," Pandora answered honestly. She had used a typewriter a few times to type up the plays that she and Virginia had performed as teenagers.

"Dictation?"

"I've never taken dictation, but I'm a fast learner."

"That's odd, most employers give dictation." Miss Patterson frowned. "What kind of filing systems have you used? Mr. Maisel is particular about his filing."

"Well, none, but . . ."

"Miss Carmichael," Miss Patterson interrupted. "What have you done at an office?"

Pandora pulled at her gloves. "I haven't worked in an office, but I know everything about dress design. I've been designing dresses since I was fifteen. I can show you my sketches if you like."

Miss Patterson leaned forward in her chair. She had narrow cheekbones and brown eyes that seemed too large for her face.

"I don't care if you're the protégé of Coco Chanel." Her tone grew impatient. "Do you know what a girl Friday is?"

"I had to look it up," Pandora admitted.

"It means a secretary who also does all the other things in an office. Mr. Maisel is very busy; he needs someone who can make his lunch reservations and pick up his tickets to shows on Broadway and type and file. The one thing he doesn't need is a girl who aspires to be a fashion designer. Secretarial skills are the main requirement of the job, and you don't have any."

Pandora looked past Miss Patterson to the framed photos on the wall. She had to get this job. She had no other options.

"I plan to use part of my salary to take night courses in typing and dictation," she said. "I know I can do it. You just have to give me a chance."

Miss Patterson wrote something on her notepad.

"I was your age once; getting that first job seems impossible. How can one gain experience if one doesn't have any to begin with?" she sympathized. "But I wouldn't be doing my job if I hired you over more-qualified applicants." She handed the piece of paper to Pandora. "This is the address of a dress factory on Thirty-Ninth Street. They're always looking for girls to work on the assembly line, and you don't need any previous experience."

Pandora slipped it into her purse and stood up. She had to maintain her dignity.

"Thank you, that's very kind."

"Don't thank me yet. The hours are long and the pay is low." She glanced at Pandora's lace-up pumps that had once been Virginia's. "You might want to get more comfortable shoes. Good luck, Miss Carmichael. I hope it all works out."

Pandora walked out into the street. The feeling of rejection washed over her. She couldn't work in a factory—the salary wouldn't cover her rent for a room in New York, and if she commuted, all the money she earned would go to train fare to Hyde Park, and there would be no time to work on her designs.

She had been so sure she'd get the job, now she didn't know what she'd do. No matter how many places she applied, she'd get the same response. She supposed she could work as a cook or a maid, but she'd have the same difficulties that she'd have working in a factory, long hours, low pay, and no time to pursue her dreams.

She wondered if this was what her mother faced before she worked in the department store. But Laura hadn't needed to work, she preferred being in the department store with other women rather than taking care of Pandora at home. Yet in a way, their situations were similar. Laura wasn't good enough to have the life she wanted, and neither was Pandora.

The doors that Pandora thought had opened to her during the Winthrops' house party were still as firmly closed as the lids on Esther's cookie jars.

There was a coffee shop on the corner, and she longed for a cold drink or an ice cream. But she couldn't afford it. She tossed the folded-up newspaper advertisement in the garbage and waited for Daniel to pick her up. She had no idea what to do. Her father wasn't speaking to her, she had no job, no funds, and even secretarial school was out of reach now.

~

That afternoon, Pandora sat at the table in the Van Luyens' kitchen and read the invitation again.

ADELE AND MILTON ENRIGHT REQUEST THE PLEASURE OF PANDORA CARMICHAEL'S COMPANY AT THEIR ANNUAL SUMMER PARTY, JULY 23RD–JULY 25TH, 1926, BLYTHDALE, HYDE PARK.

The beautifully embossed invitation had arrived that morning. Even the envelope was lovely, thick parchment sealed with red wax.

But she wished she had never received the invitation, that Owen had never mentioned it to his mother. Now she had to go; it would be impolite to refuse.

She ran her fingers over the lettering. How could she spend another weekend listening to Lillian debating whether her bouquet should have roses or lilies of the valley? And she'd have to see Owen. The thought of having to engage him in conversation made her heart contract as if someone had cut off her circulation.

The door to the Van Luyens' kitchen opened, and Virginia entered wearing a drop-waisted floral dress and T-strap sandals. She had a head-band wrapped around her dark, wavy hair, and she carried a brown paper bag.

"You're clever, sitting here in the nice, cool kitchen," Virginia said to Pandora. She set the bag on the table. "I've been shopping, and it's so hot. I'm desperate for something cold to drink."

The kitchen, with its light-colored stone floors and slab-marble counters, was the coolest room at Riverview. Double-sash windows let in the breeze from the river, and copper pots and pans hung from the ceiling.

Virginia poured a glass of water and took the items out of the bag. Two slim books and three chocolate bars.

"Why did you buy poetry by Christina Rossetti and Elizabeth Barrett Browning?" Pandora picked up a book. "And there's plenty of chocolate in the pantry."

"These are Baby Ruth bars." Virginia opened one and handed half to Pandora. "They're new at the grocery stores, and they're already the most popular candy bar in America."

Pandora bit into one. It was delicious, loaded with peanuts and caramel and nougat.

"And the poetry?" Pandora asked.

"It's for Wolfgang. He's read all the male poets, Ralph Waldo Emerson and Longfellow and Walt Whitman," Virginia said. "He isn't familiar with any female poets. It got me thinking." She ran her fingers over the cover. "Men control the publishing houses and literary magazines; it's so difficult for female authors to get noticed. I want to host my own salons in New York. Anyone can come and listen, but it will feature female authors and poets. Similar to what Gertrude Stein is doing at her salons in Paris."

"Your mother would never allow it," Pandora reminded her.

"I won't tell her. I'll use money from my trust to rent a space, and I'm taking classes at Barnard. When my mother is staying at the townhouse in New York, I'll say I'm going to study with a friend in the evenings." She looked at Pandora. "Wolfgang thinks it's a wonderful idea. We're going to talk about it this weekend."

"You're going to Byrdcliffe again?" Pandora's brow creased.

Last Saturday, Virginia had borrowed Archie's car for the whole day. She'd begged Pandora to go along with her little white lie, saying that she was going to New York to buy shoes for Felicity Dinsmore's wedding. Everything would have worked out, except that Virginia wasn't back by evening, and Archie had a date.

Archie hadn't minded. His date was with Lucy Vanderbilt, and he had only agreed to it to make his mother happy. He was content to send his regrets and spend the evening listening to his favorite radio programs and playing Louis Armstrong records on the phonograph.

But Lucy was very disappointed, and her aunt, Louise Vanderbilt, was furious. Lucy had been staying with Louise and her husband, Frederick, for the summer, and Louise thought Archie would make the perfect suitor for Lucy.

Archie brought Lucy two dozen roses the next day to apologize, and Virginia promised Archie she would never return his car late again.

"Where would you find a space you can afford, and what kind of people would come to the readings?" Pandora asked.

Virginia ate her candy bar. She suppressed a smile.

"You're afraid it will be somewhere sordid; uptown in Harlem or down in Greenwich Village," she said. "But Harlem is one of the most exciting places to be. A few weeks ago, I saw Zora Neale Hurston walking down the sidewalk with the poet Langston Hughes. I'd just finished reading Zora's short story 'Spunk' in *The New Negro* anthology."

"What were you doing in Harlem?" Pandora asked uncomfortably.

Pandora had never been to Harlem, but she had read about it in the newspaper. It wasn't the kind of place that young women in Virginia's social circle went.

"The whole point is to be around new voices in the arts," Virginia continued on. "I'm not going to discover them at the Dinsmores' afternoon teas, where the most risqué conversation is about whether to spend a week in the fall in Palm Beach or wait until winter."

Pandora reflected on how different she and Virginia were. Virginia was like a bird, continually fluttering her wings to escape its cage. Pandora was the opposite; she loved everything about Hyde Park. The stately mansions perched on the riverbank, the apple orchards and country lanes. Fall, when the weather grew cooler and the sun-dappled trees formed arches over the pavement. She even loved Main Street, with its dress shops and library, and the pharmacy where the owner had known her since she was a child and allowed her to buy things on credit.

And yet in some ways they were the same. Virginia felt trapped by her own future. Just as Pandora's father wanted her to go to secretarial school, Virginia's parents expected her to get married and run a large household just like her mother.

That's why Virginia was so adamant that young women have choices.

"Wolfgang knows everyone in New York. We're going to make a list of people to invite. Don't worry, I'm not going to borrow Archie's car. I'll take the train. I'll be back by Sunday at dinnertime."

Pandora's eyes widened.

"You're going to spend the night at Byrdcliffe?"

Pandora had never asked Virginia whether she was a virgin, but she assumed she was. For all Virginia's love of the arts, she attended church every Sunday. And like Pandora, she was only twenty.

"Don't look at me like that, I'll have my own cabin," Virginia said in response to Pandora's horrified expression. "I'm not going to sleep with Wolfgang. I'm not going to sleep with anyone until I'm ready." She gave a small smile. "Sex should be a woman's choice, like everything else. I'm not interested in sex right now; I'm much more excited about literature."

Pandora breathed a sigh of relief. In a way, it would have been nice if Virginia was more experienced. Then Pandora could ask the questions that spun around her head. At the same time, she didn't want to picture her dearest friend doing things she couldn't imagine doing herself.

"You'll be in New York in the fall too. You can attend my salons," Virginia urged. "There won't be anyone to stop you."

But Pandora wouldn't be in New York in the fall. She hadn't told Virginia about her failed attempt to get a job.

She picked up the invitation and sighed. Maybe she should attend the Enrights' house party. Perhaps something good would happen; she had run out of other ideas. And she had to think about her father. Everything he had saved was gone. If she didn't do something soon, he might never talk to her again. And she couldn't blame him.

Something inside her turned over and clicked into place. Like the motor on Archie's car.

"I have to respond to this invitation." Pandora set the envelope on the table. "Then I'm going to sew a new bathing suit; the Enrights have a swimming pool. I saw the design in *Harper's Bazaar*. Yellow and blue stripes with a blue belt."

~

Blythdale was even more spectacular than she had imagined. The house was three stories built in the Italianate style, with a low-pitched roof and overhanging eaves supported by stone brackets. Belvedere towers afforded views of the river, and Pandora was charmed by the marble cupola and pedimented doors and windows. Pine trees lined the approach to the house, and a stone fountain stood in the middle of the circular driveway. The grounds boasted a separate garage, stables, and proper English garden.

"Are you sure you'll be all right?" Archie asked Pandora as he parked his car behind a black Rolls-Royce Phantom. A young man in a straw boater hat jumped out and opened the passenger door for a girl wearing a yellow summer dress and cloche hat. The man took the girl's hand, and Pandora felt a twinge of envy. They both seemed so happy and in love. They probably did this sort of thing every weekend: drove their fancy car to house parties and enjoyed swimming and dancing.

"Don't worry about me, I'll be fine." Pandora pulled her attention back to Archie. "I don't expect you to take care of me."

"There's nothing I'd like better." Archie grinned. "But I promised Lucy we'd go swimming as soon as I arrived," he said as he turned off the ignition. "Apparently two dozen roses from the most expensive florist in Hyde Park wasn't enough to make up for breaking our date." His expression turned serious. "Owen is a fool; he doesn't know what he gave up. You're worth a dozen Lillian Clarksons."

"Archie, there you are!" Lucy strode toward them. "Everyone's waiting for us at the swimming pool."

A straw hat was perched on Lucy Vanderbilt's blond curls. She wore a cotton caftan with a wide sash tied around her waist that showed off her long, shapely legs.

"I haven't unpacked my bag," Archie said to Lucy. "I need to get my bathing trunks."

"The Enrights have a drawerful in the pool house," Lucy replied as she took his arm.

Archie turned to Pandora.

"Are you coming?"

Pandora gulped. She wasn't ready to face Lillian and Owen together.

"Go ahead, I'll be right out," Pandora said brightly. "I'm going to find the powder room first."

Inside, the house was cool and dark; thick curtains shielded the furniture from the sun. The entry had stone floors painted with pink flowers. The walls were the exact color of an avocado, with recessed molding and gold trim. A huge chandelier dangled from the ceiling.

Pandora took what she thought was the hallway leading to the powder room, but it brought her to a library. She poked her head inside. Walnut bookshelves holding leather-bound books lined the walls. A rolltop desk took up the center of the room, and a chandelier hung from the ceiling. A spiral staircase led to a second floor of books, where there were leather chairs and a great stone fireplace. The walls were painted a red that was so rich it was almost plum colored, and the floors were covered with floral rugs.

"It's a wonderful room, isn't it," a female voice said. A woman stood next to the window. She looked to be in her late forties. She had light brown hair, wide green eyes, a warm smile, and the smooth complexion of a film star.

"I didn't mean to barge in," Pandora said. "I was looking for the powder room and took a wrong turn."

"I'm happy to have company," the woman said as she held out her hand. "I'm Adele Enright."

"Pandora Carmichael." Pandora shook her hand. "What a beautiful room! I'd love to have a library like this one day, filled with books on fashion. My dream is to be a fashion designer and open my own boutique."

Pandora stopped. She was babbling to a woman she just met.

"Do you study fashion design at school?" Adele asked.

Adele sat down and motioned for Pandora to do the same.

Pandora was certain that all the other guests at the house party came from wealthy families. She couldn't tell Adele that her father had wanted her to attend secretarial school, but she couldn't hide who she was.

Pandora shook her head. "Not at the moment. I live at Riverview; my father is the Van Luyens' tennis instructor."

"That's right." Adele's eyes lit with recognition. "Your father is Willie Carmichael. Milton and I saw him play at Wimbledon years ago. All the other players were terrified of his serve."

She expected Adele to react the way that Lillian did, with a touch of disdain. Instead, Adele's smile broadened.

"All my children played tennis," Adele said. "Harley wasn't very keen, he preferred performing plays," she said fondly. "I spent a great deal of his childhood watching home productions of *The Tale of Peter Rabbit.*"

Adele's gaze turned to framed photographs arranged on the desk. There was a photo of four children wearing tennis whites and holding racquets. The older two boys had Adele's light brown hair, and the girl had pretty blond curls and round cheeks. The youngest boy looked awkward and gangly, like a puppy that hadn't grown into its paws.

"Are these your children?" Pandora asked.

Adele moved to the desk.

"The oldest is Alistair. He never stopped exploring when he was a child, he got in all sorts of trouble. When he was four, he climbed into his sister's dollhouse and got stuck. When he was eleven, he decided to take the car for a drive. He thought driving would be as simple as turning on the engine." She laughed. She pointed to the boy next to him. "That's Frank. He was born sixteen months after Alistair. He could never sit still long enough to finish his homework. But he was wonderful at sports."

Adele turned away from the photograph. She walked to the window.

"Alistair and Frank were killed in the war. Alistair died at the Battle of Cantigny and Frank was killed four months later in the Somme Offensive," she said slowly. "When they were young, I never thought any harm would come to them. Milton was so proud when they shipped off, shiny as new coins in their khakis and smart caps. Somehow, I knew differently. I suppose it was mother's intuition. All those months of praying to keep them safe didn't help."

Pandora's father had been badly injured in the war. Willie spent months recuperating at a hospital in the South of France. His wounded shoulder still bothered him, and the arthritis only made it worse. But at least he'd made it home.

"I'm so sorry for your loss," Pandora said.

Adele moved back to the photograph.

"The girl is Annie. She's five years older than Harley, and she always behaved like a mother to him. She loved to bathe Harley when he was a baby, and she insisted on feeding him. Our poor maid was always washing food stains from her clothes. Annie, her husband, George, and their two children live in San Francisco. I miss her, I hardly see them.

"The youngest is Harley. He's at Princeton with Archie and Owen. He was the kindest child, always bringing in stray dogs and giving fruit from our trees to neighbors. The cook would go to make an apple pie, and all the apples would be gone from the pantry." She touched the photo. "He's still the same. He goes with me to deliver food at the shelters in New York."

"It must have been great fun when they were children." Pandora reflected on her own childhood. "I never had brothers and sisters. Someday, I want my own family."

Adele turned to Pandora. She seemed to make an effort to put away the past.

"You will. There's no reason why you can't have a family and study fashion and open a boutique. I was married at nineteen, I didn't know what I wanted. It's different these days. Young women can attend college or go abroad. They have time to figure out what's important to them. So many things are changing, but there's still a long way to go." Adele changed the subject. "I don't believe in class distinctions. Young men or women shouldn't be limited by their birth station, only by their aspirations. I feel the same way about marriage. Marriage shouldn't be about merging dynasties. The only reason two people should get married is because they love and respect each other."

Pandora listened to Adele with interest. She had never heard anyone in the Van Luyens' social circle talk this way. At Maude Van Luyen's afternoon teas, the discussion was often about who was getting engaged to whom and whether their names were in the New York Social Register.

But Pandora didn't believe that a society woman like Adele could really be so open minded. She thought about how her mother had been treated. After Willie lost Wimbledon, and then was injured in the war, she received no more invitations to cocktail parties at the Astors' mansion in Newport. And now Pandora was seeing the same pattern play out in her own life.

She had to figure out how to make it on her own. Perhaps Pandora didn't need to attend fashion school. Instead, she could keep teaching herself from books and magazines. But if she went to secretarial school like her father wanted, she'd have no time to work on her designs—and she still needed to earn back the tuition money she'd spent on fabric.

And even if she did fall in love and get married, her husband probably wouldn't be able to afford a maid or nanny. In the evenings, she'd be at home, supervising the children, cleaning the house, cooking the meals.

Marrying Owen would have solved all her problems and given her everything she wanted: love, marriage, a family, and the means to pursue her fashion-design dreams. She didn't know what she would do now.

It was easy for women like Virginia and Lillian Clarkson. They could throw money at their problems. It was different for Pandora. Her dreams would fade away. She'd be left with a few pretty dresses stored in a closet, like her mother's rack of dresses.

"I'm being the worst hostess," Adele said. "I've talked on and on when you're just looking for the powder room." She led Pandora to the door. "I'll show you where it is, and then you should go out to the pool for refreshments."

After Pandora brushed her hair and reapplied the lipstick that Virginia insisted she wear, she walked back down the hallway. She heard voices from a room at the end. The door was half open, and two young men stood close to each other. Their expressions were serious, and the taller man crossed his arms, as if they were having an argument.

They moved apart when they saw her.

"I'm sorry," she said from the doorway. "I didn't mean to interrupt."

The door opened wider. The taller man waved her inside.

"You're not interrupting, we're glad you're here," he said. "We need someone like you."

"Someone like me?" she repeated.

"A woman. We're rehearsing a play, and we don't have anyone to read the female lines," he explained. "You can do it for us."

Both of the men were about her age. The taller one looked familiar. He was very fair, with blond hair that flopped over his forehead, and he had a smattering of golden hair on his arms. He wore white trousers and a white V-necked vest with a blue bow tie, and two-tone Oxford shoes.

Perhaps she had seen him at the Winthrops' party.

"I'm not good at acting," Pandora said.

"You just have to read from the script." He held out a thin book. "It's for the Triangle Club. That's the theater troupe at Princeton." He pointed to the other man. "This is Preston Stevens, the playwright, and I'm Harley Enright."

Pandora realized why Harley looked familiar. He was the youngest child in the photograph. He must have inherited his blond hair and lean build from his father, but his green eyes and high cheekbones were from Adéle.

"Pandora Carmichael." She introduced herself. "Are you sure you don't want someone else? Some of the girls here must have taken drama classes."

Harley handed her the book.

"You'll do perfectly," he said with a smile. His teeth were very white. Pandora noticed how handsome he was, and a warm spark shot through her body. "Don't overdo the love scene." He waved at Preston. "Preston tends to use flowery language."

They rehearsed for thirty minutes. Pandora enjoyed reading the lines; it reminded her of the plays she and Virginia and Archie performed as children. Then Preston said he was hungry.

"Would you like to join us?" Harley asked. "We're going to raid the kitchen."

"Isn't there food by the swimming pool?" Pandora wondered.

Harley leaned forward conspiratorially. "Preston tells everyone he's too pale to go in the sun, but the truth is, he can't swim," he confided. "I promised I'd stay with him. Our cook is protective of her kitchen. She doesn't like guests rearranging the dishes."

Harley had an infectious smile. She found herself smiling back at him.

"I'll remember that if I want a cup of warm milk at night."

She was tempted to join them, but she had to face Lillian and Owen sometime.

"Thank you, but I'll go out to the pool," she said.

Harley held out his hand. His expression was playful as if they now were members of some secret club.

"It was nice to meet you, Pandora Carmichael. If Preston's play gets produced, I'll be sure to send you a ticket."

~

The swimming pool was at the end of the gardens, overlooking the Hudson River with a pool house and a large area for sunbathing. The grounds were stunning. A walkway lined with statues led down to a marble pergola. Stone benches were scattered around a manicured lawn, and clipped hedges framed a clock garden made entirely of pink carnations.

If only the weekend was about to unfold the way Pandora had imagined when Owen had first mentioned it. She and Owen would have been planning their honeymoon. After everyone had gone to bed, they would have strolled through the clock garden. It wouldn't matter if anyone saw them; they'd be engaged.

"Pandora, come join us." Owen's voice interrupted her thoughts. "Lillian and I were talking about you. We're planning on putting in a tennis court at our new house. Could your father advise us?"

Owen stood with Lillian and a few other young people in front of the pool house. They all wore bathing suits and held French 75 cocktails. Pandora was glad she was wearing her new bathing suit. She had paired it with one of Virginia's scarves, and she felt stylish and confident.

"Owen wants a clay court, but I prefer grass," Lillian put in. "Grass courts are more attractive, and you can use them for outdoor parties."

Lillian's tone was as sugary as the penny bags of candy Pandora used to buy at the pharmacy, but Pandora saw through her. Everything about Lillian—the casual way she linked her arm through Owen's, how she waved her left hand in the air—claimed her victory.

"You already found a house?" Pandora asked, hoping her voice didn't show the pain that welled up inside.

"We started looking," Lillian corrected her. "Not for anything in Manhattan. Daddy is buying us a townhouse on Park Avenue. We want a place in New York so we can expose our children to museums and theater. The summer estate is where they can run and swim and be with their friends." Her mouth formed its signature pout. "Owen speaks so fondly of his summers at Rosecliff and Riverview; I almost feel left out."

If Virginia were there, she would whisper that Lillian had probably never stepped foot in a museum, and the only reason she attended the theater was to show off a new dress. But Virginia was at Byrdcliffe, and

Pandora had to face Lillian alone. She wasn't going to play Lillian's game anymore. It was time she stood up for herself.

"I'll ask my father to help you once you find a house," Pandora offered. She brushed an imaginary thread from her scarf. "That is if he's not in the South of France."

"The South of France," Lillian repeated, as if Pandora had announced her father was taking a boat to Antarctica.

"Didn't I mention it?" Pandora asked sweetly. "His old pupil Suzanne Lenglen wrote and begged him to visit. She spends the winters at Beaulieu-sur-Mer on the Riviera. She won Wimbledon six times. They call her la Divine, that's French for 'the goddess.' She's more popular in Europe than Marlene Dietrich."

Lillian's face turned as pale as the creamy stone flanking the swimming pool.

"My parents tried to get her autograph at Wimbledon years ago, there was too much of a crowd," Lillian said. "I didn't know your father knew her."

Pandora took her time answering. She wanted to make sure she had everyone's attention.

"He coached her when he was living in the South of France. She sends a telegram before every tournament to thank him."

Pandora didn't mention that Willie had been in a rehabilitation hospital when he worked at the tennis club in Nice. His shoulder hurt so much from the gunshot wound he received during the war that sometimes he could barely hold a racquet. But he had no choice. He had to send money home to Laura and Pandora. It didn't do any good, though. Laura left him days after his ship docked in New York.

Lillian took Owen's arm. This time it seemed more out of fear than possession.

"We'll find a house before Christmas," Lillian said firmly. "Or we could build one. Then it would be exactly the way we want." She turned to Owen. "Don't you agree?"

For the first time, Owen seemed slightly hesitant.

"I'm not sure, architects are expensive, and my father gave us a budget."

Lillian squeezed Owen's arm more tightly. Pandora could see the veins on his wrist.

"Don't be silly, your father will do anything we ask," Lillian persisted. "I'll talk to him about it tonight."

Pandora took a sip of her drink, content.

~

Pandora spent the rest of the afternoon sitting by the pool by herself. Archie played Marco Polo with some of the other guests, and Pandora watched them. In the early evening she returned to her guest room to get ready for dinner.

The guest room reminded Pandora of an illustration of a Renaissance palazzo in Italy. The floor was black and white marble squares, and the velvet wallpaper had a gold-and-silver pattern. A ceramic pitcher stood on a stand next to a little sink, and the bed had a heavy wooden headboard.

Outside the window, cars came and went in the driveway. Two men emerged from the house that Pandora recognized as Harley and Preston. Preston got into the driver's seat of a red car. Harley leaned into the window, and they had an animated conversation.

Pandora was about to turn away when a woman caught her attention. It was Adele Enright, hurrying from the side of the house to the driveway. She linked her arm through Harley's, and they walked up the steps. They paused for a moment at the door, and Adele looked up at Harley's face.

Adele had spoken so fondly of Harley, Pandora expected to see love and affection in her expression. Instead, she saw something different, something peculiar. It was worry mixed with fear.

Chapter Six

Pandora descended the staircase to the living room for cocktails. Tonight, nothing about her gown was understated. She was determined to outshine Lillian.

She was very proud of her dress. She'd gotten her inspiration from one of Jeanne Lanvin's earlier designs, a robe de style, which she was famous for. The pink satin bodice had cap sleeves shaped like oysters, and the narrow waist and dropped skirt complemented her slim figure. The skirt was fuller than the popular flapper gowns, almost like a ballerina's tutu. Pandora added a gauze sash around the waist and gold appliqués to the skirt. The finished effect was worth every penny that the fabric had cost her. Just a touch of lipstick offset her creamy complexion. She glowed.

All eyes turned to her when she entered. She knew they would. She resembled the actress Gloria Swanson in the movie *Beyond the Rocks*, with Rudolph Valentino. Sleek and elegant.

Her intention wasn't to make Owen jealous or even to attract other men. She wanted to prove something to herself. Pandora might not have Lillian's father's money or Lucy Vanderbilt's pedigree, but she had her own intelligence and talent, her own beauty and charm. Tonight, that had to be enough.

She glanced around the room to see whom she wanted to talk to. Harley Enright stood next to the punch bowl. He looked very handsome in a single-breasted black topcoat with shiny faille cuffs. His bibfront dress shirt was smooth and stiff, the buttons made of black onyx.

Pandora walked over and joined him.

"Pandora, how nice to see you!" Harley greeted her warmly. "Would you like a cup of fruit punch? I made it from my own recipe. Gin and shredded pineapple with orange juice and a squeeze of lemon."

Pandora accepted the cup of punch. It was delicious, sweet but with a touch of tartness.

"Is that the sort of thing they teach you at Princeton?" she asked, smiling. "I thought college boys were supposed to learn economics and finance."

Harley's face clouded over, and Pandora wondered if she'd said something wrong. But he quickly smiled.

"Learning to be a bartender is more important than any classroom lecture." His tone had the same light manner. "Every Princetonian is guaranteed to be able to fix a gin Rickey and a southside by graduation."

"I almost feel sorry for you," Pandora said with a laugh. "Between football games and the eating clubs, it's a wonder anyone goes to class."

"Some people don't, especially athletes." Harley nodded. "The professors give them As anyway. The theater set don't get the same privileges. I pored over my economics textbook every night and still got a C; my father was very disappointed."

That's why Harley's face had clouded over. His father was unhappy with his grades.

"He can't blame you as long as you studied," she countered.

"It's different when your father owns a bank and expects you to take the office next to his after graduation."

"Is that what you want?" Pandora wondered.

"I'd make a terrible banker." Harley sighed. "I'm not quick with numbers, and I'm worse at sports. My father believes most business deals happen on the tennis court or at one of his clubs. I thought he'd be happy when I joined the Triangle Club at Princeton, but I even got that wrong. Most of the athletes like Archie and Owen belong to the Tower Club and the Ivy Club. The Triangle Club is for theater people."

"What's wrong with theater people?" Pandora inquired.

Harley finished his cup of punch. He poured another and continued talking.

"According to my father, they take investors' money and fritter it away as if it's confetti on the stock market floor. He has more respect for the janitors than the actors. He says at least they're doing something useful." He looked up from his drink. "I'm grateful to the janitors, of course, but it's not the same. The stage is the most thrilling place in the world."

"Do you want to be an actor?" she asked curiously.

Pandora didn't know any actors. She had only been to the theater in New York once, with Virginia and Archie last year.

"God, no. I only practiced with Preston because he needed someone to read lines." Harley shook his head. "I want to be a director and producer. There's nothing like putting on a show: Watching the audience take their seats expecting nothing more than a couple of hours of entertainment. Then, when the play is good, the lights go on and there's a hush over the space. You can tell by their faces that they've been transformed."

Harley seemed about to add something else. But he stopped talking and finished his drink instead.

"I know what you mean," Pandora said to fill the silence.

As they stood there taking in the crowd, she allowed herself to imagine designing gowns for the women at the party. They'd come to her boutique in Hyde Park or to her private atelier in Manhattan. She'd provide a little sitting area in front of the dressing room so customers could rest and drink tea when they got tired. Once a month, Pandora would hold a fashion show that was invitation only. The women wouldn't need to travel to Paris anymore. Pandora Carmichael's dresses were the only ones they would wear.

But she had tried to sell her dresses by word of mouth, and she had failed. She felt the pain deep in her chest. Harley was very good looking, and he seemed interested in her. She recognized something similar in him. A drive to achieve his goals despite the obstacles standing in his way. A new thought settled over her, as soft and luxurious as the sable cape Maude Van Luyen wore to the opera. Perhaps she would see Harley again.

"There's nothing like doing the thing you're passionate about," Pandora agreed, letting the image dissolve.

Harley set down his cup next to the punch bowl.

"I don't have a dinner partner yet. Would you join me?"

"I'd love to."

He nodded as if something else, something more important, had been decided between them.

"My mother has the best taste," he commented. "She's never wrong."

"What do you mean?" Pandora inquired.

"She told me that she met you in the library. She said you were by far the most interesting girl at the party," he reflected. "She forgot to add something. You're also the loveliest."

~

Pandora was seated at one end of the dinner table next to Harley. Milton Enright sat on her other side at the head of the table, and Adele, resplendent in a white straight tabard-style dress and diamond tiara, sat across from her.

Lillian couldn't stop glaring at Pandora. She was obviously jealous.

Besides the fact that Pandora was in the bosom of the Enright family, Harley was arguably the most handsome man in the room. His blond hair looked almost white under the chandeliers, and his eyes were the same green as the emeralds on his cuff links.

"Adele tells me your father is Willie Carmichael," Milton said to Pandora after the soup was served. "We saw him play at Wimbledon years ago; it was the highlight of our trip."

Milton Enright was an older version of Harley, but with salt-and-pepper hair. He was the kind of man that commanded any room. Pandora could imagine him closing business deals at the bar in the Metropolitan Club, his name on a plaque as one of the founding members.

"I've always been envious of athletes' talent, but I admire them at the same time. Athletes have to work hard for their success," he continued. "Lou Gehrig prides himself on never missing a baseball practice since he was at Columbia."

Pandora noticed Harley wince. He looked down at his plate and concentrated on his soup.

"My father is the Van Luyens' tennis instructor now," Pandora said to Milton. "He still practices every day. He's getting older and he wants to keep up with his students."

"Nothing wrong with being a tennis instructor," Milton replied. "My grandparents emigrated to America from Ireland when my father was three. They couldn't afford to send him to school, so he got a paper route. He taught himself to read by reading the newspaper every night. He started the bank with money from his paper route.

"At his retirement dinner, he looked out at the sea of faces in the ballroom of the Plaza Hotel and said he was grateful for his years at the bank, but he still missed the paper route. There's nothing like ending the day with a pocketful of coins and a hunger in your stomach."

Pandora wanted to reply, but she was afraid of hurting Harley's feelings. Even though Milton was talking to her, she guessed he was addressing Harley.

"There are other ways to work up an appetite," Harley said sharply. "And I know plenty of actors who practice their lines for ten hours a day. You can't learn Shakespeare by reading it once."

"No one works harder than Harley at his schoolwork," Adele cut in as if she was used to being the referee between her husband and son. She changed the topic. "Pandora is interested in fashion. She wants to be a fashion designer."

Milton studied Pandora thoughtfully.

"I don't know anything about women's fashions except that Adele looks beautiful in everything she wears," Milton said. "There's nothing wrong with women having hobbies, as long as home and family come first."

Pandora flinched inwardly, but she didn't say anything. Harley caught her eye, and in that moment, she knew that he was on her side. Milton was of the older generation; he wouldn't believe in women having careers.

The rest of the dinner passed more easily. Archie was seated in the middle of the table, in between two pretty girls. Pandora had to laugh. The girls kept interrupting each other, trying to get Archie's attention. The entrée was cranberry-orange roasted duckling with creamed spinach and duchess potatoes. For dessert they had lemon-filled coconut cake and vanilla ice cream.

After Milton and Harley had a few glasses of wine, they both relaxed. Pandora wondered if it was always like this between father and son. A push and pull like a playground game of tug-of-war and then a truce. At least Milton seemed to care about Harley, and he was obviously in love with his wife. He hung on Adele's every word.

Pandora could tell that Milton and Adele Enright liked her. Conversation bounced easily between the four of them. Pandora couldn't help casting the occasional glance at Lillian, who was trying to engage her dinner partners with a story about a Cordon Bleu cooking course she took in Paris. Even being near Owen didn't faze Pandora.

She couldn't help but notice that he seemed slightly bored and kept refilling his wine glass.

After dinner, Harley led her into the ballroom. The band had started playing, and guests were already dancing. Harley was a wonderful dancer, even better than Archie. He led her in a spirited Charleston, and then took her in his arms and twirled her around in a tango and a foxtrot as if they had been dancing together forever.

Other men asked her to dance too. Archie and George Baker St. George, whose grandfather, George Fisher Baker founded the First National Bank of New York City. Even Milton claimed one dance. Owen approached her, but to her relief, Harley cut in and said that Pandora had promised him the next three dances.

It was hot inside the ballroom, and she needed some air. She slipped outside, down the steps, and into the garden to enjoy the cool breeze and the sky full of stars.

She allowed herself to reflect on the day. Her triumph over Lillian at the pool house that afternoon and being seated opposite the Enrights at dinner. Harley's attention, and the way every young man on the dance floor seemed to take a new interest in her.

She heard a rustling sound and turned around.

Harley stood on the lawn, two glasses of champagne in his hands.

"I thought I saw you step outside." He handed her a champagne flute. "Do you mind if I join you?"

Pandora was surprised to see him. She accepted the champagne even though she didn't want any more to drink. It would be impolite to refuse.

"Aren't you supposed to be dancing?" she inquired. "You *are* the host."

"Most of the girls aren't really interested in dancing," Harley reflected. "They're more concerned with learning my intentions after I graduate from Princeton. Whether I intend to join my father's bank right away, or if I'll spend a year abroad first." He sipped his champagne, and his eyes were dull. "They worry that if I go abroad, they'll have to suffer through a long engagement."

"Don't you have to propose first?" she teased. "Or at least ask them for a second dance?"

"The girls and their mothers make these decisions." Harley sighed. "I'm just the guy whose family belongs to the right clubs and who can provide the correct size diamond ring."

Pandora remembered Adele's comments on marriage. It was easy to say that kind of thing, but the reality was often different. Even if Adele was more progressive than other women of her set, she might feel differently when it came to her son.

Harley dug his shoes into the grass.

"I'm not being a good host. I'm talking about myself instead of asking about you," he apologized. "I hope you're having a good time."

"I'm having a wonderful time," Pandora said truthfully. "I was imagining how I was going to describe it to Virginia, Archie's sister. She's my best friend. Though we're nothing alike. Virginia isn't fond of house parties; she prefers literary readings and lectures."

"You don't always choose your friends for what you have in common," Harley commented. "Sometimes you choose them for how they make you feel about yourself. A real friend is someone you can be yourself with, no matter what that's like. And they won't desert you."

Harley was right. Pandora and Virginia disagreed on so many subjects.

But they supported each other through everything.

"That's how it is for Virginia and me." Pandora nodded. "We can tell each other anything. Sometimes, talking to her is the only way to figure out what I really want."

Beside her, Harley finished his champagne. His face took on a thoughtful expression.

"The luckiest people, I think, discover the same type of friendship in marriage. I think my parents have that despite their differences. My mother was nineteen when my parents married, and they're nothing alike. Now that their children are grown, she spends most of her time doing charity work, and my father is only interested in his work at the bank.

"My mother isn't like other women in Hyde Park, who believe charity is hosting luncheons and attending galas. She founded the Grand Street Settlement House on the Lower East Side."

"I've never heard of it," Pandora replied.

"Settlement houses have been around for twenty years. They're in the poorest sections of New York: Brooklyn and the Bronx and Lenox Hill. Local residents can go there and hear lectures and get advice. Or simply have a clean, pleasant place to be away from their everyday lives.

"The settlement committees help get better street lighting and garbage collection for the neighborhoods. Lately she's been petitioning to replace tenement buildings with public housing."

"Your mother does all that?" Pandora asked, wide eyed. Adele seemed so refined; she couldn't imagine her arguing in front of a meeting hall. And yet, Adele had surprised Pandora with her views on social standing. Pandora had never met anyone like her.

Harley nodded.

"She also helps the women who work at the factories. She donates all my old clothes, and she takes the women gloves and stockings. The women work all day; they don't have time to sew clothes for their children. And they can't afford extras for themselves."

Harley shuffled his feet from side to side.

"My father is the opposite; he's only interested in the bank and his private clubs. But when they're together, they're happy. They often eat in the dining room just the two of them, and they can talk for hours. A few times this summer, I've seen them out here dancing." He waved at the terrace. "They're good friends, and they love each other; you can tell by looking at them."

"They did seem fond of each other at dinner," Pandora affirmed. "Your mother is very beautiful."

Harley studied Pandora. He touched her wrist.

"So are you, Pandora."

Harley's eyes shone in the moonlight. Pandora told herself it didn't mean anything. She had allowed herself to be swept away by Owen's small attentions, and she'd ended up with a broken heart. Harley was merely tipsy from the champagne.

"I'll get in trouble for keeping you to myself," he joked, as if he needed to break the mood. He held out his arm. "Shall we go inside and dance?"

She linked her arm through his.

"I'd like that." She nodded.

"I'm glad you came, Pandora Carmichael," he said with a smile. "I'm having a much better time than I imagined."

Chapter Seven

July 1926, Hyde Park, New York

The Monday after the Enrights' house party, Pandora spent the morning in the Van Luyens' kitchen, chopping celery and cabbage for Esther's Jell-O Perfection Salad. It felt strange to be bending over the sink when two nights before she had been sipping champagne with Harley on Blythdale's terrace. She wondered what he would think if he could see her scrubbing vegetables. Would she still be the kind of woman he would ask to rehearse his play? She knew she was only invited because of the Van Luyens. But what if Harley was different? Perhaps he'd still notice her when she wasn't wearing an evening gown and Virginia's borrowed jewelry.

Virginia was in New York with her mother, and Archie and Willie were playing tennis. Pandora had planned on spending the day sewing a new dress, but she couldn't concentrate. The fabric kept slipping from the sewing machine, and twice she'd pricked her finger with a pin. She told herself she was tired from staying up late and dancing. But it was something else.

She had enjoyed Harley's company and wondered if she'd see him again.

The back door opened, and Archie entered. He had a towel draped over his shoulder, and his forehead was damp with sweat. His cheeks were tan from the house party, and Pandora could see the muscles under his shirt. He looked very handsome.

"Pandora, the star of the weekend," Archie said, wiping his brow.

"I don't know what you mean." Pandora looked up from the sink.

"Every young man at the Enrights' house party was taken with you, some that are not so young," Archie replied. He grabbed an apple from the fruit bowl. "I heard Milton Enright comment to Adele that Harley finally found a worthy girl. Milton Enright doesn't have a nice thing to say about anyone unless that person is about to deposit money into Enright's Bank."

"Milton Enright is lovely. He suggested I bring my father over for a tennis match sometime. And there's nothing going on between me and Harley. We just met."

"I've known Harley for three years at Princeton, and he's never paid attention to a girl. He's too busy with theater productions on the weekends." Archie polished the apple on his vest. "The Enrights are good people. Adele Enright isn't like the other women in her circle; she's trying to change things."

"Since when do you want the world to change?" Pandora arched her eyebrows. "You're going straight from graduation into your father's real estate company. By the time you're forty, you'll have a summer estate and your own set of billiard cues at the Union Club."

"I'm looking forward to working in the real estate firm as much as a goldfish about to join a household with an inquisitive cat." Archie sighed.

"I thought you wanted to work with your father," Pandora said, surprised.

"I loved my childhood, and I'm grateful to my parents for everything they've done, but that doesn't mean I want the same future," Archie admitted.

Pandora always assumed the children of wealthy parents—Archie, Virginia, Owen, and their friends—were doing exactly what they wanted. It was only people without money like Pandora who had to struggle to achieve their dreams.

"What do you want to do?" she asked curiously.

"I'd like to be a history and politics professor," Archie confided. "I've never felt so inspired as at Princeton. It's as if the answers to my most burning questions are in the bricks of Nassau Hall."

Archie looked so serious, Pandora had to stifle a giggle.

"I thought the only places in Princeton you were interested in were the games room and the dining hall at your eating club," she said, smiling.

Archie frowned at Pandora. He took another bite of the apple.

"You're not the only one who wants something different out of life," he retorted, his voice gruff. "I'm going to be chained to my father's company for the next fifty years. Real estate is fine if you're only interested in buildings. I want to know how we got where we are and use that knowledge to make the world better."

"I don't understand." Pandora put down the sticks of celery.

"It's not just the poor in this country who lead difficult lives, it's also the Jews and Negroes. Black singers might be applauded at night clubs in Harlem, but there's still public lynching of Negroes all over the South. And have you heard of the Jewish quota? Universities like Princeton and Yale only allow a few Jews in each class.

"None of that will change if the rich keep building taller buildings so they can lock themselves in their penthouses. Why should it? They don't care a fig about anyone who the doorman doesn't let inside.

"There's only one Jewish student in my class at Princeton. His name is Aaron Rabinowitz, and whenever the professor calls on him, everyone laughs at his name." Archie bit into his apple. "He's not invited to the eating clubs, and his roommate throws out his mother's care packages because he claims the matzo ball soup makes the room smell like onions."

Archie was right. So much in the world remained unfair. Women were allowed to vote, and they could work outside the home but for far less pay than their husbands.

Sometimes Pandora read Willie's newspaper when he left it on the table. She reminded herself that positive changes happened too. Recently, she learned that Nellie Tayloe Ross became the first female US governor when she won the election in Wyoming. And in May, Ford Motor Company became the first American company to institute a forty-hour work week.

She wondered if her own dreams of opening a boutique were important compared to Adele's desire for social change and Archie's determination to improve the lives of Jews and Negroes. But perhaps by opening a business, she could help others. She would employ young women in her atelier and pay them a good salary. Perhaps one day, she could teach fashion to girls who didn't have enough money to attend design school.

Archie tossed his apple core into the garbage, snapping her out of her reverie.

"Anyway, I have to go. Lucy Vanderbilt invited me to go rowing. Though I'll do all the work. She'll sit in the boat, eating strawberries prettily and saying she's glad she wore a wide-brimmed hat." His shoulders heaved, and he took a long breath. "I'm sorry, I didn't mean to take my frustration out on you. Just don't get too serious with Harley." His smile returned, and Archie was once again the golden boy she had known since childhood. "You're a lovely young woman, Pandora. Lots of men would be interested in you."

The door closed, and Archie's footsteps sounded on the stairs.

Pandora recalled what Harley said about the settlement houses, and the women working in the factories. Pandora was so sheltered. She couldn't remember ever seeing the poverty in New York when she was young, and she had since been shielded by the gates of the estates along the Hudson. If Pandora was ever in Adele's financial position, she'd find a way to help others.

After she finished making the Jell-O salad, she'd sew a new dress. How many times had her father said that if he were still young, he would have another chance at Wimbledon, and this time he'd win? Pandora was young; she couldn't give up. She had to find a way to follow her dreams.

The phone rang as she was sewing on the last button. She went into the kitchen and answered it.

"I'm calling for Pandora; this is Harley Enright." The sound of his voice sent a thrill down her spine.

"This is Pandora."

"Pandora," he said, "it's my mother's birthday next week, and I need to buy her a present. I wondered if you'd help me. I'd pick you up and drive us to Hyde Park."

"You want me to help choose a gift?" Pandora said in surprise.

"I don't know many girls, and I'm sure you have good taste," he shared. "If you're too busy, I can figure it out myself."

Esther's Jell-O Perfection Salad was ready and sitting in the icebox.

"I have time, and I'd love to come."

"Excellent. I'll pick you up in an hour."

Pandora hung up the phone. She should be wary after what happened with Owen. What if Harley only saw her as the help and wasn't interested in her? But she couldn't deny the small flutter of attraction.

She went to her room to choose what to wear.

~

That afternoon, Pandora and Harley strolled along Main Street in Hyde Park. Pandora wore a red cotton dress with a matching cloche hat. She was glad that women weren't required to wear gloves during the day anymore. It was too hot.

"Tell me about yourself. Have you always lived at Riverview?" Harley inquired.

"What do you mean?" She turned to Harley.

Harley was dressed casually in a beige V-neck sweater and tan linen trousers. His boater hat had a jaunty sash in the Princeton colors of orange and black, and he wore brown-and-white Oxford shoes.

"We spent the house party talking about me," Harley replied. "I don't know anything about you or how you grew up."

"I don't remember a lot from before my mother left," Pandora said.

She didn't want to talk about Laura. It was too painful, and the last thing she wanted was for Harley to feel sorry for her. It was likely that most of the other young women Harley knew had doting parents. It was better if she presented herself in the same way.

"My father is wonderful, but he's quite private; he doesn't talk a lot. Esther, the Van Luyens' cook, has always been kind, but she's not like a mother. She's only ten years older than me and she's busy. She has a serious suitor."

She stopped. She didn't want to sound ungrateful.

"Maude and Robert Van Luyen have always been good to me. And Virginia and Archie are as close as a proper brother and sister."

"What about Pandora Carmichael?" Harley questioned. "What makes you happy?"

No one had ever asked Pandora that before.

"Beauty makes me happy," she said. "Beauty in the normal things: flowers and houses and gardens. Beauty in fruits and colorful vegetables and the sky on a summer day." She flushed, embarrassed. "I suppose that's why I love fashion. To me, beautiful dresses are a type of art."

"I'm sure a young woman as lovely as you is talented," Harley said gallantly.

"And I love children," she said earnestly. "I've always wanted a family."

Pandora kept talking. Harley had prompted something to open inside her, and she found she couldn't turn it off.

"It's become acceptable for women to have careers, but they can't want a family too," she continued. "Virginia is against marriage; she wants to lead a life of the mind. Your mother is terrific. She's the first person I've met who understands you can want both at the same time."

Pandora stopped to look in a store window. She was afraid she'd said too much. Harley was easy to talk to, but she didn't want to bore him. She needed to turn the conversation back to him.

"What about you? What makes you happy?" she inquired.

Harley took off his hat and wiped his forehead.

"I love plays and the theater, but I also love nature. That's why I love Princeton. I can spend all day at the Triangle Club hashing out a script and then take a walk or go rowing on Lake Carnegie." He put his hat back on. "I like games—charades and croquet. My brothers were much older than me, but my sister, Annie, and I were very close. She's in San Francisco. I wish I could visit her and her children more often. I count my mother as a friend as well. When I'm at school, we often meet for lunch in New York."

Pandora was enjoying talking to Harley so much she almost forgot about Adele's birthday present.

"Then we'd better find her a gift," she said, stopping in front of a dress shop. "Why don't we go inside and look around."

They didn't find anything at the dress shop. Adele probably bought her clothes at Lord & Taylor, and Pandora didn't know her style. A florist delivered flowers to Blythdale every week. And it didn't seem right for Harley to buy his mother jewelry.

A stationery store stood on the corner. Pandora went inside.

She moved past the table of glass paperweights and silver letter openers and a rack of notecards with embossed envelopes. Pandora pulled a burgundy leather notebook with lined pages from a shelf.

"This is perfect." She handed it to Harley.

"A notebook?"

"Usually when a man gives a present, it's a reflection of himself. A dress so his wife looks more elegant than the other women at a dinner party, a piece of jewelry to show off his wealth. Perfume is lovely, but often the saleswoman suggests a scent the man likes himself.

"Women should have those things, but they can buy them for themselves." She warmed to her theme. "A notebook to write down her private thoughts is different. You'd be giving it to her for her own enjoyment. She'll keep it locked in her drawer; you'll never see it again."

Harley's eyes lit up. Pandora could tell that he was impressed.

"That's astonishing. How did you think of it?"

"Women do everything for their husbands: they make sure their shirts are ironed and their meals are prepared; they even plan their social schedules. Maude Van Luyen calls her husband's secretary twice a week to coordinate his appointment book.

"It's the same with the children. Once a woman has children, her time is spent choosing the right schools, taking them to lessons, arranging birthday parties.

"Women need something of their own to be happy. A private notebook isn't much, but it's a start."

Harley took the notebook to the counter.

The salesman wrapped it in tissue paper and tied the package with a satin ribbon.

Pandora and Harley walked onto the sidewalk. It was midafternoon, and children played in the park. A family licked ice cream cones, and two women in floral dresses passed by with hat boxes.

"Can I buy you an ice cream to thank you?" Harley asked.

She liked being with Harley. It felt different from being around Owen. She'd always had a slightly anxious feeling with him. And there was none of the spirited banter she had with Archie. She felt comfortable with Harley. And he was so handsome women turned around to get another look.

She nodded and took his arm. "It's so hot, an ice cream sounds perfect."

Pandora thought Harley would order from the Good Humor wagon parked on the corner. But he walked past the ice cream truck to Finley's drugstore. Inside, there was a soda fountain and a row of high-backed stools. A huge mirror stood behind the soda fountain, and there was a selection of glass bottles arranged in front.

"Prohibition is the best thing that happened to soda fountains," Harley said, sitting on a stool. "People can't go to bars to drink, so they go to soda fountains instead." He picked up a menu. "It's all the craze after the theater. In New York the fountain drinks have the same names as regular cocktails. Hippodromes and Buster Browns and Gibson Girls. Except a Buster Brown is made with chocolate ice cream and pineapple sherbet with poured-over caramel nut sauce and catawba syrup. And a Gibson Girl is two sliced bananas and oranges, chilled in a punch bowl and served with vanilla ice cream and crushed pineapple."

Pandora burst out laughing.

"How do you know these things?" she inquired.

"The Triangle Club often goes to New York to see plays. It's great fun. There's nothing like the camaraderie of actors and playwrights."

Harley ordered an ice cream sundae, and Pandora had a banana split with whipped cream and chopped nuts.

"My mother couldn't stop talking about you after the house party," Harley said. "I worry about her when I'm at Princeton. She must get lonely. Perhaps you could go to lunch with her or go shopping. Maybe even see a movie. My mother loves Mary Pickford, but she doesn't like going to the movies alone."

The ice cream suddenly tasted gummy in Pandora's mouth. She found it hard to swallow.

Harley was just like Owen. He saw her as someone he could use. But instead of using her to help him win at tennis, Harley was looking for a companion for his mother. It didn't matter how many beautiful dresses Pandora wore or what witty things she said. Men of Harley's social class would never treat her as an equal.

She plunged the spoon into the banana split. Even if she did fall in love again, it would come to nothing. The Lillian Clarksons and Lucy Vanderbilts would always live in estates on the Hudson, with their banker husbands and English setters and children dressed in pinafores and sailing suits. Pandora would remain on the sidelines, grateful to be invited to the occasional house party with Archie and Virginia.

Even Virginia was like the other young women. At any moment, she could change her mind about starting a literary salon and marry whomever she liked. All she had to do was appear in a Worth gown and one of her mother's tiaras, and suitors would line up to ask her to dance.

Adele Enright might be open minded, but it wouldn't make a difference. Milton was old fashioned; he might not accept someone from Pandora's social station as a daughter-in-law. And Harley himself had likely learned to choose a certain type of bride at Princeton and his eating club.

Pandora's father was right. She had ruined everything by throwing away her chance to go to secretarial school. Now her future was as bleak as the women Adele Enright helped at the factory.

Pandora brought her eyes up to meet Harley's. She forced herself to smile.

"Of course," she said with a nod. "I'd be happy to spend time with your mother."

~

Later that day, Pandora sat in the kitchen at Riverview. She stirred a cup of tea.

She'd have to keep searching for a proper job; she couldn't help Esther forever. But what was she qualified to do? The thought of becoming a maid at Rosecliff or Beechtree was too awful to contemplate, and she'd already discounted the idea of working in a factory. She could work behind the counter at the bakery, but it would hardly pay enough to get the food stains out of her dresses.

Through the window, she noticed a delivery boy. He held a box of chocolates in one hand and a bunch of lilacs tied with a pink ribbon in the other. Pandora smiled to herself. Esther's suitor, Ronald, often sent flowers or chocolates, but never both. He must be close to asking Esther to marry him.

Pandora opened the back door.

"Esther isn't here, but you can leave them on the counter."

"They aren't for Esther." The delivery boy handed them to her. "They're for Pandora Carmichael."

Pandora's eyes widened. The chocolates were from a confectionery, and the flowers were from the florist on Main Street. A card was tucked inside the ribbon.

She waited until the delivery boy left. Then she opened the card and read it aloud.

"Dear Pandora,

Forgive me, I don't know which you like better, flowers or chocolate, so I sent both.

They're staging a production of George Bernard Shaw's play *The Devil's Disciple* at the Poughkeepsie playhouse next Tuesday. It's one of my favorites; the Triangle Club performed it three years ago.

I hope that you'll join me.

Warm regards,
Harley"

Pandora's cheeks flushed with pleasure. Harley wanted to see her again! He wasn't only interested in her as a companion for his mother.

She wondered why he hadn't called and invited her. Perhaps he was shy when it came to dating and wasn't comfortable talking on the phone. Archie said that Harley hadn't had any girlfriends before.

Outside the window, the sun slipped behind the Catskill Mountains. The lawn shimmered pink and gold in the evening light, and the river glinted as if it were scattered with diamonds.

First, she'd put the flowers in water. Then she'd call Harley and say she'd love to go to the play with him.

Chapter Eight

August 1926, Hyde Park, New York

At the end of August, the Vanderbilts would hold the last house party of the summer. There would be golf and games and afternoon tea served on the lawn. The grounds boasted two thousand rosebushes, and Frederick had commissioned New York's leading landscape architect, Charles Platt, to design the pergolas and swimming pool. Guests could visit Frederick Vanderbilt's farm, and the invitation promised a tour of the mansion and the multitiered gardens, each with its own type of plant.

The Roosevelts and Dinsmores would attend, as well as Archie and Virginia and their parents and the Winthrops and Enrights. Harley had invited Pandora as his guest.

Pandora had seen Harley twice a week for the past month. It wasn't like when Owen used to come to Riverview to lounge around and play tennis. Harley took her boating and on drives. He brought her little gifts—roses from the Enrights' garden, a jar of jam made by the cook. His mother sent small things too—a book on influential women Adele thought Pandora might like, a scarf she happened to see at the dress shop.

Milton Enright kept his promise and invited Willie to play tennis at Blythdale. Pandora and Harley and Adele watched from the sidelines, and Pandora could have kissed her father when he let Milton win. After the match, they drank lemonade and talked about current tennis stars: the French player René Lacoste, known as the Crocodile for never letting an opponent get away, and the American hero Bill Tilden.

Harley was so sweet to her. He wasn't like other young men who treated dates as something to get out of the way before the real fun of the evening began: playing poker and billiards with their friends and seeing who could drink the most old-fashioneds.

Her favorite thing to do with Harley was to see plays at the playhouse in Poughkeepsie. Afterward, they would dine at a restaurant and talk about how Harley would have directed the play or what the playwright was trying to say. It was during those times, sharing large plates of spaghetti and drinking frosty Coca-Colas, that Pandora felt something she had never felt with Owen. A friendship as well as an attraction.

Harley asked her opinion about the costumes, and Pandora drew sketches on the napkins. Often their arms brushed, and a frisson, like some kind of electric shock, shot through her.

It was a thirty-minute drive from Poughkeepsie to Hyde Park. On the drive home, Harley hummed show tunes, and Pandora gazed at the mansions sleeping behind iron gates. For the first time, she felt like she belonged.

In the beginning, Pandora had been attracted to Harley for his good looks and the attention he lavished on her. Now she realized that she was falling in love with him. Her heart seemed to beat faster when she was with him. When she wasn't with him, she was distracted and had to pull her mind back to her chores. It frightened her. She didn't want to get hurt the way she had been by Owen.

The week after the party, Harley would return to Princeton. He hadn't kissed her yet. He was raised too properly to do anything impolite, but it made Pandora anxious. At Princeton, Harley would be busy with classes and the theater. She worried the whole thing might fizzle out.

And she had so enjoyed being with Adele. Adele was everything a mother should be. She talked about Harley incessantly. And she was so kind to Pandora. Offering Pandora her scarf or a pair of gloves when Harley and Pandora went to the theater. If Harley lost interest in Pandora, she'd lose Adele too.

Pandora was in her room in the cottage at Riverview, packing her overnight bag, when a knock came at the door. She assumed it was Virginia seeing if she was ready.

Except it wasn't. It was her father, and he looked concerned.

"Can I come in?" he asked.

With his height and strong physique, her father had always looked young for his age. But over the past few months he had grown older. His shoulders were slightly stooped, and his blue eyes were watery. The laugh lines around his mouth had deepened and were visible even when he wasn't smiling. It was Pandora's fault. If only she could fix it.

"I wanted to talk to you about something." Willie sat on the chair that stood at her dressing table.

"I'm going to pay you back soon. I started looking for jobs in the newspapers. It's just . . ."

She couldn't tell her father the truth. That she had been rejected for the girl Friday job in New York. That every advertisement she had seen—as a telephone operator at Macy's department store, as a clerk in a flower shop—required experience she didn't have. It was demoralizing, and since she'd started seeing Harley, she'd stopped looking.

"I'm still angry, but it's not about that." Willie waved his hand. "I want to talk to you about Harley Enright."

The color rose to Pandora's cheeks. She never talked about men with her father. The only person she confided in was Virginia.

"What about Harley?" Pandora wondered.

"You're out with Harley all the time, and he's always sending flowers and boxes of chocolates."

Pandora twisted her hands nervously. She couldn't let her father believe she was enjoying herself when she had lost his money and should be looking for a job. Perhaps if Willie knew that she and Harley were serious about each other, he would feel differently.

"It has been a nice summer; Harley is kind and funny, and he's interested in what I say."

"Harley is still in college; perhaps he's just having fun."

"Harley isn't like that; he's different than other young men," she persisted. "I'm sure he'll declare his feelings soon, and then I'll be able to pay you back. You could buy a house or take a holiday," she said earnestly. "You haven't taken time off in years."

In the autumn and winter when the Van Luyens only came to Riverview on weekends, Willie helped around the estate. Someone had to keep an eye on it, and he never felt he could get away for any length of time.

"I don't need a vacation, we live in one of the most beautiful spots in the Hudson Valley," he countered. "And I wouldn't know what to do with myself in a bigger house."

"You like Harley. You told me so when the Enrights invited you to play tennis."

"Harley is a fine young man," Willie affirmed. "That doesn't mean you should jump into something, even if he does have good intentions. Marriage isn't worth anything without love."

Willie hunched forward in the chair. He paused for a moment, as if he wasn't sure he should continue.

"When your mother and I met, Laura was eighteen, and I was a couple of years older. She grew up on a farm and came to New York to be an artist's model.

"I used to play at the tennis club in Central Park. One day Laura sat with some friends in the front row. I looked up from a serve into those blue eyes. I was so distracted I served the ball straight into my opponent's racquet. It was the only match I lost all season."

Pandora tried to imagine her mother, young and carefree in New York. She must have been so beautiful.

"After the match, we took a stroll through Central Park and got pizza at Lombardi's. She came to all my matches, and I started winning. First the Davis Cup in Boston, then the US National Championship in Newport. She loved the excitement of being in the stands, the buzz of the applause." He paused for a moment. "And I was in love with her."

Her father told her the whole story of their marriage. Three months after the wedding, he was scheduled to play in France and England, and they planned to make the trip their honeymoon. But Laura got pregnant and was too sick to go. Two years later, when he advanced to the semifinals at Wimbledon, Pandora was a toddler, and there was no question of Laura joining him.

He lost at Wimbledon, and after that he quit the amateur circuit—there was no money in it. He took a position at the tennis club in New York, but Laura wasn't happy.

She missed Willie being a celebrity, and she wasn't fond of keeping house and being a mother. She got a job at a department store so she didn't have to stay home, and Willie looked after Pandora between coaching sessions.

Then the war started, and Willie was injured in France. By the time he returned, Laura had had enough of the marriage and left.

"It wasn't your fault that she left," Pandora said urgently.

Her father looked so broken up; she couldn't bear to see him hurt. And there was no point in saying what she really felt—that Pandora was the reason that Laura left. That might hurt Willie even more. They had been a family, and Laura hadn't felt they were worth staying for.

"The doctors wouldn't let me leave the rehabilitation hospital, and the army wouldn't discharge me," Willie went on. "If Laura had truly been in love with me, she would have waited. That's what I'm trying to say. When we got married, I thought my love for her was enough for both of us. You can only marry Harley if you both love each other; otherwise it won't work."

Pandora flung her arms around her father. It felt good to be talking to each other again. She felt closer to him than she ever had before.

"You could be worrying for nothing; Harley hasn't kissed me yet. If he doesn't, I promise I'll get a job." Tears sprung to her eyes, and she blinked them away. "Harley is special, but I've already got the best man in the world."

Willie stood up. He returned the chair to the dressing table.

"I hope you're right. At least you can learn from my mistakes."

~

Virginia was already in Archie's car when Pandora appeared downstairs. She looked summery in a floral dress with butterfly sleeves and a huge floppy hat.

"I've been waiting for ages," Virginia chided. "You're getting as bad at being on time as Archie. Don't tell me that's what happens when you fall for someone."

"It has nothing to do with Harley," Pandora protested.

"Of course it does. You were choosing what to wear," Virginia said. "Tonight is the last night for Harley to declare his intentions."

"That's not why I'm going to the party," Pandora said stubbornly. She didn't want Virginia to think she expected anything from Harley. It was bad enough when Owen proposed to Lillian. She couldn't face that humiliation again, even with her best friend.

"I have wonderful news." Virginia waved away her comment. She patted the back seat. "Get in and I'll tell you."

Pandora threw her bag in the back and climbed into the car.

"I found a space for my poetry salons. It's on Christopher Street, opposite the Greenwich Village Theater."

Pandora's eyes widened. Greenwich Village was as scandalous as Harlem. Bohemians lived there, along with actors and artists and vaudeville players. Virginia couldn't host her salons there.

"Your mother would never allow it—and rightly so," Pandora said, shocked. "It's not the kind of place for a young woman to be alone."

"Who says I'll be alone?" Virginia said gaily. "The point of the salon is to be surrounded by people. Wolfgang is going to help me fix it up. I'll put in heavy drapes so no one can see us from the street, and big sofas so people will be comfortable while they're listening to poetry. And a bar of course, stocked with gin and whiskey.

"Wolfgang and I are making a list of poets to give readings." She ticked off names on her fingers. "Nella Larsen promised to read from her new poems. And Jessie Fauset, who's the literary editor of *The Crisis* and a friend of Langston Hughes. And Gwendolyn Bennett—I met her in Harlem. She's as beautiful as an artist's model, and a talented poet too."

Pandora hadn't heard of any of them. But she loved seeing Virginia so excited.

"What did I miss?" Archie appeared. He dropped his bag in the seat next to Pandora and hopped into the driver's seat.

Virginia glanced quickly at Pandora. Archie was terrible at keeping secrets; he didn't know anything about Virginia's salons.

"We were talking about you and Lucy Vanderbilt," Virginia said airily. "If you marry her, you'll inherit the Vanderbilt estate someday. A hundred and sixty acres of parkland and another five hundred acres of the farm." Her eyes twinkled. "You'll have your own sheep and pigs."

"I'd rather dip my feet in cement than own pigs." Archie shuddered. "I don't need an estate. I'm happy with my room at Princeton."

"What about Lucy?" Virginia wondered. "You've been seeing her all summer; she's in love with you."

"With Lucy it's all about herself, her own entrance at a party." Archie sighed. "She wouldn't notice if I sent someone else in my top hat and tails."

Just as Archie knew nothing about Virginia's salons, Virginia knew nothing about Archie's dream to be a professor. Pandora felt slightly guilty that Archie confided in her rather than his sister, but Virginia loved to tease Archie; she'd never take him seriously.

~

Pandora had seen the Vanderbilt estate from the river, but she'd never been inside the gates. The parkland stretched on forever with bridges and stone benches and a mill attached to a pond. When the mansion appeared on the hill, Pandora's mouth dropped open.

The house was grander than Riverview and almost twice as large. Pandora had read an article in the *New York Times* declaring it "the finest place between New York and Albany." Frederick Vanderbilt loved to entertain, and he often rented a private train to bring guests to the estate from New York. The house had fifty-four rooms designed in the Beaux-Arts style. The exterior had perfect symmetry and Greek columns that were so tall Pandora had to crane her neck. It was four stories with a flat roof and featured a circular portico and pedimented doors decorated with stone gargoyles. Smaller buildings surrounded it: stables, living quarters for the gardeners, and even a separate sports pavilion.

"It's quite nice; you could enjoy living here," Virginia said offhandedly to Archie when they pulled into the driveway.

"That's easy for you to say," Archie grumbled, turning off the engine. "Lucy isn't happy unless she gets her way about everything." He jiggled his blazer pocket. "I brought my own flask. It's the only way to cope with her and still enjoy myself."

For the first time, Pandora felt sorry for Archie. He was only dating Lucy to make his mother happy. The Vanderbilts were the most important family in New York, even Pandora noticed how often Maude Van Luyen dropped their name into conversation at every opportunity.

Archie wasn't like Pandora who had to use every scrap of drive and ambition to rise above her station. Or even like Virginia who had to tell her mother little white lies to achieve her goals. Young men like Archie were handed everything in life from an early age. Private tutors and athletic coaches so they got the best grades and excelled at sports. When they graduated from college, they had careers waiting for them, and when they got married, they were given a townhouse on Park Avenue and trust funds for their children.

If the Van Luyens wanted Archie to marry Lucy Vanderbilt and join the family real estate firm, that's what he would likely do. Perhaps she'd talk about it with Archie later. Make him see that if he wanted to lead his own life, he had to fight for it.

Pandora followed Archie and Virginia inside.

A butler led them into a crescent-shaped vestibule. Pandora admired the animal-skin rugs and potted palms and long, low sofas upholstered in velvets and rich satins. A stone fireplace took up one wall, and another wall was lined with marble statues.

"I heard the entry has sofas because the dinner parties go so late guests fall asleep while they wait for their cars," Virginia whispered to Pandora.

Pandora's eyes widened in awe. She'd heard that many of the furnishings—the floor-to-ceiling mirrors in the dining room, the eighteenth-century rolltop desk in the library, the Italian marble in the bathrooms—had been taken from the grand historic houses of Europe: Versailles in France, Villa Carlotta in Lake Como, Inverness Castle in Scotland. The green marble pilasters in the entry were a thousand years old. And the annular clock was crafted in France in the nineteenth century.

She was reminded how much she enjoyed house parties. She loved the beauty of the mansions themselves and the feeling of fun and frivolity when everyone arrived. The thrill of descending the staircase in her evening gown, and the pleasure the next morning of a delicious breakfast served in brilliant sunshine.

A maid in a black uniform led her upstairs to her guest room. Orange silk drapes hung at the windows, and the four-post bed was surrounded by orange curtains. An orange-and-white chaise lounge stood next to the fireplace, and towels were folded neatly and stacked at the washstand. A dart of hope, as delicate as the lace thread on her dress, shot through her. Perhaps today Harley would declare his feelings. Then, not only would she have the man she loved, but the lifestyle she loved so much would be hers too.

~

By late afternoon, Pandora and Harley had finished a game of croquet and were sitting on the lawn. So far, the house party was even better than Pandora had hoped. She and Harley had won two games of croquet and toured the farm. Pandora even got to hold a lamb. It was as small as a puppy, and when she put it next to her chest, she could feel its heart beating.

Cocktails would start soon, followed by dinner and dancing. Pandora would never be able to convince Harley to be alone with her after dark. It would be too compromising. If she wanted him to kiss her, it had to be now.

"I forgot my tennis racquet." Pandora turned to Harley. "Lucy said there's a cupboard of racquets in the sports pavilion. Will you come and look with me?"

"We're not going to play tennis tonight." Harley frowned. "Shouldn't we get ready for dinner?"

Most of the others were walking back up to the house. The sun made pink-and-orange ribbons on the lawn, and the milky scent of gardenias wafted through the air.

"We promised Archie and Lucy we'd play doubles first thing in the morning," Pandora reminded him. "If I don't find a racquet now, I might not get a chance."

Harley stood up. He straightened his boater hat.

"All right." He nodded.

They walked down the hill to the pavilion. Pandora wondered what she would do when they arrived. She couldn't just reach up and kiss him. It had to be Harley's idea.

The pavilion felt cool and inviting after the afternoon heat. One long room held a Ping-Pong table and a selection of dumbbells. From there, a hallway led to changing rooms and a kitchen.

Pandora rummaged through a storage closet.

"I see one up there," she said, pointing to a shelf. "I'm not sure if I can reach it."

Before Harley could stop her, she climbed onto a shelf. With one hand, she reached for the racquet, and with the other she kept herself steady. Just as the racquet came loose, she lost her footing and started to fall. Harley's arms encircled her, and she dropped into his embrace.

Their faces were so close together, Pandora could feel his breath on her cheek. She brushed her lips against his. Harley froze and Pandora worried she had made a terrible mistake. But then he kissed her back. His mouth was warm and sweet.

"I'm sorry." Harley pulled away. "I shouldn't have done that."

"It was my fault," she assured him. She didn't want Harley to feel guilty. "You were so close and"—she let the color rise to her cheeks—"I couldn't resist."

Harley studied her intently. She had never seen his eyes such a bright shade of green.

"I wasn't going to come today," he admitted.

"You weren't?" Pandora repeated, her heart beating faster.

If Harley hadn't come, they might not have seen each other before he returned to Princeton. She couldn't be wrong again, Harley had to have feelings for her.

"It's the eighth anniversary of the Somme Offensive."

"I don't understand." Pandora frowned.

"August 27, 1918. The date my brother Frank was killed. American and Canadian and Australian troops fought together. They pushed the Germans all the way back to the Hindenburg Line. It was one of the greatest victories of the war." Harley hung his head. "Except my brother didn't make it. Frank was hit by a grenade and blown up in front of his whole unit."

Adele had mentioned the battle of the Somme. Pandora should have remembered.

"I'm sorry," she said.

Harley shrugged. "Frank was ten years older than me. I don't remember him that well. But every year, my father takes the anniversary badly. My mother is visiting a cousin, so he's alone today."

"You must go and be with him," Pandora insisted. "The Vanderbilts won't mind. I'll find another dinner partner, and . . ."

"My father wouldn't have let me stay if I asked. He doesn't like to show his emotions," Harley cut in. "I'm glad I didn't suggest it. I wanted to see you before I leave."

Harley moved closer to kiss her again. His lips had barely touched hers when a door opened and they heard footsteps. Archie appeared in the room.

"Lucy sent me to get blankets for the fireworks after dinner," Archie explained. "What are you two doing here?"

Harley's cheeks turned red. Pandora quickly answered for both of them.

"I needed a tennis racquet"—she waved one in the air—"so Harley and I can beat you and Lucy tomorrow."

Archie gave Pandora a peculiar look. Perhaps he had seen the tennis racquet stuffed in her overnight bag. He pulled a stack of blankets from the closet and handed them to Pandora and Harley.

"I'm glad you're here. You can help me," Archie instructed. "I can't carry everything myself."

It was clear that Pandora and Harley wouldn't get any more time alone.

"We'd be glad to." A small sigh escaped her. She reluctantly accepted the blankets. "Though I'm sure you could have managed. They hardly weigh a thing."

~

Archie appeared in Pandora's guest room while she was getting ready for dinner. She had hoped it was Virginia. She would have shown Virginia her dress and confided in her about Harley's kiss.

"What are you doing here?" Pandora demanded. "Someone might have seen you come into my room."

"You don't care about that sort of thing," Archie declared, settling on an armchair. "Or you wouldn't have gone to the pavilion with Harley alone."

Realization dawned on Pandora. She faced Archie angrily.

"You didn't come to the pavilion for blankets, you were following us!"

"I had to; I couldn't let you stay in the pavilion with Harley by yourself."

"It was still daylight, and I'm perfectly capable of taking care of myself," Pandora snapped.

"I see that now." Archie took off his straw hat. He pulled fretfully at the brim. "Since you're the one who kissed Harley."

"How did you see? You must have been spying on us!" Pandora had never been so furious. Her blood boiled, and rage surged through her chest.

"I didn't mean to spy, and I wasn't going to follow you," Archie said, looking the slightest bit guilty. He recovered himself, and his own anger returned.

"When you and Harley took off across the field, I was going to ask if I could join you. Lucy was prattling on about visiting me at

Princeton," he explained. "I was worried about you. You went inside, and I had to see what was going on. As I walked through the door, you slipped from the closet shelf, and I saw you kiss Harley."

Archie's liquid eyes settled on Pandora, and she could see why he was successful with girls. His tender expression was impossible to resist.

"I'll tell you what was going on." She walked to the window and gazed out. "Harley was about to express his feelings for me, and you interrupted. Who knows if he'll get another chance."

Archie was silent for so long, Pandora wondered whether he'd left.

"You can't marry him, Pandora. You hardly know each other."

"Of course I can't marry him." She whirled around. "Because he hasn't proposed."

"You were hoping he would; that's why you kissed him," Archie responded.

"You like Harley." Pandora frowned. "And he genuinely cares about me."

"Harley isn't self-centered like Owen, and he's one of my best friends," Archie conceded. "It's something else. I can't say exactly—it's more a feeling. Trust me, it wouldn't work out."

Pandora searched Archie's face for a clue to what he was talking about. His closed features reminded her of one time when they were children and Archie ate a pudding cake meant for a dinner party. Archie told Esther that his dog Speckles took the cake, but Speckles's paws and nose were clean. Archie finally admitted it when he was doubled over in bed with a stomachache from eating the whole thing.

Suddenly she knew why Archie was discouraging her relationship with Harley.

"You don't want me to marry well! You want me to stay poor Pandora, grateful for any attention you and Virginia give me. You'll marry Lucy and have all this"—she waved out the window at the English-style gardens—"while I'm taking dictation from a middle-aged boss who expects me to work twelve-hour days and let him get under my skirts.

"You say you'd rather be a professor at Princeton, but you don't have to choose. You can have that too. Some honorary position after you and Lucy donate a building. Even Virginia will end up marrying a Dinsmore or an Astor after she's had her fun of playing benefactress to the arts. After she's married, she'll keep supporting a few poets and authors. It will give her the same thrill other society women get from having a lover."

Pandora stopped, horrified at herself. Archie and Virginia had always treated her like a sister. Every birthday they carried out the same traditions they did for themselves: flapjacks for breakfast followed by opening presents and a game of Marco Polo in the swimming pool. And they supported her accomplishments. When she was in the finals in a school tennis tournament, Archie had come home from boarding school to watch her play.

No one could have been a better friend than Archie when they were children. She thought about the leaves they collected every fall. Whenever she felt dejected, she'd pull down the box from its hiding place in the nursery and read their wishes and hope they would come true.

And she knew what his parents wanted for him wasn't what Archie wanted for himself. She felt terrible, as if she had been trying to hurt him.

But she had to stand up for herself. There wasn't any reason for her not to marry Harley.

"You don't mean that, you're upset," Archie said.

"If you think I don't love Harley, you're wrong," Pandora said. "And I know he loves me too."

Suddenly she had a rushing sensation, as if she were swimming in a cool, clear river. Today was the anniversary of his brother's death, yet Harley was attending a house party because he didn't want to miss seeing Pandora. He must have feelings for her.

Her mind went over all the times they spent together during the past month. Buying cherries from a fruit stand, picking flowers along the riverbank. Making a pie together in Blythdale's kitchen and afterward sitting on the lawn with Adele, while Taffy, the Enrights' cocker spaniel, ran circles around them. The plays at the Poughkeepsie playhouse and the ice cream sundaes at Finley's drugstore in Hyde Park.

Being with Harley was so relaxed and easy it was almost like they were already married.

And he valued her opinion. Harley was the first person besides Virginia and Archie who was truly interested in what she said.

"You better go," Pandora said to Archie. She walked purposefully to her closet and took out her gown. "I have to dress for dinner. Lucy wouldn't approve if she walked in while you were here and found me in my slip."

"Forget I said anything," he huffed. His jaw clenched and he strode to the door. "Don't worry, I won't offer my advice again."

Pandora decided then and there to forget about her disagreement with Archie and enjoy the night.

The evening felt torn from the pages of Edith Wharton's novel *The Age of Innocence*. Dinner was served in the Vanderbilts' dining room. The coffered ceiling came from an Italian palazzo and had a mural in its center. The Persian rug was one of the largest in existence and stretched twenty by forty feet. Each guest had their own server. Additional waiters formed a line like toy soldiers in *The Nutcracker*.

The women wore couture gowns bought in Paris and London, complemented by sapphire and ruby pendants. Pandora remarked to Virginia that it looked like there were more precious jewels in the room than at Tiffany's. Virginia whispered back the Vanderbilts could buy Tiffany's with the household money in their cookie jar.

Pandora's own dress had a metallic lace bodice and gradually tiered skirt. She had found the fabric in a chest in the Van Luyens' attic, and she'd accentuated it with hand-sewn beading and embroidery. The finished effect resembled an Asian lacquered screen that Coco Chanel kept in her workroom, which Pandora had seen in one of her fashion books.

Virginia had lent her a shimmery evening bag and long white gloves. Rhinestone clips held back Pandora's hair, and she had dusted her cheeks with pale pink powder. When she descended the staircase, she felt as beautiful and confident as any woman in the room.

Harley barely left her side all night. He sat opposite her at dinner and made sure her wine glass was never empty. He claimed the first dance and dissuaded other men from dancing with her when they cut in. The few times he danced with other girls, he left Pandora with someone to talk to and a full glass of champagne.

It was the first time Pandora had seen Harley in a top hat, and it suited him perfectly. His wing-tipped shoes were polished to a gleam, and his tuxedo shirt had a wonderful smell of laundry soap and cologne.

During a lull in the dancing, they stood near other couples on the balcony. The sky was thick with stars, and Pandora could hear crickets and frogs.

"I'll miss all this at Princeton." Harley sighed, leaning his elbows on the ledge. "There's nothing like the Hudson Valley. It's the most beautiful spot in the world."

"You won't have time to miss it," Pandora said lightly. "You'll be busy with your eating clubs and theater productions."

Harley fiddled with his pocket handkerchief.

"I'm quitting the Triangle Club; I'm not going to be involved with theater this year."

Pandora was shocked. Harley had been looking forward to it so much.

"You can't do that!" she exclaimed. "The Triangle Club is your favorite thing about Princeton."

"I won't have time for it and my finance classes," Harley continued. "Finance is important if I want to join my father at the bank."

"That's not what you want. You want to be a director and producer and open your own theater on Broadway," she reminded him.

Harley's voice slowed as if he was making an effort to talk.

"I've decided that's not practical. My father is right; someone needs to take over the bank. One day I'll inherit Blythdale too. I won't be able to afford its upkeep on ticket sales and newspaper reviews."

Pandora couldn't have been more shocked if Harley had said he was taking a ship to Antarctica.

"Theater is your passion," Pandora said urgently. "You can't spend your life in an office if that's not where you want to be."

Harley turned to Pandora. His green eyes were luminous under the light of the balcony.

"That is where I want to be, especially if . . ." He took her hand. He had never held her hand before. His palm was smooth against her glove.

"We haven't known each other long, but I feel as if I've been looking for a woman like you forever," Harley began. "You're lovely and bright, and you accept me as I am. It might be presumptuous to think you share my feelings, but—" He stopped, and it took all of Pandora's willpower not to press him to continue.

She heard the strains of the band starting up again in the ballroom. The moon was bright and white over the Hudson. Fireflies flickered on the lawn, and the air was thick with the spicy almond scent of hawthorn.

Harley dropped to his knee. He reached into his pocket and drew out a velvet box.

"Pandora, will you marry me?" he said finally.

She gasped at the brilliant round diamond on a gold band.

"It's my mother's stone, but I had it reset. If you don't like it, I could get something else."

Pandora's eyes widened, and she could feel her heart pounding. She had been dreaming of this moment. But now that it was happening, somehow it didn't feel right.

All the plays they had enjoyed this summer, many of the discussions they'd had at Finley's drugstore, revolved around Harley's love of the theater. Pandora loved Harley's passion for the theater. She understood that sort of passion, and it made her feel special that he included her in it.

If Harley worked at his father's bank, he'd be miserable all the time. What would happen if at some point Harley decided it was Pandora's fault that he'd had to abandon his dreams of becoming a producer? Could she live with herself if everything Harley did—the dinner parties they would give to entertain clients, the endless hours he would spend in a board room, the private clubs his father would make him join—was because of her?

Pandora was in love with Harley, but she couldn't let him marry her if it meant giving up his hopes and dreams.

But if she declined his proposal, she'd lose Harley and never be able to repay her father. Willie had put his trust in Pandora, and Pandora had failed. And everything Pandora longed for—the grand estate, the children, the chance to open her own boutique—would disappear as surely as an ice sculpture melting on a summer night. Just like with Owen, Pandora would lose the man she loved. Except this time, it would be her fault.

She looked into his green eyes. Harley was so handsome. She wanted to gaze at him across the breakfast table every morning and go to sleep beside him every night.

Harley made a coughing sound; he squeezed her hand tightly. He was waiting for her to answer. Perhaps he thought the trade-off in careers was worth it if it meant they could be together. His expression was so loving and hopeful she couldn't turn him down.

They could discuss his career later, once they were married.

"The ring is perfect," Pandora breathed. It really was perfect. Elegant and timeless and not too large. She held out her finger. "The answer is yes."

Harley took her in his arms, and his mouth found hers. His kiss was long and deep, and she felt warm and cherished.

"I promise I'll be a good husband," Harley said when he released her.

Pandora pushed her fears from her mind. She and Harley were a team now; nothing would get in the way of their happiness. The future was as bright and silvery as the moon shimmering on the Hudson.

"Let's go inside before it gets chilly." Harley took Pandora's arm.

The minute they entered the French doors, Virginia swooped down on them. She glanced from Pandora's radiant expression to her left hand.

"I wondered where you two went," Virginia gushed. She pointed at Pandora's hand. "Is that what I think it is?"

"I asked Pandora to marry me, and she agreed," Harley answered for both of them.

A champagne flute was pressed into Pandora's hand. Couples crowded around them. The men thumped Harley on the back and offered their congratulations. Pandora held up the ring for everyone to see, and all the guests clapped.

Only one person held back. Archie stood at the bar, downing a cocktail. His expression was dark and brooding. Instead of coming over to join them, he finished his drink and poured another.

Chapter Nine

Pandora and Harley decided on a June wedding, to be held a few weeks after Harley's graduation from Princeton. Pandora was so happy she kept pinching herself to make sure she wasn't dreaming. She'd be able to pay her father back and take care of him when he was older. Already Willie had almost forgiven her, and he was thrilled about the wedding.

The reception would be held at Blythdale. The wedding would take up the entire weekend. They'd start with a picnic on the lawn on Friday, followed by an intimate dinner for the wedding party. There would be a prewedding breakfast on Saturday, then the church service, and then dinner and dancing in the gardens.

Adele hired the band Paul "Pops" Whiteman and his orchestra. Pandora couldn't believe it when Adele told her. Pops Whiteman was the most popular band leader in New York. Adele said Harley was her last remaining son, and she already felt like Pandora was her daughter. She wanted them to have the best of everything.

One of the happiest parts of planning the wedding was the time Pandora spent with Adele. Pandora didn't care that much about seating arrangements or which car would transport them to the church. But she loved Adele's company.

They spent hours together in the morning room at Blythdale. Their conversation moved easily from centerpieces and bridal bouquets to Adele's involvement with the settlement houses and the women working in factories.

Adele sat on a committee that met monthly at the Grand Street Settlement House to address social issues. The committee was advocating for public restrooms to be installed in the neighborhood and starting a kindergarten so that young children had somewhere to go while their mothers worked. Adele promised she'd take her to a committee meeting when Pandora returned from the honeymoon.

Adele was becoming the mother that Pandora never had. She no longer envied girls like Lillian or Lucy. Just being with Adele made her happy.

Milton Enright was kind to Pandora too. He was so relieved that Harley was joining the bank that nothing was too good for the couple. He insisted on paying for the wedding and wouldn't take any money from Pandora's father. Harley and Pandora could honeymoon wherever they liked, and when they returned, they would live at Blythdale until they moved into their own home.

Unlike Lillian, Pandora was in no rush to find a house. She wanted it to be perfect, and looking at estates—the brick mansions that dotted the river between Hyde Park and Poughkeepsie and stone farmhouses that had been added on to since the Civil War—was one of the things she enjoyed most.

And being with Harley, of course. During their engagement, they hadn't seen each other as much as they wanted. Harley was busy with classes, and Pandora was wrapped up in wedding planning. But they spent hours on the phone. They talked about Harley's economics professor, who had been one of Woodrow Wilson's advisors before teaching at Princeton. And about the young British fashion designer Norman Hartnell, who was making a name for himself in London. Her favorite moments, better than the trips to the bakery in Hyde Park to taste wedding cakes, better than the hours spent with the florist choosing bouquets, were the moments spent on the phone with Harley. Pandora loved hearing Harley's voice, loved knowing he was thinking about her.

Harley believed in Pandora's talent, and it made her work even harder. She stayed up all night sketching new designs so she could show them to Harley when she saw him. His praise was better than all the chocolates and flowers he gave her; it made her dreams feel real and important.

~

One weekend, Harley invited Pandora to Princeton to see Preston's play. Pandora chose her dress with care; she wanted to make a good impression on Harley's friends.

She was inspired by the French designer Madeleine Vionnet's new bias cut, which hugged the waist and skimmed over the thighs. Instead of using a monochrome fabric like Madeleine Vionnet used in her designs, Pandora chose a gold organza patterned with blue butterflies. Virginia said it was Pandora's prettiest dress.

When Pandora arrived at Princeton, Harley showed her all his favorite spots on campus. They strolled along the banks of Carnegie Lake, and he showed her the lawn in front of Nassau Hall where George Washington pushed back the British during the Revolutionary War. In the afternoon, they shared a picnic in the quad, and Pandora felt radiantly happy.

That evening, Pandora worried that Harley would miss being part of the production. But he seemed to enjoy the play immensely. Afterward, they attended the cast party, and Harley introduced her to everyone as his fiancée. She kept searching for a hint of unhappiness in his manner. But he stood with his arm around her and whispered in her ear that he was the luckiest man in the world.

Now that they were engaged, Pandora longed for their kisses to progress to something more. They were rarely alone, and neither of them felt comfortable necking in the car. She thought they'd get their chance at Princeton. But women weren't allowed in the rooms, and Harley could get in trouble. For now, they had to be content to continue as they had.

The only blight on her happiness was Archie. Their close camaraderie was gone, and she didn't know how to get it back. She wanted to talk to Archie about his dreams of becoming a professor, but he hardly spoke to her. At Christmas services, he sat in the pew in front of Pandora and didn't turn around. Pandora recalled Christmas services when they were teenagers. Archie would draw funny pictures in the hymn book and pass them to Pandora. Pandora would have to bite her lip to stop from bursting out laughing.

She missed Archie; she didn't know how to get back in his good graces. But she couldn't ask Harley his opinion, and it wouldn't be fair to involve Virginia. Pandora told herself it was part of growing up. It was natural that everything was changing, and she had to be grateful for what she had.

~

Today, Adele and Pandora were going into New York for a dress fitting. At first, Pandora had planned on sewing her wedding dress herself. She envisioned a tulle gown with miles of petticoats that spun around when she danced. Or a satin sheath with lace accents and silver tassels.

But Virginia argued that Pandora's wedding dress had to come from a bridal salon. Lillian Clarkson had already been to London twice to be outfitted for her gown. If Pandora made her own dress, no matter how beautiful it was, Lillian would likely spread a rumor that Pandora sewed her wedding gown because she couldn't afford to buy one.

Adele had been thrilled to go dress shopping with Pandora. She pored over fabrics as if she were the bride herself. They finally settled on a scoop-necked crepe de chine gown with a ten-foot lace train. Her gloves would have diamond buttons, and Adele would lend Pandora her diamond earrings.

The car pulled up in front of Lord & Taylor. Adele waited for the chauffeur to open the door. She wore a calf-length pleated skirt and matching jacket, with a fur cape draped over her shoulders, and a cloche hat decorated with a felt flower.

"I'm afraid you'll be alone tonight; I have to attend Milton's bank dinner." Adele stepped onto the sidewalk. "You won't have to cook, though. The icebox in the townhouse is full, or you can pick up something from the deli on Fifty-First Street."

Pandora had been to the Enrights' Park Avenue townhouse a few times before. It was three stories of elegant rooms decorated by the designer Elsie de Wolfe. The first time Pandora entered the living room, done all in white—white rugs, white sofas, even the grand piano was white—she fell in love. She had never seen anything so perfect.

"Virginia is in town; I'll have dinner with her."

Virginia had started holding her salons and had been begging Pandora to come. So far, Pandora had refused. She didn't feel comfortable socializing with Virginia's circle of bohemian friends. Perhaps it would be different if Harley were with her. It wasn't the kind of thing she would do alone.

Lord & Taylor featured eleven floors of dresses and shoes and housewares. One floor was devoted entirely to restaurants and there was a gym, solarium, and men's smoking room. The wedding dress department was tucked into a corner of the sixth floor. The designer, Madame Dupree, was a tiny woman in a severe black dress and large white glasses. A small black poodle followed at her heels. Assistants flitted between the worktable and dressing rooms, balancing silver trays of petite sandwiches on Wedgwood china.

Pandora's wedding gown, with its scalloped hem sewn with pearls and a train attached by a satin headpiece, took her breath away. She stared in the mirror, her blond hair smooth at her shoulders, her blue eyes somehow larger than ever, and wished her mother could see her. If her mother saw how lovely she looked, how much Pandora resembled her, she might realize how much she had missed out on. Then Pandora deliberately pushed the thought away. Her mother had left because she wanted to. On her wedding day, Pandora would be surrounded by people who loved her. Her father would give her away, and Virginia would be the maid of honor.

Once the fitting was completed, Pandora and Adele ate lunch in the Mandarin Room on the tenth floor. Pandora had never eaten Chinese food before. She couldn't wait to tell Willie about the huge bowls of noodles and chop suey. She even saved him a fortune cookie, a sugary sweet, golden cookie with a paper message tucked inside.

After lunch, Adele wanted to visit a factory to drop off a donation. The car delivered them to a men's shirt factory on Thirty-Ninth Street in the Garment District. It wasn't far from Lord & Taylor, but inside it was the exact opposite of the posh interiors of the department store. Instead of the spacious elegance and polished surfaces of Lord & Taylor, the factory was crammed with machinery and fabric and yarn. Workers were packed as tightly as sardines, and the click-clack of the sewing machines was deafening. Pandora was overwhelmed by the many smells—the glue, the ink for the labels, and even the women's perfume. Adele told her that many of the women were so glad to be out of the house and at work they wore perfume, even though it was only to stand in an assembly line.

The chauffeur unloaded packages that Adele gave to the foreman. She had gathered stockings and biscuits and magazines for the women to read during their lunch break.

"It's not much, but it helps," Adele said to Pandora. "Women won the right to vote six years ago, yet in some ways their lives haven't improved. They traded impossible conditions at home for longer, more-grueling days at a factory. What the suffragettes accomplished is admirable, but there's so much more to be done."

Adele was right. Pandora had attended a lecture about women in the workforce one weekend while she was visiting Harley at Princeton. Eight million women in America were earning salaries, but most of them were seen as unskilled workers and kept from high-paying jobs. The jobs open to women were often drudgework in cotton mills and rubber factories or telegraph operators. Pandora had experienced this herself when she tried to get a job as a secretary. Without dictation or typing skills, she wasn't qualified to do anything besides be a maid or work in a factory. Even with teaching, the pay and conditions were terrible. Teachers could lose their positions for being over forty or having the wrong hairstyle. After women were married, they were expected to stay at home, and if they did work, they were paid half as much as their husbands.

Adele introduced her to a woman named Gladys who had been the factory's first female employee and was still confined to the factory floor. She met Phyllis, a woman who was Pandora's age and pregnant with her third child. Phyllis had terrible morning sickness but couldn't take time off because she was afraid she'd get fired. Adele promised to bring her a special tea and instructed her to take naps during lunch.

"This is Millie Grimes." Adele introduced Pandora to a woman of about thirty. Millie wore a faded cotton dress and plain black shoes.

"It's nice to meet you." Pandora shook her hand. Millie's fingers were covered with little cuts from the machines, and her fingernails were round and short.

"Millie went to secretarial school; she's the fastest typist I know," Adele continued. "She was going to start work in an office, but her husband was injured at the docks. Millie's salary is half what her husband's was, and now she has to support her family."

"Wouldn't secretarial work pay more than a factory?" Pandora turned to Millie, recalling her own attempt to get a job as a girl Friday.

The salary advertised in the newspaper had been quite a bit higher than what women earned in a factory.

"Much more." Millie nodded.

Pandora didn't understand. Millie was well spoken and pretty, with brown hair and hazel eyes.

"I can't afford a nice dress for the interview," Millie said matter-of-factly. "My husband's medicine costs a fortune. We have three children to feed and clothe. There isn't money for anything else."

Pandora was about to reach into her purse to give Millie money for a dress, but something in Adele's expression stopped her.

"Surely a dress can't be the only reason Millie doesn't apply to be a secretary," Pandora said to Adele later in the car on the way to the townhouse on Park Avenue.

"I've offered her money for a dress, but she won't accept it." Adele pulled at her gloves. "She won't take anything that isn't given to all the women."

Pandora suddenly had an idea.

"Could I use the car this afternoon?" Pandora inquired.

"Of course. Stephen will take you anywhere." Adele patted Pandora's hand. "I must be getting old. All I want to do is take a bath and lie down before dinner."

~

That afternoon Pandora gave Stephen an address and sat back against the upholstery. She wondered if she was making a mistake. But girls like Millie deserved a chance; she had to do something.

Levi Dresses occupied a two-story building on Broadway a few blocks from Penn Station. A gold sign stood above the door, and in the window was a display of skirts and blouses.

Just a few days ago, Pandora read about Levi Dresses in an article about the New York fashion industry. More women were buying dresses ready to wear. The custom-made tailors were being replaced by dress shops that had a showroom and factory in the same space.

Levi Dresses wasn't anything like Thomas Maisel Dresses, which had occupied a small set of rooms on the second floor of an office building. Inside were countless metal racks crammed with dresses. Pandora had never seen so many dresses. Bolts of fabric were stacked against the walls, and through a door she could hear the click-clack of sewing machines.

A middle-aged man wearing a dark suit approached her. He had thinning hair and a long, angular nose.

"Can I help you?" he asked.

"I wonder if I could speak to the owner."

"I'm the owner." He held out his hand. "Levi Rosen."

"Pandora Carmichael." Pandora shook his hand.

Levi led her to a quiet corner, and Pandora told him about Millie—how she was so bright, but she couldn't afford a dress for a job interview, and she wouldn't accept a dress as a gift.

"I was wondering if you could extend to her a store credit. Millie would pay for the dress when she gets a job. I'll sign a guarantee, of course." Pandora pulled at her gloves. "My fiancé's father owns Enright's Bank."

Levi nodded in recognition. Pandora could tell he was impressed. Enright's Bank was one of the most prestigious in New York.

"I admire what you're doing," Levi said. "But I've never met you. And I can't let customers take dresses without paying for them. I have salaries to pay and business expenses."

Pandora had been so hopeful that her plan would work. She supposed she could go home and sew a dress for Millie. But she was so busy with wedding planning, and she wanted to help Millie today.

Suddenly she had an idea. She unclipped her gold earrings. They had been a present from Harley, but Harley gave her gifts all the time. And she was certain she'd get them back.

"What if I gave you these earrings to keep until Millie pays for the dress?" She handed them to him.

Levi turned them over. He studied them carefully.

"I suppose that would work."

Pandora was already scribbling her address on a piece of paper.

"You can return them to me here." She handed it to him.

"All right, you have a deal." Levi slipped the paper into his pocket. He smiled for the first time. "You're a persuasive woman, Miss Carmichael. I'll make sure Mrs. Grimes tries on our best dresses."

~

Adele was still lying down in her room when Pandora returned to the townhouse. She picked up the telephone in the living room and dialed Virginia's number.

"Pandora!" Virginia said when she answered. "You didn't tell me you were in town."

"I wondered if you're free for dinner," Pandora said. "Somewhere that Harley would approve of."

Virginia's light laugh came down the line.

"Don't worry. I won't corrupt you by taking you to a speakeasy," Virginia promised. "We'll go to Sardi's. It's in the Theater District, so there will be interesting people."

Sardi's was located in the basement of a brownstone on Forty-Fourth Street. When Pandora arrived, only a few diners were scattered at the tables. A short while later a play must have let out, because suddenly the interior was full of men carrying theater programs and women waving cigarette holders and hovering around the entry. It was so crowded that Pandora worried Virginia wouldn't see her when she arrived.

"You shouldn't let the waiter seat you in the back." She heard Virginia's voice ring out.

Pandora glanced up from the menu. She almost didn't recognize Virginia. Her long, luxurious curls were gone, replaced by a sleek helmet of hair that stopped just below her chin.

"You got your hair bobbed!" Pandora said in shock.

Virginia pulled out a chair. "The hairdresser said I look exactly like Louise Brooks. He probably says that to all the women when they leave the salon."

Virginia did resemble Louise Brooks. The short hair made her eyes seem larger and accentuated the curve of her neck.

"You're prettier than Louise Brooks. But I can't believe you cut your hair!" Pandora exclaimed. Pandora would never get a bob; she thought it would feel practically like walking around naked.

Virginia waved her hand dismissively.

"All the women in New York are doing it. Wolfgang and I went to Chumley's the other night. F. Scott Fitzgerald was there with his wife, Zelda, whose hair is almost as short as a boy's."

"I heard there was a police raid on Chumley's last week," Pandora cut in. She didn't want Virginia to get arrested.

Virginia smiled cheekily. She picked up a menu.

"Everyone who goes to Chumley's knows the police enter from the Pamela Court entrance," she proclaimed. "So the customers go out the Bedford Street door."

Pandora was about to respond when a group of young men entered. One of them looked familiar. It was Preston Stevens, Harley's playwright friend at Princeton. Another man followed him, and Pandora gasped. It was Harley. He wore a top hat with a silk scarf draped over his shoulders.

Harley caught Pandora's eye, and he walked over to their table. He seemed even more shocked than Pandora.

"Pandora"—he leaned down and kissed her—"what are you doing here?"

Pandora didn't know why she was so surprised. New York was only an hour from Princeton by train; Harley probably came to Manhattan all the time. But he never said anything about visiting New York when she was at Princeton. Seeing him here, unannounced, was unsettling.

"I came into New York with your mother," she replied. "Virginia and I are having dinner."

"I'm thrilled to see you." Harley recovered himself. He waved at his friends. "We're a large group; you have to join us."

They followed Harley and joined his friends at a round table beside the window.

"This is much better. Last time I was at Sardi's, this table was occupied by George Gershwin and his crowd," Virginia said as she slid into a chair.

"Harley is a regular at Sardi's," Preston piped in. "He can get any table he likes."

The color rose to Pandora's cheeks. She told herself it was the rum in the fruit punch, but she knew better. Harley was acting differently than he did at Blythdale or even at Princeton. He passed around a gold cigarette case and had no problem ordering a second and third pitcher of punch. He was even dressed differently, in one of the new tuxedo jackets instead of the traditional tails.

"We saw the musical *Castles in the Air*," Preston said. "The audience never stopped clapping."

"It really was wonderful," Harley enthused. "The costumes alone were worth the price of the ticket."

"It's the fifth musical we've seen this semester," Preston said. "That's all Broadway is about these days. Every show we see has more showgirls and more feathers."

Pandora felt close to tears. She averted her gaze so Virginia wouldn't notice. Pandora and Harley had grown so close; she thought she knew everything there was to know about him. Tonight, Harley seemed foreign to her. As if they were viewing each other from miles away instead of across a dinner table.

They talked on the phone almost daily. Why had he never mentioned that he saw plays in New York?

"Harley better bring you to my play in New York in the fall," Preston said to Pandora.

"You have a show opening on Broadway?" Pandora asked in surprise.

"Didn't Harley tell you?" Preston inquired. "It's not Broadway, but it's close enough. We just started rehearsals."

"Of course, we wouldn't miss it," Pandora said.

"I should hope not." Preston reached for a bread roll. "After all, Harley is bankrolling the production."

Harley's skin turned pale, and he busied himself with cutting his steak.

Pandora looked at Harley, but he avoided making eye contact. She remained quiet through the rest of dinner. The others talked about the young new directors and the growing movie industry in Hollywood. After dinner, Virginia suggested they all go on to the Cotton Club. Pandora claimed she had a headache and said she'd go back to the townhouse.

She walked out to the sidewalk to find a taxi.

"Pandora, wait, I can explain." Harley rushed out after her. Preston and the group waited a little farther down the block.

"You don't have to explain anything," Pandora said unsteadily.

Harley took her gloved hand and held it in his.

"I didn't tell you I invested in Preston's play because I didn't want my father to know," he admitted. "It's only a little money from my trust. I'm hardly funding the whole production."

"It's none of my business," Pandora said.

She couldn't tell him the real reason she was upset. It sounded childish. She knew Harley loved her; he showed it all the time. And she shouldn't expect him to tell her everything. After all, she didn't tell him everything. For instance, Harley knew nothing about her losing the money for secretarial school. And she hadn't mentioned Virginia's poetry salons. That wasn't her secret to share.

But there was something different about Harley tonight. This was a new Harley. One who drank fruit punch spiked with rum in public and attended musicals with showgirls wearing feathered headdresses.

Harley put his arms around her. He drew her close and kissed her.

"I don't care if I ever see a play again, as long as we're together," he whispered.

His lips were warm and familiar, and she let herself fall into his embrace. The uneasy feeling she had must have been caused by the rum combined with the cigarette smoke inside Sardi's. Here, kissing on the sidewalk, Harley seemed exactly the same.

It felt good to have his arms around her. As if her closest confidant had disappeared and suddenly returned.

"I'm behaving like an anxious bride." Pandora laughed it off. "All I need is a couple of aspirin and a good night's sleep."

Harley waited until she got inside the taxi. He closed the door and leaned in the window.

"I mean it, Pandora." He touched her hand. His green eyes were bright as emeralds. "I need you. You're the only person I can talk to. If I don't marry you, I'll never survive."

She watched him through the window as her cab pulled away, and she couldn't help but wonder where he was staying that night.

Chapter Ten

Three days before the wedding everything was going perfectly. The weather had been gorgeous: a mild spring gave way to a temperate early summer with cool, clear evenings. Pandora walked around the Van Luyens' and Enrights' gardens and felt something rich and warm curl up inside her. Everything that was dear to her would soon be hers forever.

Not even the night she ran into Harley in New York could spoil her happiness. Pandora and Harley didn't talk about the dinner at Sardi's. The next time she saw him, he brought her thoughtful gifts: a book of fashion illustrations he knew Pandora wanted, a box of chocolate-covered nougat for Willie. They took long walks and talked about life after the wedding, the upcoming play season in Poughkeepsie, whether they should get a dog or share Taffy with Adele and Milton. Whenever she felt uneasy about it, when she recalled how much fruit punch Harley ordered, how easily he and his friends discussed feathers and showgirls, she told herself she was too sheltered. Not every play was a serious production, reviewed in the *New York Times*. Harley was like any young man who liked enjoying himself. He loved her, and they were getting married.

She hadn't even minded attending Owen and Lillian's wedding at the end of May. The lawn at Rosecliff looked lovelier than Pandora had ever seen it, and Lillian made a breathtaking bride in a satin gown from the House of Worth in Paris.

At the reception, she overheard Owen comment to Harley that he was a lucky man, that Pandora was beautiful and intelligent. Even Lillian was friendly. Though she did boast to Pandora and Virginia that they were having a two-part honeymoon: three weeks in Palm Beach followed by a small break and then two months in Italy and the South of France. Virginia whispered to Pandora that if Pandora pushed her own wedding back a couple of weeks, Owen and Lillian would already be in Europe and then they couldn't attend.

Pandora felt that everything was falling into place as it should. She was thrilled to receive a letter from Millie. It was typewritten on formal stationery with "Corning & Sons Inc." printed on the letterhead. Pandora could have hugged the letter when it arrived.

"Dear Miss Carmichael," Pandora read aloud.

"I received my first paycheck and paid Levi Dresses the $6.88 for the interview dress. I'm now the secretary to William Corning, chairman of Corning & Sons. My salary is twice what I earned at the factory, and I'm home in time to cook dinner for my husband and children.

I sent Mr. Rosen a thank-you with the payment, but I thought you would like to know.

Sincerely,
Millicent Grimes"

It was almost lunchtime, and Pandora was sitting in the Enrights' morning room, working on place cards for the reception. The door opened and Harley entered.

"Harley." Pandora looked up. "I didn't know you were here."

Recently Harley had been staying at the Park Avenue town-house and joining his father at the bank. Harley's first official day of work would be after the honeymoon, but Milton wanted him to get acquainted with his duties sooner rather than later.

"I took the train; I just arrived," Harley answered. He stepped forward and kissed her on the cheek. He looked handsome in a yellow V-neck sweater and beige trousers.

"I'm starving. I haven't eaten all day," he said. "Could we go into the kitchen? There's something I want to talk about."

They made baked-bean sandwiches and took them out to the pergola.

"Pops Whiteman and his orchestra will set up on Friday," Pandora said when they were seated. "They'll play 'It Had to Be You' for our first dance, and 'The Man I Love.' I can't wait to see my father dance a waltz." Her face broke into a smile. "Your mother and I decided on my bridal bouquet. It's so large you won't be able to see my face. Everyone keeps telling me that's the fashion." Pandora stopped sheepishly. "I'm prattling on like every bride. No wonder men escape to their private clubs and smoking rooms."

"I have news on the honeymoon," Harley announced. "We won't have to take the train and steamboat to Lake George after all."

It had been Pandora's idea to honeymoon in Lake George. She didn't want to leave her father for the months they would have been away in Europe, and Harley's father was eager for Harley to start work at the bank. Lake George was the perfect destination. It had boating and fishing, and in the last twenty years, many prominent families had built grand houses along the lake. Pandora and Harley could have the days to themselves and join friends for dinner parties in the evenings.

"My father is giving us a new car for the honeymoon. We went to the showroom yesterday. A 1927 Winthrop Double-Six roadster." He bit into his sandwich. "When we get back, you can keep my car."

Pandora's eyes widened. Her own car meant she could drive to Riverview and see her father and Virginia whenever she liked.

"I never dreamed of having my own car." She gasped. "I'll have to thank him."

"He has another surprise for us. We'll find out at the wedding." Harley put down his sandwich. "There's something I need to tell you. I was at a party on Friday."

"What kind of party?" Pandora asked.

"It was at the 300 Club. Preston was there and some actors and playwrights."

Pandora had heard of the 300 Club. It was a speakeasy on West Fifty-Fourth Street. Every time it was shut down, the name changed, and it moved a few blocks and opened again.

"There's nothing wrong with theater parties," Pandora said. "Someday, you'll have to tell your father that you invested in Preston's play. It is your money."

"It wasn't a theater party." Harley avoided Pandora's gaze. He pushed his blond hair over his forehead. "It wasn't a bachelor party either."

Harley's face took on a pained expression, and for some reason Pandora felt frightened. Her heart hammered uncomfortably, and she felt a tugging in her chest.

"What kind of party was it?" she asked uneasily.

Harley stood up. He shoved his hands into his pockets and paced around the pergola.

"I've wanted to tell you for ages, but at the same time I'd rather go our whole lives without mentioning it," he began. "I'm trying so hard, and it just takes time. Pandora, you're so lovely. You're everything I could ask for . . ."

Pandora didn't want to listen.

"Are you saying you don't love me anymore?" She jumped up.

She had been right about Harley when she ran into him at Sardi's. There had been something different about him. He was in love with another woman and was afraid to tell her.

Harley took her hand in his. "I do love you," he said adamantly.

"Then what's the matter?"

Pandora forced herself to smile. She could face anything as long as Harley was in love with her. She tried to sound like a modern woman. "If something happened at the party with another woman, I would be horrified. But if everyone was drinking, I might understand."

"It wasn't another woman." Harley's voice was low. There was a tremor around his mouth. "It was a man."

Pandora's sandwich dropped on the ground. She let out a gasp and put her hand over her mouth.

She knew a little about homosexuals. In England they were still sent to prison. It wasn't a crime in New York, but it was almost as bad. Clubs where homosexual activity took place were raided by the police for obscenity and disorderly conduct.

"It was a one-time thing," Pandora said quickly. "Wedding nerves or fears about your new job. Perhaps you can tell your father you need more time. You need a rest; you can join the bank next year."

"Pandora." Harley stopped her. "I've known I'm this way for years. I fell in love with a boy when I was at boarding school. I knew it was shameful; I did everything I could to ignore it."

He had never looked so anguished. He sank onto the bench and rested his elbows on his knees.

"You can't imagine what it's like to be fifteen years old and know you're about to do something that will change your life forever. From then on, you'll always be afraid. Afraid of being ostracized by your community, hated by your own family. Even afraid of being sent to jail."

"Lots of boys have homosexual experiences at boarding school. It's a phase, and they grow out of it." Pandora sat beside him. She tried to stay calm. "It all makes sense. You're anxious about the wedding;

it brought up certain feelings. Everything will return to normal once we're married."

"This is normal for me, Pandora." Harley's voice became harder. "You don't understand. It wasn't a phase for me at Andover. It was the first time in my life that I was true to myself. Being homosexual isn't just about the physical act. It's who I am."

Pandora glanced up at him. His eyes were dark and hooded. She saw new lines on his forehead.

Her whole world felt off-kilter. Harley couldn't mean any of it. Willie told Pandora that after the war, many soldiers suffered episodes of trauma. Something reminded them of the war—a rifle shot in the woods, the smell of gun powder, and they felt like they were back on the front lines. Perhaps it was the same with Harley. Something at the 300 Club triggered a memory of boarding school. None of what he was saying could be true. It wasn't possible.

"You said you loved me. You asked me to marry you."

"I do love you." He pressed her hand. "I want to marry you more than ever."

Pandora wrenched her hand away. She inched back on the bench.

"So I can be some kind of veil to make you look respectable. While you carry on with men?"

Harley turned to face her.

"It's not like that. I want the same things you do. A house, children, a family." He waved his hand. "This other thing would become something pushed to the side. It wouldn't have anything to do with us. Our lives would go on the way we planned."

Pandora recoiled in horror.

"Why did you choose me?" she demanded. "Is it because I'm poor? Because I wouldn't have Lucy or Lillian or any of those other young women to stand by my side when you broke my heart? Or were you doing me a favor? 'Pandora Carmichael will marry me because she'll never have other prospects.'"

Her eyes filled with tears; she blinked them away. She couldn't let Harley see her cry. She had fallen in love with him. And he'd betrayed her.

"I love you, Pandora. I loved you from the moment I saw you. You walked into the study when Preston and I were rehearsing, and it was if I had a new chance at life." He twisted his hands. "You're bright and intelligent and lively. The more time we spent together, the more I felt like I discovered my best friend."

A sharp pain pierced her chest. She felt the same way about Harley—that she had found the person she belonged to.

But how could she trust him? In marriage you had to be honest with each other about everything. Yet Harley was being honest with her now. He could have waited until she found out, and even then he could have denied it. Pandora believed he was trying to turn over a new leaf. If Pandora loved Harley, she would help him.

He sensed the change in her. He reached for her hand.

"I'll be a good husband. You can open your boutique in Hyde Park. I know how talented you are; the boutique will be a huge success. We'll get a townhouse in New York, and you can open another boutique in Manhattan."

The mention of New York brought it all back.

"So you can sneak off to a speakeasy with another man," she retorted. "I'll sleep with a wad of twenty-dollar bills on the bedside table so if there's a police raid, I can get you out of jail."

"There won't be other men, and if there are, I'll be discreet."

"You weren't discreet this time," she snapped. "You could have been arrested."

"In a way, I'm glad I went to the party. I realized I couldn't go into the marriage with a secret." Harley touched her wrist. "I need you, Pandora. Without you, I'd be completely lost."

Pandora's thoughts spun like the carousel at Coney Island. Many married couples didn't have sex: the husbands had been wounded in the war or injured in an accident. Some wives already had six children and were so afraid of getting pregnant, they stopped making love with their husbands.

But this was different. Harley was asking her to live a lie. What if they never made love—could she live without passion? All the times Harley had kissed her, her body instinctively wanted more. She had been looking forward to her wedding night, to a lifetime of making love with her husband. Now she would have to get used to possibly living without it. If they did make love, it would be something else entirely. It would be Harley doing what was expected of him.

He'd put her in a terrible position. If Pandora and Harley didn't get married, she would lose Adele. Pandora adored Adele; she was almost like a mother. They had grown so close. And there was Willie. Willie would eventually live with them when his arthritis grew worse and he could no longer teach tennis. Lately, he had to cancel more lessons because of the pain in his shoulder. In a few years, he might not be able to teach at all.

"How would it work?" she asked doubtfully.

"Nothing would be different. My parents must never know. They've endured so much with my brothers dying in the war. It would destroy them." He took her hand. "And you're right. I'll be so busy with the bank and entertaining friends I won't have time to think about anything else."

Pandora sat back and looked around. It was a perfect summer day. The sun glinted on the river, and the air smelled of hyacinths. In three days, the lawn would be transformed for the reception: round tables set with huge vases of scarlet and white roses, a platform filled with musical instruments, a separate table with an ice sculpture and a six-tier wedding cake with chocolate fondant icing.

She and Harley had promised themselves to each other. She couldn't flee at the first obstacle she encountered. But she needed time to think.

"I need some time," she said. "We can talk about it later."

"Of course." He nodded.

~

Later that same afternoon, Pandora sat at a table in the public library in Hyde Park. She'd spent the last two hours reading everything she could about homosexuality. The only treatments were terrifying. In Austria, doctors administered something called aversion therapy, where the patient was given electric shocks and chemicals to make them vomit. She could never subject Harley to such terrible things.

She read newspaper clippings about homosexuals congregating at public bath houses and gathering at nightclubs in Greenwich Village. The February before, fifteen hundred people attended a masquerade ball at the Renaissance Casino in Harlem, and the newspaper reported that you couldn't tell the men, in their elaborate evening gowns and painted faces, from the women.

She wished she could confide in Virginia, but then Virginia would have to keep Harley's secret too. She had to make the decision by herself.

The door to the library opened, and Vivian Clarkson entered. She wore a green chemise dress. A small hat was perched on her head, and she wore white gloves.

"Pandora," Vivian said when she recognized her. "What a pleasant surprise."

Pandora hastily covered the newspaper. She didn't want Vivian to see what she was reading.

"Vivian," Pandora responded. "It's nice to see you."

"I came in to pick up the new Dorothy Sayers mystery book," Vivian said brightly. "Why don't I get it, and then we can have coffee?"

Vivian had been so nice to her. At Lillian's wedding, when the lawn at Beechtree was crowded with guests, she had made a point of coming over and talking to Pandora and Harley.

"Of course, I'd love to." Pandora stood up, slipping the book she had checked out into her bag.

They sat in Hilda's Coffee Shop and ordered two coffees and a plate of ladyfingers. They talked about the upcoming wedding, how anxious and excited Pandora was. Vivian assured her that she would do fine; young women were so capable these days.

Pandora pondered how a woman as warm as Vivian could have Lillian for a daughter.

"There is something I wanted to ask you." Vivian interrupted her thoughts. "Lillian mentioned that you design dresses."

"Harley and I have to find a house and get settled first," Pandora answered. "After that, I hope to open a boutique."

Vivian sipped her coffee thoughtfully.

"Leland and I aren't going to Europe this year, and I'd love a new gown for the opera. Perhaps you could make something for me when you return from your honeymoon. I'd pay whatever you like."

Pandora gulped her coffee in excitement. Vivian Clarkson asked her to design a dress! She knew it was partly because she was about to become Mrs. Harley Enright. That didn't matter. It was still flattering.

"I'd love to," Pandora said happily.

"Wonderful." Vivian set down her coffee cup. "I should go. I'm getting my hair done for your wedding. Leland and I are thrilled to be invited."

After Pandora finished her coffee, she drove back to Blythdale. She had to find Harley and tell him her decision.

The newspaper articles and books proved it would be pointless to try to change him. She had to accept Harley the way he was. She would approach the marriage on practical terms. Marrying Harley meant she'd have a family and could open her boutique. In return, Harley would be protected from gossip.

Harley was in the library when she arrived. She was reminded of the night they met. Harley had been so handsome and sweet; she had instantly been attracted to him.

"You're back." Harley glanced up from the desk.

He pushed his hair across his forehead. Pandora could see fear and trepidation in his eyes.

"I think we can go through with the wedding, but we have to promise to be faithful to each other. If you were involved in any kind of scandal, it could ruin everything." She took a deep breath, wondering if Harley would agree.

Harley walked to the window. The lawn was freshly mown, and the gardeners were clipping roses in the rose garden.

Pandora could see the uncertainty in his expression, as if he was weighing her suggestion. He paused for another moment, then he turned and crossed the floor.

"You have my word. I promise I'll be faithful."

Harley put his arms around her and pulled her close. Pandora buried her face in his chest.

She had to believe him.

Chapter Eleven

Pandora spent the following day at Riverview. She had spent so much time at Blythdale in the weeks leading up to the wedding, it felt nice to be at home. She tidied the cottage's small living room and sorted the fashion books on her bookshelf.

She spent a whole hour in the kitchen, arranging the spices. When she stepped back to admire the rows of bottles and jars, she had to laugh. For as long as she could remember, she had dreamed of attending the Van Luyens' dinner parties and never having to serve again. Now she had an afternoon to herself, and she spent it in the pantry.

After she finished the spices, she sat at the kitchen table with a basket of peas and a bowl in front of her. The kitchen door opened, and Archie stood in the hallway. He wore his tennis whites and held an overnight bag. His cheeks were smooth, and his eyes looked as pale blue as Maude Van Luyen's china. She caught the scent of his aftershave.

Pandora was about to go give him a kiss on the cheek, but she remembered they were hardly speaking.

"I just drove up from New York; your father said you were home." He entered the kitchen.

"Esther had to run some errands; I'm helping with tonight's casserole."

"Mrs. Harley Enright shouldn't be shelling peas." Archie pulled out a chair.

"I'm not married yet, and I wanted to do it," Pandora replied.

Archie picked up a pea pod and snapped it open. His expression was warmer than she had seen it in months.

"Do you remember when we used to do this together? I always wanted to make the pea pods into boats and sail them in the sink," he said cheerfully.

"You were no help at all." She laughed.

"It was more fun than piano lessons." He rummaged in his bag and brought out a slim book. "I brought you something."

Pandora couldn't have been more surprised. It was a dog-eared copy of *The Adventures of Tom Sawyer* by Mark Twain.

"I found it on my bookshelf. The first time I read it was the summer you and your father arrived at Riverview," Archie went on. "Tom Sawyer wasn't the most stand-up guy in the beginning, but he turned out all right in the end. And he was loyal to his friends." He handed her the book. "I wanted you to have it as an apology."

Pandora glanced curiously at Archie. She had never heard Archie apologize in his life. Whenever he was wrong about something, he found a humorous way to wriggle out of it.

"An apology?"

"For the night you got engaged to Harley. You didn't ask for my advice, and I shouldn't have given it to you."

"I don't understand," she said, frowning.

"Harley is one of my closest friends. But people talk, especially at college." He picked up another pea pod. "I heard rumors."

"What kind of rumors?" she asked cautiously.

Archie's cheeks turned red. He emptied the peas into the bowl.

"At Princeton, Harley was only interested in the theater. The theater attracts a certain kind of man." He stopped and looked at her searchingly.

Pandora's heart beat faster. Had Archie heard rumors about Harley's homosexuality? She couldn't admit anything to him.

"If you're talking about showgirls and actresses, you're worried about nothing," she said airily. "Harley is completely loyal, and he's not involved in the theater anymore."

"That's when I realized I was wrong," Archie reflected. "I should have apologized sooner."

"Harley is my best friend. We're perfect for each other." She emptied the peas into the bowl.

"I'm glad." Archie looked at Pandora. "I care about you, Pandora. I only want you to be happy."

Pandora took a deep breath. She had to regain her composure. She turned the conversation to Archie.

"What about you? Are you happy with Lucy?"

"It doesn't matter if I'm happy," Archie said with a shrug. "I'm probably going to marry her anyway."

"That's ridiculous; you should marry whomever you like."

"I've told you, that's not how it works." He took an envelope out of his bag. "I received an invitation for a two-year fellowship at Oxford. It's only awarded to top students. But I could as easily accept it as I could become a janitor in one of my father's buildings."

He crumpled the envelope in his hand.

"My future is all planned out. I've been invited to the Vanderbilts' summer house, Sonogee, in Maine. Then our family will spend Christmas at the Vanderbilts' estate, Biltmore, in North Carolina. I'll probably propose on New Year's Eve, and Lucy and her aunt will spend months planning the wedding. We'll honeymoon in Rome and Venice and then move into the Vanderbilt mansion on Fifth Avenue."

"You have to stick up for yourself," Pandora said hotly. "Accept the fellowship, marry someone you love."

Archie looked at her heavily. He slipped the envelope back into the bag.

"Easy for you to say. No one is counting on you to keep the family name in the New York Social Register," he remarked. "My parents mean well, and I understand. What's the point of building a real estate empire if there's no one to carry it on?"

Pandora hated seeing Archie upset. But she didn't have an answer.

"I came to apologize, and yet here we are having this bleak conversation." Archie stood up and smiled. "That's why they invented tennis. It's impossible to worry about life when I'm concentrating on my serve."

~

Three hours later, Pandora crossed the gardens from the cottage to the main house. The lawn was dark, and the only sound came from the crickets on the riverbank. She had spent an hour in the bath and another two hours curled up in her bed reading. She was hungry.

She saw a light on in the study. She wondered who was there. The Van Luyens were out to dinner, and Archie was spending the evening with Lucy. The door was open, so she poked her head inside. Archie was sitting at the desk. A plate of casserole was in front of him, along with a glass and a bottle of whiskey.

"Pandora." Archie greeted her with surprise. His eyes were slightly glassy. "I thought you were dining at Blythdale."

"Harley doesn't get back until tomorrow," Pandora replied. "I decided I needed a quiet night at home."

"You can join me if you like." He waved at the tray. "I thought I'd try the casserole, but I'm not hungry." He picked up the glass. "The whiskey works much better."

Archie hardly ever got drunk. When he did occasionally get tipsy, he merely ambled upstairs and went to bed. He'd appear at breakfast the next morning, freshly shaven and smiling, without the slightest trace of a hangover.

He seemed tipsy now. She could see a line of sweat on his forehead, and his words were slightly slurred.

"Are you feeling all right?" she inquired.

He attempted a smile. He picked up the bottle.

"Your father beat me at tennis. Then Lucy invited me to a private opera performance." Archie grimaced. "I don't like opera. So I decided to stay here and eat casserole and drink whiskey instead." He refilled his glass. "Do you remember when we were children and Virginia made us put on plays? Her favorite was *Peter Pan*."

"I remember."

"I never liked playing Peter. I was afraid the same thing would happen to us as in the play." He gulped the whiskey. "That we'd grow up and never be together again."

"We're still together," Pandora said.

She recalled when Archie spontaneously added a scene to the play and gave her a peck on the lips, sealing their closeness forever. The kiss had surprised her. She hadn't thought of that in years.

"We have other people in our lives. Even Virginia has someone, though she doesn't talk about him."

Pandora's throat burned. She felt suddenly thirsty.

"I wouldn't mind a glass of whiskey." She pointed at the bottle.

Archie moved to the other side of the desk and handed her a shot. She drank it quickly. Then another. The burning persisted, and he poured her another.

Their hands touched, and she glanced at Archie. She saw something new in his eyes, but it took a moment to recognize what it was. It was something she hadn't seen before.

Archie wanted to kiss her. She was sure of it.

She wanted to kiss him too. She wanted more than a few kisses; she wanted to make love. Not for the reasons she would likely sleep with Harley in the future—in order to conceive a child. She wanted to make love because they were a man and a woman who were so consumed by desire they couldn't do anything else. Making love with Archie would restore something to her, it would prove that she was a desirable woman. But Archie never would. He was too good, too honorable.

She reached forward and kissed him. Archie pulled back in surprise. She kissed him again, and this time he returned her kiss.

The kiss felt different from Harley's. Archie's kiss was insistent and probing, and a warmth spread between her thighs.

"I shouldn't have done that," he apologized, moving away.

Pandora picked up the bottle and poured another shot of whiskey. Archie glanced at her in surprise.

"You're not a good drinker, Pandora," he said gently. "Haven't you had enough?"

Pandora swallowed the whiskey. She looked at him squarely. "What if I asked you to make love to me?"

Archie's mouth dropped open. He gasped in shock. The fork fell on the floor, and he picked it up.

"What did you say?"

Pandora walked to the other side of the study. She turned and faced Archie.

"You heard me correctly. I want you to make love to me, tonight, while no one is here."

Archie's brow creased. He put the fork on the plate.

"It's my fault; I've been acting maudlin all day," he apologized. "What you're asking is impossible. I'd never do anything to hurt you. And Harley is my friend."

Pandora's cheeks colored. In two days, she was getting married, and she'd never break her wedding vows. Tonight was her only chance to know what true passion felt like. Yet she couldn't tell Archie that Harley was homosexual.

"I can't tell you the reason, but it would mean so much to me," she said.

Archie was so handsome. His blond hair flopped over his forehead, and the rolled-up sleeves of his white shirt displayed the golden hair on his arms. The muscles on his shoulders were tight, and his body was long and lean.

"You're supposed to be getting married in two days," Archie reminded her.

"I am getting married," Pandora said firmly. "I would never be unfaithful to Harley." Her eyes were wide. "It would only be tonight; I'll never do anything like this again."

Archie sipped his whiskey. When he gazed at her, she saw the longing in his eyes. It would only take one more kiss to put him over the edge.

She crossed the room and kissed him. His mouth was warm. He kissed her back and then pulled away.

"We can't do this, Pandora. We're both drunk and not thinking straight," he begged. "I'd never forgive myself if you regretted it."

Archie was right, it was madness.

But she didn't want to stop. She wanted Archie to take her in his arms, to touch the places that would make her gasp with pleasure.

Didn't she deserve one night of passion when she was about to marry a man who would never truly desire her? She wanted to surrender herself to Archie.

He stood so close she could smell his shaving soap. She reached up and kissed him again. This time he wrapped his arms around her. A groan escaped his mouth.

"Pandora, we have to stop," Archie choked out.

She could tell by the heat in his expression that he didn't mean it.

"It will be our secret," Pandora promised.

Archie's eyes traveled down Pandora's body. His gaze was imploring. He leaned forward and kissed her. His mouth was hungry this time. His hands caressed her breasts. Her nipples stood on edge; a delicious tingling started between her thighs.

"Not here," he whispered. "Let's go up to my room."

Pandora hadn't been in Archie's room in ages. It still had the same striped wallpaper and a sitting area near the fireplace. A desk stood by the window, and he had flung his overnight bag on the dresser.

Archie took her in his arms and kissed her. He fumbled with his shirt, and she stopped him and unbuttoned it. It felt strange and exciting to have her hands on a man's chest. She opened his shirt and pressed her cheek against his skin.

Archie turned her around and unbuttoned her dress. Her slip fell from her shoulders, and she stepped out of her panties. She turned back so she could see his face. His eyes traveled over her naked body, taking in her small, pert breasts, the golden tuft between her thighs.

Finally, he took her hand and led her to the bed.

"Are you sure?" he asked when they lay down. She ran her hands along his well-muscled arms and the smattering of blond hair on his chest.

"Completely sure." Pandora nodded.

Archie kissed her slowly. His kisses were probing; she felt them in her stomach, between her thighs. A moan caught in the back of her throat.

"I don't want to hurt you," Archie whispered.

Pandora guessed that Archie sensed she was a virgin. It didn't matter. Every part of her body was on fire; she wanted him more than ever.

"I want you," she whispered. "Please, now."

He kissed her again, harder this time. She was drowning in his kisses; she wanted them to last forever.

"I love you; I have always loved you." The vow escaped Archie's lips. But she decided she had imagined the words. Then he gently rolled on top of her. She felt a pleasure and pain that was almost too much to bear.

Her body arched to meet his, and she couldn't remember feeling so light and free. Archie began to move, and Pandora rose higher, then tumbled down an invisible cliff.

Afterward, they sat against the headboard. Archie pulled the sheet around them.

"Are you all right?" he asked anxiously.

"I'm fine. More wonderful than I could imagine," Pandora said truthfully.

Archie was silent. He touched her cheek and kissed her head.

"I'm lucky to have you in my life," Pandora said.

She wiped a trickle of sweat from his chest. He turned to her and smiled his boyish smile.

"Tonight, I'm the lucky one," he replied. "You're a beautiful woman, Pandora. I'll never forget this."

Pandora thought of the perfectly planned life with Harley that lay ahead of her. It seemed so removed, as if she were gazing at a painting. But she was now ready. Nothing had changed, and she would move forward into her bright future.

Chapter Twelve

Everyone warned Pandora that her wedding day would pass in a blur. She had not stopped thinking about her night with Archie, but now she would set the memory aside. Later, she would examine her feelings of guilt mixed with passion. But not now. She was determined not to miss a single minute of the day.

She woke up to the breakfast tray that Willie left at her door, with a note that the bride shouldn't eat in the kitchen on her wedding day. Virginia joined her, and together they packed her suitcase for the honeymoon.

Before the service, a Rolls-Royce Phantom picked up Pandora and Willie and took them to the church. Milton had imported it from England. It was the same make of car that drove King George and Queen Mary and their children around at Buckingham Palace. Virginia's jaw dropped when she saw it. Pandora would certainly make the wedding pages in the *New York Times* now.

Later, Pandora sat in a dressing room behind the chapel, enveloped by more chiffon than she had ever seen in her life. She couldn't believe the day had actually arrived. When Adele gave her the diamond ear-rings she had worn on her wedding day as something borrowed and a sapphire brooch as something blue, Pandora burst out crying and ruined her makeup. Adele had to reapply Pandora's powder and fix her lipstick.

"The best thing about your marriage isn't that Milton is so thrilled or even that you make Harley so happy." Adele stepped back and admired her handiwork. "It's that I'm gaining a daughter. Besides Annie, of course, but she lives all the way across the country."

Pandora was so touched. She would have hugged Adele, but she worried about crushing her wedding dress.

The best moment of all was when Pandora walked down the aisle. Her father handed her over to Harley, and she saw a look of such love in Harley's eyes, and Pandora thought she heard a few of the guests gasp. She cast a quick glance at Archie standing behind Harley. He smiled back, and she knew that he would always keep their secret.

She told herself that the way Archie made her feel when she looked at him, the sudden warmth between her thighs, the shiver that ran down her spine, was only natural. They had made love; she was no longer a virgin.

For a moment, she wondered if Archie felt guilty too. But Archie didn't have anything to feel guilty about. Pandora had asked him to make love to her. She cast the memory out of her mind and locked eyes with Harley. She was in love with him, and they were getting married.

~

After the ceremony, Pandora stood on the balcony at Blythdale as the band played a selection of Al Jolson songs and waiters passed around champagne and hors d'oeuvres. She was about to join Harley on the lawn when Owen and Lillian approached her.

Lillian wore a feathered headdress and held a pearl fan. Pandora noticed the diamond wedding band sparkling next to Lillian's engagement ring.

"Owen told me you're going to Lake George for your honeymoon. My parents used to own a cabin there; it's quite pleasant except for the mosquitoes." Lillian looked at Pandora with large, innocent eyes. "It's too bad you and Harley aren't coming to Europe. We could have met up and had fun."

"Unfortunately, we can't be gone all summer. Milton is eager for Harley to take over more responsibilities at the bank," Pandora explained.

"I can't wait to get to Italy; I need a change of scenery." Lillian sighed. "We spent the entire spring looking for houses and haven't found anything."

Pandora wished she could excuse herself and join Harley, but it wouldn't be polite.

"Milton and Adele are giving us a house as our wedding present," she said to Lillian. "They told us at the rehearsal. It's called Summerhill."

Summerhill was only a mile from Blythdale. The houses even shared a paddock. It was built by Richard Morris Hunt in the Gothic style with a third floor, which would make a perfect nursery.

Lillian's face turned pale. She furiously fanned herself.

"He couldn't have given you Summerhill. It's not for sale."

Pandora smiled her brightest smile.

"I can't believe it myself. The owners were clients of Milton's, and the house wasn't even on the market. We haven't seen it, but Adele said I'll fall in love. We're going to start furnishing it as soon as we return from our honeymoon."

Lillian smiled as politely as she could and pulled Owen onto the dance floor. Virginia joined Pandora.

"What did you say to Lillian?" Virginia wondered. "She's as white as the china."

"We shouldn't gossip about the guests," Pandora chided. They both giggled and turned to take in the view of the gardens.

The sun had set, the moon was full and bright. Pandora had chosen the decor herself. She had wanted the lawn to look as if the stars had dropped down from the sky. The tables were covered with silver table-cloths, and silver bows were tied around the chairs. Gold wine goblets contrasted with the sterling silverware arranged on crisp white napkins.

"I can't believe it's my wedding day." Pandora sighed, sipping her champagne. "Everything is perfect."

Virginia wasn't listening. Pandora followed her gaze and noticed a young man in a top hat and tails. He had fair hair and blue eyes with long eyelashes.

"Who is that? Men that good looking shouldn't be allowed at weddings." Virginia kept staring at him. "The married women will hide their wedding rings, and the single girls will fight each other for your bouquet."

"I haven't had the pleasure of meeting the bride and maid of honor," the man said as he approached them, making a small bow. "I'm Porter Merrill. Harley and I were at boarding school together."

At the mention of boarding school, Pandora felt a prickly sensation at the back of her neck.

"We were both in the drama department at Andover," Porter continued. "Harley was a brilliant director; he made me believe I could act."

"I'm sure you were hypnotic onstage," Virginia said coyly.

"Only until I opened my mouth." Porter smiled. His teeth were straight and white. "I could never remember my lines."

"Pandora, I see you've met Porter." Harley joined them. He seemed out of breath, as if he had rushed over to them.

"Harley, you're interrupting," Porter said cheekily. "I was going to tell them a story about our school days."

Harley was about to comment when a young woman joined their group. She wore a beaded dress, and her hair was fastened by a diamond tiara. Her eyebrows were thick and dark, and she had closely set brown eyes. She wasn't pretty; her nose was too long, but she carried herself with a certain elegance.

"This is my fiancée, Doris." Porter introduced them. "Doris's father is head of the Young Republican Club in New York. I'm throwing my hat into the ring for state senate."

"You'll be a natural." Harley beamed, turning to Pandora and Virginia. "At Andover, Porter was vice president of the drama society."

"Only because the other boys were too lazy, and you were already president," Porter remarked. "Doris has promised to write my speeches. She studied English at Vassar."

They talked about Porter and Doris's engagement and the governor's mansion in Albany. Eventually, Porter and Doris drifted off. Pandora was about to ask Harley to dance, but he had disappeared.

She finished her champagne and set the glass on the sideboard. Could Porter be the boy Harley had been in love with at Andover? That was impossible. Harley would never invite him to the wedding if so.

Milton approached her looking debonair in a fitted black jacket with a long swallow tail. His trousers had silk strips up the sides, and he had a white handkerchief tucked into his breast pocket.

"The bride shouldn't be standing alone." Milton offered her a champagne flute. "I brought you a glass of champagne."

"No, thank you." She shook her head, watching Porter and Doris talking to another couple. "I've had too much to drink already."

"You've made our family very happy, Pandora," he commented. "Harley is a lucky man."

She pulled her eyes away from Porter. She couldn't let him spoil the reception.

"On second thought, I am thirsty." She turned to Milton. "I'll have that champagne after all."

Milton handed her the glass. The band played "I'll See You in My Dreams." Pandora sipped the champagne and pretended she didn't have a care in the world. When the reception finally ended and Pandora and

Harley had waved goodbye to the assembled guests, they drove to the Beekman Arms in Rhinebeck. They would spend the night there and drive three hours to Lake George in the morning.

The room's furnishings dated back to the Civil War. The four-post bed had a quilted bedspread, and against the wall was a porcelain sink with a jug of water. A rolltop desk stood in the corner, and a vase holding sunflowers sat on the wooden coffee table.

"Porter's fiancée, Doris, invited us to dinner when we come back from the honeymoon," she said casually. "You never mentioned him before."

She waited for Harley to respond, but instead he walked to the door.

"I've got a splitting headache; I'm going outside for a smoke."

Pandora paced around the room and waited for Harley to return. She shouldn't have said anything about Porter; they were both exhausted. Harley had given her no reason for concern—he didn't talk to Porter again for the rest of the reception.

After half an hour, the door opened. Harley walked in and kissed her.

"I'm sorry; I'd forgotten how champagne affects me," he apologized. "My head is still throbbing. Why don't we go to bed?"

Pandora went into the bathroom to wash her face. She slipped on the satin negligee she had chosen for the wedding night and checked her hair in the mirror. She wondered if it would be best to get their first night of lovemaking over with and try to conceive a baby. But she couldn't help thinking about making love with Archie. What would it be like to make love with Harley instead?

When she came out, she found Harley sprawled on the bed, fast asleep. She lay down beside him, relief mixed with disappointment. Harley had made the decision for her.

When she closed her eyes, sleep wouldn't come. Instead, she saw Porter Merrill in his top hat and tails. Virginia was right. Men that good looking shouldn't be allowed at a wedding.

~

For the first two weeks of their honeymoon, they didn't try to make love. Pandora couldn't blame their surroundings, so she decided to put it out of her mind. Harley seemed happy, and they had plenty of social engagements to keep them busy. They had been invited to a dinner party hosted by a young couple, Walker and Daisy Frick, whom they met at the beach. Pandora planned to dress up, and after the party she'd ask Harley to help unbutton her gown.

Harley appeared in the bedroom. He wore a summer suit and held a straw hat.

"What a pretty dress," he commented, standing behind her at the mirror.

"Do you like it?" Pandora turned around. It was white lace with a heart-shaped collar and ankle-length skirt. "Your mother and I picked it out at Lord & Taylor."

He handed her a small box. "I picked up something for you in the village."

Inside was a gold charm bracelet with a charm of a rowboat.

"It's lovely. Where did you find it?"

"At a jewelry store," he replied. "I happened to pass the window. I wanted you to have a reminder of our honeymoon."

Pandora fastened it around her wrist. It really was beautiful. Her mind went fleetingly to Porter, and she wondered if there was another reason Harley bought the bracelet. She was being silly. Harley loved to bring her gifts, and they were newly married.

She stood on tiptoe and kissed him.

"Thank you. There's nothing I would have liked better."

"We better go or we'll be late." He put on his hat.

The Fricks lived in one of the smaller mansions on Lake Shore Drive. Daisy Frick was in her late twenties with blond hair and large brown eyes.

"It's nice to meet new people," Daisy said, leading Pandora into the drawing room. "Lake George is pleasant, but the same people come every summer. I should have known when we got married." She fiddled with a diamond ring the size of a bird's egg. "Lake George is strictly for the second son, the one who doesn't inherit the grand estate in Newport."

"What do you mean?" Pandora asked curiously.

"Walker's father is Henry Frick." She sat down and motioned Pandora to sit beside her. "He made his fortune in steel. I should have realized Walker's older brother, Henry Jr., would inherit everything. And then there's the family scandal, of course. Walker is always using his charities to try to make up for what happened."

Pandora looked at Daisy with a puzzled expression.

"Maybe you haven't heard about it," Daisy went on. "Walker's father built a hunting and fishing club in Pennsylvania. The dam wasn't shored up properly, and there was a flood. Two thousand people died, many of them Henry's employees." Daisy twisted her diamond ring. "Ever since then, his family has been involved in all sorts of charities. Walker wanted me to cochair the Orphan Asylum fundraiser." She pretended to yawn. "The meetings go on forever. So I came up with a plan." She patted her stomach. "I'm three months pregnant; I can't cochair an event that will happen a month before the baby is due." She smiled smugly. "Walker is ecstatic we're having another child, and I get out of doing charity work."

Pandora was even more puzzled.

"How did you plan to have a baby?"

Daisy leaned back on the sofa. "It has to do with your monthly cycle. Most women use the method to stop from having babies. Trust me, you don't want to get pregnant right away. You'll miss out on the fun of being newlyweds. I'll give you a tip. As long as you refrain from having relations in the middle of your cycle, you won't get pregnant."

"It's that simple?" Pandora asked in surprise. No one had ever explained it before.

"Take my advice and wait to have a baby as long as you can." Daisy patted Pandora's hand. "After I had Walker Jr., Walker looked at my body as if I were our Labrador after she had puppies. It takes more effort after a baby to keep a man attracted."

Pandora stood on the Fricks' porch overlooking Lake George. The night was still, and she could hear dinner parties at other houses. She wondered if the houses were full of happy couples, or if some of them kept secrets, like she and Harley.

Harley was enjoying himself. Walker had gone to Yale, and they talked about private clubs in New York. She heard Walker invite Harley to dinner at the Knickerbocker Club.

She couldn't get Daisy's words out of her mind. Pandora's cycle had always been regular. Which meant she should have gotten her period three days ago. But she hadn't. And there were none of the cramps that usually preceded its arrival.

A fear gripped her, and she couldn't let it go. What if she had gotten pregnant on the night she spent with Archie? She finished her cocktail and went inside to join Harley.

After the dinner party was finally over, Pandora paced around the bedroom of their cottage, waiting for Harley to join her. Finally, the door nudged open. In one hand, Harley held a bottle of gin and in the other an empty glass.

"I'm sorry I took too long," Harley said.

Pandora wondered how many glasses of gin he drank. His eyes were glassy, and he seemed much drunker than when they'd arrived back at the cabin.

"I'm not the least bit tired." Pandora kept her voice light. "I had a wonderful time."

Harley put the bottle on the desk next to the window. He refilled his glass.

"All the men said how lucky I am to have such a lovely bride," he slurred. "It's a pity I've created a mess."

"I don't know what you're talking about."

Harley gulped the gin. "Yes, you do. It's been on your mind ever since we drove away from Blythdale. I saw you this morning at the bakery."

The boy behind the bakery counter had big blue eyes and dark, curly hair. He had talked to Harley for a little too long, and when he handed Harley his loaf of bread, their hands touched.

Pandora glanced down at her wedding ring. Harley was right. She had been jealous. She needed to learn to control her emotions.

She wondered what Harley would say if he found out about her night with Archie. Would he be jealous, or would he feel relieved that Pandora found passion with someone else? The thought filled her with despair. She truly loved Harley. She never wanted to give him a reason to doubt her.

"You're imagining things." She soothed him.

Harley put his glass down and sank onto the bed.

"You wish I was like other husbands who can't wait to go home and make love to their wives." He gazed up at her. Grief and resignation were in his eyes. "Pandora, you know I love you. I want to make everything all right."

Pandora walked over to him. She leaned down and kissed him on the cheek.

Harley didn't say anything. He stood up and unbuttoned his shirt and took off his pants.

Pandora watched him. His calves were narrow and sinewy, and he had wide, muscular thighs. The hair on his arms and legs was golden, as if he spent every day of his life in the sun.

Harley drew her toward him. She thought he was going to kiss her, but instead he reached down and stroked her breasts. The exquisite tingling, the darts of pleasure she experienced with Archie, unexpectedly filled her.

She was about to kiss him, but she held back. Some instinct told her to wait.

Harley fumbled with her buttons, and the dress fell to the floor. He didn't stop to pick it up. He kissed her neck and pushed her hair from her shoulders.

Pandora let out a gasp and leaned against him. Harley pushed her down on the bed and lay beside her. She wanted him to kiss her deeply the way Archie had. Instead, his hands moved down her thighs.

Then his body was above her, and she waited for him to enter her, for the waves to begin. Suddenly he slipped and fell on top of her breasts. He lay there for a minute, and Pandora waited for him to try again. His breath became even, and she knew that he was asleep.

She thought again about her late period. If she was pregnant, and the baby was Archie's, it could destroy her marriage. How could she have done such a thing? And what made everything worse is that for the first time since her mother left, when Archie held her and whispered that she was beautiful, she had felt like she was enough.

Whatever happened, she would have to live with the consequences. Harley was so drunk; he wouldn't remember anything in the morning. All she had to do was convince him that they had consummated their marriage, and she'd be safe.

Chapter Thirteen

In early September, Hyde Park shimmered in the heat. The sidewalk outside Ruby's Ice Cream was so hot that an ice cream cone melted in minutes. Women wore large floppy hats, and the cars parked along Main Street were too hot to touch.

Pandora walked down the steps of the doctor's office. She had known what Dr. Bancroft would say before he examined her. Pandora was almost three months pregnant. The baby was due in February.

After their one failed attempt to consummate the marriage in Lake George, Pandora and Harley didn't try to make love again. The baby couldn't be Harley's.

Pandora and Harley were living at Blythdale until their new house, Summerhill, was furnished. The familiar surroundings—the gardens where they strolled during their engagement, the rowboat they used for picnics—made Harley relax, and they enjoyed each other's company. The marriage was working, and they were happy.

Harley stayed at the townhouse in New York with his father on weekdays and came to Blythdale on weekends. Pandora expected him to be miserable after working all week at the bank, but he arrived home smiling and full of stories: The little girl who came in with her father to open a savings account and got lost and found Harley's office. Harley gave her a Bit-O-Honey and told her to come see him when she was older. The young couple who asked for a loan on a house in Westchester. Harley approved the loan, and the following week they asked him to dinner.

Harley liked people, and people liked him. Perhaps he was where he belonged, after all.

Pandora herself was so busy she needed to keep a diary. Adele gave Pandora a lavish luncheon introducing her to Hyde Park society and another smaller one at the townhouse in New York. She had afternoon teas and shopping excursions to Kingston. Pandora sewed the evening gown Vivian Clarkson had requested, and in her spare time she looked at spaces in Hyde Park to open a boutique.

She also spent time with Adele and had recently accompanied her to a committee meeting at Grand Street Settlement House. Afterward they visited Millie at her new offices and took her to lunch at the Hotel Algonquin. They talked about world events, and Pandora made a mental note to read the newspapers more often so she could be as well informed as Adele and Millie. It was refreshing to discuss current events with other women. The society women in Hyde Park occupied themselves with their afternoon teas, and working women were so exhausted from long days spent in an office or factory, they didn't have time for anything else.

She thought about Virginia's belief in education for girls. Women would never have the same opportunities as men if they didn't learn about the world around them.

Pandora marveled at her own good fortune. She had a caring husband, a comfortable lifestyle, and a beautiful home.

And now she was having a baby. Except the baby wasn't Harley's.

Soon Harley would notice the changes in her body. Her breasts were larger. For the first time in her life, her waist wasn't small, and her stomach wasn't flat. Pandora would have to lie about the due date.

And then there was Archie. She'd barely seen him since the wedding. He'd been at the Vanderbilts' house in Maine with Lucy. She missed him more than she had imagined she would. She missed their easy camaraderie. She missed his mischievous, boyish attitude. Archie never took things too seriously; he always cheered her up.

The happiness that had washed over her in Dr. Bancroft's office soon disappeared. Despite the heat, she felt a slight chill. She had created such a mess; she couldn't be more ashamed of herself. If anyone discovered the truth, it would create a scandal greater than anything to do with Harley's homosexuality.

She wasn't just worried about what people would say. Archie was Pandora's oldest friend, and Harley was the man she loved. She couldn't bear to hurt either of them.

Her hand instinctively went to her stomach. The baby came first. The rest she would have to figure out.

⁓

Adele was sitting in the morning room at Blythdale when Pandora returned from her doctor appointment.

"Pandora," Adele said in greeting. "I was hoping I'd see you before I went into New York."

Pandora took out her packages.

"I bought a jar of Harley's favorite lozenges. He keeps them on his desk so his throat doesn't get dry when he talks to clients."

"Harley appreciates the little things you do for him," Adele said. She patted the space beside her. "You've made him so happy; I can't wait for you both to move into Summerhill."

"If we're in the way, we could leave sooner," Pandora suggested. "I could furnish the bedrooms first, and we'll live without downstairs furniture."

"It's not that. We love having you here." Adele shook her head. "I just thought that you and Harley might want more space." She looked at Pandora meaningfully. "Now that your family is growing."

"What did you say?" Pandora gasped.

"I should have waited until you told me," Adele apologized. Her green eyes were bright with anticipation. "Dr. Bancroft's office called while you were out. I knew right away. Wives only go to Dr. Bancroft for one reason."

Pandora spread her hands in her lap.

"I just came from there. I didn't want to tell Harley until I was certain."

"Don't worry about Harley. All husbands are shocked the first time. Harley loves children; he'll be thrilled." Adele clapped her hands. "I'll hold a baby shower next month. It will be a wonderful way to furnish the nursery."

"Isn't it too early? I'm hardly three months along."

"The pregnancy will fly by. I have to go." Adele stood up and hugged Pandora. "Wait until I tell Milton; he'll be so excited."

Pandora went upstairs to the bedroom. She sat on a chair in the small sitting area next to the fireplace. She could see her reflection in the oval mirror on the dressing table.

A wave of nausea overcame her; she told herself it was morning sickness. But she was almost three months along, and she hadn't experienced it before. It was something else; it was guilt about what she'd done and fear of being found out. What if Harley remembered more about the night in Lake George than she thought?

For a moment, she wondered if the marriage had been a mistake. She loved Harley, but that almost made things harder. She couldn't help being jealous of any attention he paid to another man. No matter what a wonderful time they had on the weekends, after seeing a play and talking about it over hot chocolates or at the end of a Sunday spent playing croquet with Adele and Milton, she still wondered if some handsome young man was waiting for Harley in New York.

And it wasn't fair that Archie didn't know about the baby. Archie loved children. But he had his own life. If she told him the truth, she might ruin whatever happiness Archie had found with his work or with Lucy. Adele was over the moon about the baby; Milton and Harley would be too. She couldn't ruin their lives with such a scandal when the Enrights had been so accepting of Pandora.

Her reflection stared back at her from the mirror. She had never felt so stricken by her actions.

Harley would be home soon, but she wasn't ready to talk to him. She'd go to Riverview to see her father. She couldn't tell him anything, but just being with him in the cottage might make her feel better.

When she arrived at Riverview, Willie wasn't home. She was about to leave when Archie's car pulled into the driveway. The windshield was covered in dirt, and a suitcase was wedged into the jump seat.

"Pandora, this is a surprise." He jumped out.

He wore a sweater vest, navy shorts, and leather driving gloves. He had a boater hat perched on his head.

"I came to see my father; I was just leaving."

"Don't go yet," Archie urged. "I've just returned from Maine. Come inside and have a glass of lemonade."

Pandora followed Archie into the kitchen. He poured two glasses of lemonade and handed her one.

"I thought you and Lucy were still at Sonogee," Pandora said, sitting at the kitchen table.

"We came home a few days early." Archie sat opposite her. "I have an announcement."

"An announcement?" Pandora repeated.

Archie took a long sip of lemonade. He set his glass on the table.

"Lucy and I are engaged."

Pandora glanced at Archie in surprise.

"Engaged! I thought you weren't going to propose until New Year's Eve."

Archie nodded. "I wasn't. But Lucy spent the whole time talking about how many wedding invitations she'd received this summer and how many times she'd been asked to be a bridesmaid." He rested his elbows on the table. "One night, Louise Vanderbilt pulled me aside and gave me the engagement ring that had belonged to her mother. A five-carat pink diamond. I couldn't refuse it; what was I to do?" He shrugged his shoulders. "I was going to propose eventually; it was better to get it over with."

Archie looked so unhappy; Pandora's heart went out to him.

"Do you love her?" Pandora inquired.

Archie gave a thin smile.

"You know how I feel about Lucy." He picked up his glass. "At least she wants a long engagement. The wedding will be at Biltmore in North Carolina a year from now, at Christmas. The Vanderbilts are going to build a chapel for the ceremony." He sipped the lemonade. "I'm going to live in London until the wedding. My father owns property there, and Frederick Vanderbilt has business interests he wants me to manage."

"What about the fellowship at Oxford?"

"I already turned it down," he replied. He tried to smile. "At least I'll be able to visit the Bodleian Library at Oxford. Lucy and Louise will spend a few months in London, picking out her trousseau."

Pandora couldn't imagine not seeing Archie lounging around Riverview in his tennis whites. A new wave of nausea swept over her. Archie was engaged to be married. She couldn't tell him about the baby even if she wanted to. Archie would never break his engagement, and Pandora wasn't free. She loved Harley and was going to stay married to him.

He glanced at her curiously.

"I've been rambling on about me. Are you feeling all right, you look a bit green."

"It must be the heat," Pandora said offhandedly.

"I've hardly seen you and Harley all summer. How is he?"

Pandora arranged her features carefully. She looked up and met Archie's eyes.

"He's very happy. Marriage is even better than we imagined."

~

Pandora drove back to Blythdale and climbed the stairs to their bedroom. She was suddenly very tired and wanted to lie down. She was about to open a book when Virginia appeared in the doorway. Her bob was covered by a large hat, and she wore a floral dress and short white socks.

"I didn't know you were coming up this weekend," Pandora exclaimed.

"I decided spur of the moment." Virginia flopped on the bed beside her. "I have so much to tell you. I'm starting my own publishing house."

"You're what?"

Virginia's salons were very successful. So many people came she now held them biweekly, and still guests spilled into the hallway. Poets and authors clamored to read their work, and the salon was written up in the *Messenger*, Harlem's most popular literary magazine.

Wolfgang had moved back to New York, and together, he and Virginia scoured the city for new writers. Last month, Dorothy West read from her short story "The Typewriter." Dorothy was only twenty, but the story won first place in a national writing contest.

Virginia handed a slim volume to Pandora. "This book gave me the idea."

The title was *The Garden Party and Other Stories* by Katherine Mansfield.

Virginia told Pandora that Katherine Mansfield was from New Zealand. She'd died two years ago from tuberculosis. She was only thirty-four and had been one of the most promising writers of her generation. Virginia Woolf proclaimed she was the only writer she was jealous of, and T.S. Eliot wrote a review calling her a "dangerous woman."

"A man can't say anything better about a woman that that." Virginia smiled mischievously.

Pandora turned the book over.

"I don't understand. She's already published."

"She led a fascinating life. She was married twice and had at least three female lovers. I'm going to publish her biography."

Virginia's publishing house would be called Riverview Press, and it would publish biographies of female poets and authors.

"Think how much readers will learn about being an abolitionist during the Civil War from reading about Harriet Beecher Stowe, and struggling poets will be shocked that Emily Dickinson wrote eighteen hundred poems but only ten were published during her lifetime," Virginia said excitedly.

"What's even better is that I'm going to hire young authors to write the biographies. Women like Dorothy West. Dorothy's money from the writing contest ran out, and she has to work two jobs."

Virginia took off her hat. She smiled triumphantly.

"It sounds expensive," Pandora remarked. "Where will you set it up, and how will you pay the writers?"

"Wolfgang has an apartment in Morningside Heights. We'll use his living room. And I already have a couple of investors." Virginia's eyes danced. "Not all the people at my salon are penniless artists. Wealthy women also attend, and they're eager to support it."

Pandora was impressed. It was a good idea.

"Wolfgang and I visited Dorothy West last week. She works nights as a hat check girl at the Cotton Club. You'll never guess who we ran into. Porter Merrill! He was walking down Seventh Avenue, wearing some sort of velvet vest and trousers."

A shiver ran down Pandora's spine. She remembered the articles she'd read about homosexual bath houses in Harlem.

"Porter Merrill?" Pandora repeated. "Was he with anyone?"

"A couple of friends; his fiancée is away." Virginia shrugged. "Porter really is good looking. I'm surprised he's engaged to Doris; there must have been dozens of girls who were after him."

Ever since Harley accused Pandora of being jealous of the boy at the bakery in Lake George, she'd been trying harder to trust Harley. But it seemed there was always someone to be nervous about. Once, she noticed Harley talking to the milk delivery boy. The boy leaned suggestively against the milk truck as Harley took the bottles from him. Another time at a restaurant, the waiter held Harley's gaze a little too long. And there was the time that a male caller rang for Harley three times and wouldn't give his name. It turned out that Harley was trying to surprise her with a bouquet of flowers, and the flower shop had called the house instead of his office. Pandora was so embarrassed that when the flowers arrived, she forgot to tip the delivery boy.

Pandora would go mad if she kept worrying. Harley had promised to be faithful.

"Porter will be off the market soon," Pandora said to Virginia. "We received their wedding invitation. It's in November at St. Trinity's Church, with a reception at the Plaza."

"Doris isn't very attractive," Virginia commented archly. "I suppose that's the price men pay for a career in politics. I've never met a senator with a beautiful wife. The spotlight has to be on him all the time."

"Since when are you hanging around senators?" Pandora smiled.

"I told you, all sorts of people attend my salons. You and Harley should come."

"Harley is too busy. Whenever he's in New York, he goes to banking dinners with Milton."

"That's funny, I saw him in Greenwich Village last week, getting into a taxi." Virginia frowned. "Anyway, enough about me. I have something to show you."

Pandora froze at Virginia's words. She sat up straight on the bed.

Virginia brought out a wooden box from her handbag. Inside was the strangest-looking thing Pandora had ever seen. A see-through rubber cap, the length and width of a coffee cup.

"It's a Dutch cap," Virginia said. "I had it fitted by a doctor in New York. I couldn't risk going to Dr. Bancroft. My mother would have found out."

"What's it for?" Pandora picked it up.

Virginia glanced at Pandora curiously.

"I forget how sheltered you are." Virginia raised her eyebrows. "It's to stop you from getting pregnant. Lots of women use them. There are even free birth control clinics in New York." She paused. "You should get one. I'll go with you if you like."

Pandora set it down quickly. She was shocked; she had never heard of such a thing before.

"Why would I need it?" she demanded. "Harley and I want children."

"You just got married; you want to enjoy yourself first," Virginia said. "That's what's so wonderful. You can decide when to start a family instead of getting pregnant by accident."

"Why do you have it? You said you're not ready to make love." Pandora folded her arms.

"Don't you see, it gives me freedom," Virginia commented. "Why should women risk pregnancy for a night of pleasure, while men can do whatever they please. It's like getting my hair bobbed or not wearing a corset anymore. I don't want to live with restrictions. It's all part of being a modern woman."

Pandora put the cap back in the box. For some reason, looking at it upset her. She was uncomfortable talking about sex, even with Virginia.

"I don't agree," she said defiantly. She stood up and walked to the window. "Anyway, it's too late. Harley and I are having a baby."

Virginia's mouth dropped open. If Pandora weren't so agitated, she would have laughed. It was almost impossible to shock Virginia. Virginia had always known everything before Pandora: how to flirt and how to wear makeup, even how to kiss. Virginia demonstrated with a pillow when they were fourteen. Pandora had been so afraid that Archie would walk in and laugh at them she took her pillow and practiced in the closet.

"You can't be pregnant so soon. You've only been married three months," Virginia exclaimed. "What did Harley say? And what about your plans to open a boutique?"

"He doesn't know yet. I saw Dr. Bancroft today," Pandora replied. "I'm still going to open a boutique, but I'll put it off until after the baby is born."

Pandora had already resolved that she wouldn't give up her career goals. She would hire a baby nurse and later a nanny.

Suddenly her anger toward Virginia dissolved. Virginia had done nothing wrong. Pandora was anxious because of her situation.

"Harley will be thrilled—all men want to be immortal," Virginia assured her.

"I hope so." Pandora nodded.

All her misery returned. She couldn't tell Virginia about what she had done. She was too ashamed, and there was nothing Virginia could do.

For a moment, Pandora wondered how her mother had felt when she discovered she was pregnant with Pandora. Was she happy, or did she feel that she was no longer in control of her life? Is that what it meant for women not to have choices? Once you were married, with children, your life wasn't your own.

Pandora would never be like her mother. She was certain she'd love the baby more than anything.

Virginia stood up and hugged Pandora. She dropped the wooden box into her handbag. "You should get one of these after you have the baby. The way you and Harley are going at it, you'll be having a baby every year."

After Virginia left, Pandora sat at the dressing table and tried to convince herself that everything would work out. She had to put Archie and her guilt out of her mind. Archie already had his life planned, and the important thing was that Harley believed the baby was his. They had to make the marriage work.

It was the best thing for everyone.

A few hours later, Pandora waited for Harley in Blythdale's living room. A pitcher of sidecars stood on the sideboard, along with a plate of deviled eggs.

Dr. Bancroft said Pandora could drink as much as she liked. All the fuss about alcohol being bad for the baby's health was a result of doctors supporting prohibition. But tonight, she couldn't afford to lose herself in the pleasant haze of cognac and triple sec and lemon juice. She had to be alert when she told Harley her news.

She heard the sound of footsteps, and Harley appeared in the hallway. She never tired of looking at him. He wore a pin-striped suit from his tailor in New York and one of his new trilby hats.

Pandora walked over and kissed him.

"Well, look at all this." He whistled, taking in the chilled cocktail glasses and floral china plates. "Makes me wish I came home every night, instead of only on the weekends."

"I've missed you," Pandora said truthfully. "This week seemed to stretch on forever."

"I'm starving," Harley said as he bit into a deviled egg. "The only drawback of driving into New York instead of taking the train is I don't get to relax and eat a sandwich. I ran into Archie at the station. He's going to come over tomorrow for a game of croquet."

Pandora wondered how it would feel to see Archie again, to tell him that she was pregnant. She couldn't give away her secret.

She handed Harley a cocktail.

"That reminds me, Virginia was here," she said cautiously. "She saw that friend of yours, Porter Merrill, in Harlem. I wondered if you'd seen him since the wedding."

For a moment, Harley didn't move. Then he took the glass.

"New York is huge," he answered. Pandora saw a flicker in his eyes "Why do you ask?"

"We received their wedding invitation, and I wondered if Porter knew what they wanted from the gift registry," Pandora said hastily. "I can ask Doris, but if you were going to see him, it would save me a phone call."

Harley seemed to believe her. His features relaxed.

"I thought women lived to be on the phone." He sat on the sofa. "Let's talk about something more interesting. I want to see the paint swatches for Summerhill."

Harley really was a good husband. Other men wouldn't be interested in the new house until they moved in.

"The reception rooms have all been painted," she said eagerly. "The most beautiful shade of topaz."

She adored the color that the interior designer recommended. It reminded her of the showroom at Tiffany's.

Pandora couldn't put off telling him any longer. She twisted her wedding ring.

"I decided we should furnish the nursery next, before we do the upstairs study or the gymnasium."

Realization at what Pandora was saying set in. Harley turned white as a sheet. His body stiffened, and he placed his glass on the coffee table.

"A baby, so soon?" he stammered. His eyes were wide, and a sheen of perspiration formed on his forehead.

"I saw Dr. Bancroft today. The baby will be born in February."

Pandora searched Harley's face for some kind of doubt about the timing. She could only hope that he knew less about conception and having babies than she did.

He walked to the French doors leading to the balcony. His hand went to the doorknob, and Pandora was afraid he'd open the door and bolt across the lawn. Finally, he turned and walked to the sideboard. He poured a fresh drink, barely finishing it before he picked up the pitcher and poured another.

"I'm thrilled, of course. I just didn't know it would happen so fast." He sat beside her. "If it's a boy, as soon as he's born, we'll put his name down for Princeton."

Harley kept talking, as if the sound of his own voice was keeping away his panic.

"You can't put off opening your boutique. We'll get a baby nurse and a nanny."

Pandora glanced at Harley. He was acting strangely. As if he was anxious to move the conversation away from himself.

Pandora nodded. "I already started looking at spaces in Hyde Park."

Harley squeezed her hand. He put his arm around her and kissed her.

"Then I couldn't be more delighted." He gulped the sidecar. "I told you we'd have everything. A beautiful home and a family and each other."

She stared at the almost empty pitcher and felt a pinprick of fear. "You're right," she agreed. "We're going to be so happy."

Chapter Fourteen

February 1928, Hyde Park, New York

Pandora was due in two weeks. She had given up wearing corsets months ago. Adele took her to Lane Bryant on West Thirty-Eighth Street, but even the maternity dresses were uncomfortable. Every month she grew bigger, until she couldn't see her ankles and felt like she was going to burst.

In October, Pandora and Harley had moved into Summerhill. Pandora spent the first month wandering from room to room imagining a life there with her baby. As a wedding present, Adele commissioned the interior designer Ogden Codman to furnish the downstairs. Ogden had designed the Rockefeller mansion in Mount Pleasant and Edith Wharton's Park Avenue townhouse.

Pandora couldn't decide which room she loved most. The living room had hand-painted wallpaper and parquet floors and a blue-and-white patterned rug. She adored the music room with its Steinway piano and the dining room with its Regency-style pedestal dining table and russet-colored upholstered chairs. And the gardens in the fall had been spectacular. The maple tree outside her bedroom window turned a brilliant orange, and a whole patch of dogwood trees turned a dusky red purple.

Today she was going to have lunch with Millie in New York. She had seen Millie a few times since Millie took the secretarial job. On every visit, Pandora was more impressed. Millie should be running her own company instead of taking dictation and picking up William Corning's dry cleaning. But Millie seemed happy. The last time she saw her, Millie couldn't stop talking about the dollhouse she'd put on layaway at FAO Schwarz for her daughter and the baseball mitt she'd bought her son.

Pandora drove herself into New York. She and Harley didn't have a chauffeur, and the train took too long. She had something important to tell Millie. If she didn't tell her now, she might not see her until after the baby was born.

Corning & Sons was located in one of the gleaming new office towers that had sprung up east of Penn Station. Pandora and Millie agreed to meet in a diner on the building's ground floor. Millie was already seated when Pandora arrived. She wore a navy dress with a white collar and navy gloves. Her hair was cut in a bob that made her look younger but more sophisticated at the same time.

"You cut your hair!" Pandora said, waddling over to the table. She took off her coat and lowered herself onto a chair.

"I had to, all the young girls at the office are doing it." Millie touched her hair. "Your hair is blond and glossy; you should never cut it. Mine is so fine, and it's the color of a dirty tea towel."

"The style is perfect on you; I never noticed your face is heart shaped," Pandora said. "I've stopped looking in the mirror."

"I was the same when I was pregnant," Millie recalled. "I was afraid my stomach would never go back to normal."

Pandora insisted on paying for Millie's lunch. They ordered French onion soup and stewed veal with stuffed potatoes.

"I couldn't wait to tell you," Pandora said after the waiter brought their plates. "Harley's bank closed a deal with a developer on an apartment building in Brooklyn Heights. It will have a playground and a school. Only tenants with steady incomes will qualify. If you lived there, you'd have more space, and you wouldn't have to share a bathroom with other families."

In the tenement building where Millie lived, three families shared the same bathroom. The stairs were rickety, and the windows didn't latch properly. Millie and her children slept in one bed. Her husband slept on a cot in the kitchen.

Millie toyed with her soup. Her mouth turned down at the corners. "We won't qualify." She shook her head.

"You've worked for William Corning for months; he'll be happy to write you a letter."

"I might not be able to work there much longer. Last month I thought I was pregnant. I wasn't, but it will happen soon enough. Then I'll have to quit and stay home with the baby."

"I don't understand." Pandora frowned.

"While my husband was injured, we didn't . . . do that sort of thing," Millie said, embarrassed. "Now Roy's back is better, and he wants it every night. I'm bound to get pregnant, and he doesn't have a job."

Pandora was shocked. Millie had worked so hard to get where she was. She couldn't lose it all now.

"You have to explain it to him," Pandora urged. "He wouldn't want you to lose your job."

"He's a man; he has needs."

Pandora recalled the box with the Dutch cap that Virginia showed her last September.

"I have an idea," Pandora said. "Let's finish our lunch, and I'll take you someplace that may solve the problem."

They ate apple pie with ice cream for dessert, and then Pandora drove to Greenwich Village. She parked in front of a drab building with curtained windows. Two women in plain dresses hovered on the steps, and another woman carrying a small child walked through the door.

"Where are we?" Millie asked when Pandora squeezed the little car into a parking space.

"It's a birth control clinic," Pandora answered. "You'll be outfitted with a Dutch cap, and then you won't have to worry about getting pregnant."

Pandora had read about birth control clinics in the newspaper. Margaret Sanger opened the first clinic a decade earlier and went to jail for providing a woman with a diaphragm. It was considered a crime to distribute anything that was considered "obscene." Since then, the law had been repealed, and birth control clinics were springing up around New York. There was one in Brooklyn, and a few on the Lower East Side and Greenwich Village.

Millie's eyes widened, and she gaped out the window.

"I can't do that! What would Roy say?"

"He'll be happy," Pandora offered. "You already have three children, and he doesn't want you to lose your job."

"What if he can feel it? If it takes away his pleasure, he might look somewhere else."

"How will you feed your children if you're both out of work?" Pandora urged. "And apartments like this won't become available often. Imagine how happy Thomas will be if he can play baseball anytime he likes."

"Thomas would do anything to practice baseball," Millie said longingly.

"And you can keep putting away money for Daisy's college," Pandora persisted. "At Christmas, she told me she wants to be a lawyer."

Pandora had taken Millie's children out to lunch before Christmas. Daisy was a bright ten-year-old who loved to read. Thomas was seven with Millie's brown hair and freckles, and the youngest, George, was a fair-headed four-year-old with unlimited energy.

"All right, I'll do it," Millie agreed reluctantly. "I can't tell Roy, though. He'll think it's unnatural."

The waiting room held just a few hard-backed chairs and a chipped coffee table on a worn rug. A bowl of Mounds bars sat next to a vase of flowers. The other women waiting to be seen were as nervous as Millie. One seemed young enough to be in high school but had three children with her: two boys and a girl who couldn't have been more than ten months.

Millie filled out some forms, and a nurse took her back to the doctor's office. Pandora offered to accompany her, but Millie wanted to go by herself. When Millie emerged, she clutched a paper bag.

Pandora waited until they were outside before she said anything.

"You see, it took no time at all," Pandora said cheerfully. "Send me Mr. Corning's letter, and I'll forward it to the developer."

"I don't know how to thank you," Millie replied. "If it wasn't for you, I'd still be putting in fourteen-hour days at the factory."

They were about to get in the car when a man hurried down the steps of a brownstone. Pandora recognized the trilby hat and navy overcoat. It was Harley. She was about to call out to him when another man hurried down the steps. Pandora only saw his face for a few moments, but she recalled those long eyelashes and fair hair. Porter Merrill.

Harley had promised to be faithful. What was he doing meeting Porter at a brownstone in the middle of the day?

"Are you all right?" Millie's voice came from far away. "You're very pale."

It took all Pandora's strength to look away. Her mouth wobbled and her hands were shaking.

"I'm perfectly fine," she said, reaching for the car door to steady herself.

Pandora took Millie to her office and drove back to Hyde Park. She couldn't help thinking about Porter. How Virginia always commented on his good looks, the way Harley changed the conversation when Pandora mentioned him. The pains began as she turned off the exit. At first it came as a dragging feeling in her back, and she thought she had sat too long in the car. By the time she pulled into Summerhill's driveway, the pains had moved to her abdomen.

She made her way into the living room as a new pain came, stronger than the last. She debated calling Dr. Bancroft, but she thought it was probably a false alarm. She'd call Adele instead.

"I'm coming over," Adele said when Pandora explained how she was feeling.

"I'm sure it can wait if you're busy," Pandora said, her stomach tightening into a hard ball.

"Babies don't wait for anything," Adele remarked. "Try to relax until I get there."

Pandora leaned against the sofa cushions, and tears welled in her eyes. Over the past few months, she and Harley had been happy. She had thought their agreement would work. Archie was in England, and she and Harley had grown closer. They had spent a whole weekend working on the nursery. Pandora learned to make flapjacks the way Harley liked them, with whipped cream and extra butter. On Sundays, after church, they strolled through Hyde Park and admired the babies in their prams. And Harley was always so enthusiastic about her designs. Sometimes in the evenings, he'd bring Pandora her sketchbook and a pitcher of lemonade and sit beside her while she made new sketches.

And yet Harley was willing to risk everything they had built to be with Porter. Her mind went to her night with Archie before the wedding. Wasn't she guilty of the same thing? If Harley found out, he might never trust her again. The scandal could ruin all of them.

But that had been only one night, brought on by too many brandies and feeling like she wasn't good enough. Harley was meeting Porter on a regular basis.

Adele arrived and hung her coat in the closet. She wore a checkered wool dress with a scarf knotted around her neck.

"Put your feet up on the coffee table," Adele instructed her. "I'll make some tea."

When Pandora moved, she found something wet on the cushion. A pain stabbed her, and she cried out.

"What's wrong?" Adele rushed in from the kitchen.

"I must have sat on something," Pandora said, catching her breath. "The cushion is wet."

Adele put down her tea towel. She studied Pandora closely.

"Your water broke, you're in labor."

"I can't be in labor, I'm not due for two weeks."

"I've given birth four times. You are in labor," Adele replied. She walked to the phone. "I'll call Dr. Bancroft."

Another pain shot through her, sharper this time. It went through to her back, and she arched over and groaned.

"Please call Harley at the bank," she said through gritted teeth. "He won't want to miss out."

"Dr. Bancroft will be here soon," Adele said when she hung up the phone.

"And Harley?" Pandora asked, another contraction catching her unaware. The last one had barely finished when the next one began.

"I called the office. He hasn't returned from lunch; he had afternoon meetings."

Meeting with Porter at the brownstone in Greenwich Village. Pandora wouldn't think about that now. The contractions seemed almost on top of each other. Each pain felt like a giant wave, dragging her down and refusing to release her. She grabbed the arm of the sofa and moaned.

"Hold on to me and count to fifty." Adele offered her arm.

Dr. Bancroft arrived, accompanied by a nurse. There wasn't time to get to the hospital—the baby would be born at home.

He carried her upstairs and laid her on the bed.

The contractions came faster, and her cheeks were sticky with sweat. Every time she thought she couldn't face another, it bore down on her, and she groaned in agony. Adele didn't leave her side. She wiped Pandora's forehead and assured her she was doing fine.

When it came time to push, Pandora longed for Harley. Dr. Bancroft assured her that women had babies without their husbands all the time. Pandora shouldn't worry about Harley, she had to use her strength to get the baby out.

"It hurts too much and I'm too tired." Pandora moaned, the pain encompassing her whole body.

"You can do this." Adele's voice came from somewhere. "You're stronger than you know."

Then a different kind of pain filled her, fierce and cutting her to the core. She gripped the side of the bed and pressed against it.

She heard a whooshing sound and felt a surge of relief.

"Congratulations," Dr. Bancroft announced. "It's a girl."

Pandora didn't know how long it took for the baby to be placed in her arms. But when she held her, when she breathed in the sweet baby scent and admired the dewy baby cheeks, she had never been so overcome with emotion.

"She's beautiful," she gushed.

"She has to be." Adele stood beside the bed. She touched Pandora's arm, and her green eyes shone with delight. "She looks just like her mother."

The baby opened her eyes, and they were the same shade of blue as Pandora's. Her few wisps of hair were blond, and even the shape of her face was the same as Pandora's.

Pandora glanced from Adele to the baby in awe. She had done it. She was a mother, and everything was going to be all right.

A few hours later Pandora rested against the headboard. Adele had gone home to Blythdale, and the baby was sleeping.

There was a knock at the door. Pandora hoped it was Harley, but it was Virginia.

"Virginia!" she exclaimed. "What are you doing here?"

"Adele called me at the townhouse." Virginia entered the room. "I just arrived."

"I didn't know you were coming," Pandora said.

"I would have gotten here sooner, but I've already gotten two speeding tickets." Virginia grinned. "Can I see her?"

Pandora pointed at the bassinet next to the bed.

"She's lovely." Virginia admired her. "Does she have a name?"

"Esme Adele Enright," Pandora announced. "You already promised to be her godmother."

"Of course I will." Virginia nodded.

"Having a baby is harder than I imagined," Pandora admitted. "I didn't think I would survive."

Virginia took off her hat. She smiled at Pandora cheekily. "Do you remember when we were sixteen and I had so many questions about sex? I never considered the outcome; I only wanted to know how to kiss."

"Pregnancy is wretched, but it's worth it," Pandora said ruefully. She gazed at Esme. "I've never felt so much love."

"I brought you something." Virginia disappeared into the hallway and returned with a huge box.

Inside the box was the biggest teddy bear Pandora had ever seen, a silver rattle from Tiffany's, and a chemistry set.

"I stopped at FAO Schwarz," Virginia said. "The teddy bear is from Archie. I sent him a telegram, and he said to buy the biggest teddy bear I could find. The rattle and the chemistry set are from me. Esme might want to become a scientist."

"I'll keep it in her chest for now," Pandora answered, smiling.

"I should go," Virginia said when the nurse placed Esme in Pandora's arms. "I'm interfering with your feeding schedule."

"Would you like to hold her first?" Pandora offered.

Virginia gingerly took Esme from Pandora. She cradled her in her arms.

"I'm glad it's you and not me," Virginia said with a grin. "But I'll be the best godmother Esme could ask for."

Pandora fed Esme and then took a nap. When she woke, it was nighttime. The sky was dark, and the maid had lit the fire in the bedroom fireplace.

While she was sleeping, Harley had called. He was waiting for Milton to finish a dinner engagement, and they would drive up together.

Willie appeared in the doorway. He held a bunch of daffodils in one hand and a small container in the other.

"It's so late you could have waited until tomorrow," she said, her eyes alight with pleasure.

Willie strode over to the bed and kissed Pandora.

"I wouldn't have slept a wink," he answered. "The daffodils are from Maude Van Luyen, and Esther made strawberry gelatin."

He glanced around the room eagerly. "Can I see her?"

Willie picked Esme up without waiting for a reply. He held her expertly, cooing to her while pacing around the room.

"Do you remember before Harley proposed? I said marriage isn't anything without love," her father began. "I was wrong. Holding Esme reminds me of when I first held you. Marriage can give you the one thing that will bring you joy your whole life: a child."

"Harley and I are in love," Pandora assured him. "We're very happy."

Willie placed Esme in the bassinet.

"I know. I saw it in the way you looked at each other at the ceremony." Her father nodded. "I mean you have everything now; no one can take it away."

The last visitor was Harley. He arrived just after she finished feeding Esme before bed.

"I wanted to stop and get flowers, but I was already so late. I ordered them to be delivered instead." Harley kissed her.

It felt good to see Harley. She had missed him during the birth.

"I have flowers." Pandora waved at the vase of daffodils. "I'm just glad you're here."

Harley was too choked up to answer. He stood at the bassinet and gazed at the tiny blond head wrapped in a pink blanket. When he turned around, his eyes were wet.

"She's perfect. There's nowhere I'd rather be than here with my beautiful wife and daughter."

Her father was right. Pandora and Harley had everything they wanted: a beautiful house, each other, a child, the means to open her boutique. Their lives were about Esme now. Pandora wouldn't let Porter Merrill or anyone else destroy their family.

Chapter Fifteen

February 1929, Hyde Park, New York

The day of Esme's first birthday party was an unusually sunny day for February. A few hours before the party, Harley still hadn't arrived. He hadn't called, and when Pandora rang the townhouse in New York, no one answered.

Pandora tried not to get upset. She figured that Harley had probably taken clients to dinner, and it was so late when they finished, he went straight to bed. Perhaps he drove up this morning and stopped to buy Esme a present. He'd appear any minute, and she would have worried for nothing.

After Esme was born, Pandora had debated for weeks if she should mention seeing him with Porter the day she went into labor. At first, the image of them on the townhouse steps haunted her, and she could think of nothing else. But it wouldn't do any good to confront him. At best, Harley would make up an excuse: they were discussing Porter's political campaign or Harley happened to be in the neighborhood and they caught up over a late lunch.

Or what if Harley didn't try to cover it up? What if instead he proclaimed he couldn't live without Porter and was leaving her. Pandora still loved Harley. She couldn't imagine life without him.

Over time, Pandora convinced herself that whatever happened between Harley and Porter was in the past. Harley had made a promise; he wouldn't risk everything by being involved in a scandal. He was a doting husband and father. On the weekends, he couldn't tear himself away from Esme. He read her picture books and took her for long walks in her pram. Monday mornings before he left, he kissed Pandora deeply. During the week, he sent flowers and chocolates, and he was always happy to see her on Friday evenings.

Pandora was happier than she had imagined she could be. Esme grew from a serene baby to an energetic toddler who walked at eleven months and loved to sing. She adored her parents equally, and even though she was spoiled by a succession of adults: Adele and Milton, Willie, Virginia, and Archie, who sent presents from England, she never had tantrums and was sunny and good natured.

Pandora set aside her guilty secret and concentrated on being the best wife and mother. If sometimes she caught herself looking at Esme and wondering whom she would look like when she was older or if she had inherited her happy disposition from Archie, she quickly thought about something else. In time, Esme would develop her own looks and personality.

Esme wasn't the only thing that made Pandora happy. Summerhill became lovelier every day. During the winter, every room had a roaring fire, and Pandora loved nothing more than sitting in the morning room with the pale sun streaming onto the geometric-patterned rugs, sketching dresses in her notepad. They planned to build a pool house that summer, and Pandora was busy furnishing the guest wing.

Even more exciting, next week was the grand opening of her boutique. Instead of Hyde Park, she'd chosen to open the boutique in New York. Pandora couldn't be more thrilled. It was everything she dreamed of. It had been Vivian Clarkson's idea. Pandora told her about wanting to open a dress shop, and Vivian advised that she'd find a bigger clientele in Manhattan, so why not start there?

Vivian showed her the perfect space a few blocks from the Bergdorf Goodman building on Fifth Avenue and Fifty-Eighth Street. Pandora worried that it was too far uptown for the clientele she wanted to attract, but Vivian assured her that Bergdorf's was the most elegant department store in New York.

Pandora took the shop on the spot. When she wasn't with Esme, she spent every waking moment over the next few months choosing the decor for the boutique. Thick white carpet so that women's heels didn't click-clack on the wood floor. Pale blue velvet chairs for the sitting area, textured wallpaper that was elegant but wouldn't upstage the clothes.

At the same time, she worked tirelessly on her designs. She wanted to keep her first collection small, so every piece had to be perfect. She bought the most expensive fabrics, buttons, and threads. She made smart day dresses for women's lunches at Hotel Astor and the St. Regis, sumptuous evening gowns for the ballet and the opera. When she finally hung the garments on the store's satin hangers, they shimmered like peacocks under the chandelier, and she knew that she had achieved her vision.

She also started a scholarship to send girls to college. Millie's children inspired the idea. Millie's son Thomas hoped to win a baseball scholarship to Columbia, like his idol, Lou Gehrig. Millie's daughter, Daisy, was a fast runner, but no one encouraged her to compete, and there were no sports scholarships available for girls. Besides a few female tennis stars, like Willie's pupil Suzanne Lenglen, women didn't pursue careers in sports. The scholarship would be called the Willie Carmichael Scholarship for Women in Athletics and Academics, and Pandora was searching for the first recipients.

She had been busy this last year, but so very happy. She couldn't let her doubts about Harley spoil Esme's birthday. He'd be home soon, and she would have worried for nothing.

Footsteps sounded in the hallway. Pandora heard Virginia's voice.

"You'd never know you have a maid," Virginia entered the living room. "You spend half your time polishing the furniture."

"The party will be inside because it's too cold on the lawn." Pandora put down her polishing rag. "I want everything to look perfect."

Virginia sat on the crimson-colored velvet sofa. As usual, she was dressed in the latest style. A cloche hat covered her bob, and she wore one of the sailor-inspired new middy blouses over the most daring thing of all: wide-legged trousers.

"I've never been so happy to be home for the weekend." Virginia sighed. "I'm going to spend tomorrow in the bathtub and try not to even think about book jacket copy or bookstore receipts."

Virginia's publishing company was a huge success. Riverview Press had published three titles and had four more scheduled for the fall. The *New York Times* reviewed the biography of Katherine Mansfield and praised both its subject and author. Virginia had already commissioned five biographies for the following year and spent her days dealing with writers and booksellers.

"I love every minute of it, but there's so much to do." Virginia pulled off her driving gloves. "Wolfgang handles the printing press and cover designs. I do the office work and visit authors and bookstores. The phone is always ringing, and I'm slow at typing. If only I had someone to run the office, I'd have more time for everything else."

It struck Pandora that Millie could be a perfect fit for Riverview Press. She told Virginia about Millie and her sharp secretarial skills.

"She sounds like exactly what we need," Virginia said excitedly. "I could pay her more than she's earning now. If she's good, in a year we could make her a part owner. That's the best way to win an employee's loyalty."

Pandora smiled at her best friend.

"You sound like a proper businesswoman."

"I'm not going to stop there," Virginia reflected. "We're going to publish books of literary criticism written by women. The literary critics at the *New York Times* and the *New Yorker* are men, so of course they review books written by men. I'm going to change that." Virginia adjusted her hat. "Before I forget, Archie sent a present. I'm supposed to tell you what it is if it hasn't arrived."

A few months earlier, Lucy's father had become ill, and Lucy had moved back to St. Louis to take care of him. Archie was still in London, and the wedding had been postponed until Lucy's father recovered.

Archie wrote to Pandora saying he was enjoying London more than he imagined. He spent his weekends at Oxford and his evenings attending concerts and lectures. Pandora missed him, but she was pleased that he was happy. It reassured her that she had done the right thing by not telling him that he was Esme's father.

"We haven't gotten any packages from England," Pandora said to Virginia.

"It's the new Winnie-the-Pooh book, *The House at Pooh Corner*," Virginia answered. "It was released a few months ago; Archie got a signed copy."

"Esme will adore it," Pandora replied, picking up her rag. "I'll have to write and thank him."

Guests began to arrive, and Harley still wasn't home. Pandora called the townhouse again, but there was no answer. She tried the bank even though it was Saturday, but the switchboard confirmed that the offices were closed.

Harley had been so excited about Esme's birthday party. He'd planned to make pitchers of gin Rickeys, which were all the rage since F. Scott Fitzgerald described them in *The Great Gatsby*. Milton would have to fix the drinks when he arrived.

Pandora wore a dress she designed especially for the party. Pink wool with a white bow-tie neckline and pleated skirt. She surveyed the living room. The nanny, Sally, stood in the corner, holding Esme's hand. Just seeing Esme—her round blue eyes, the blond ringlets that framed her face—made her feel better. She was about to go over to them when Owen and Lillian approached her.

"There's our hostess," Lillian remarked. "We were beginning to worry that neither you nor Harley were here."

Lillian wore a drop-waisted velvet dress with a green shawl. Her diamond ring sparkled on one hand and a sapphire ring on the other.

"Harley got held up in the city," Pandora said, hoping she sounded convincing. "There's plenty to eat and drink. Milton is going to make a pitcher of gin Rickeys when he gets here."

"Gin Rickeys remind me of Princeton," Owen reflected. His skin was more pallid than the last time Pandora saw him, and his trousers were snug around his waist. "Someone was always making a pitcher of some kind of cocktail."

"Owen is always talking about Princeton," Lillian chided. "He spends almost as much time at the Princeton Club as he does at home. I suppose all young husbands are the same. I heard that Harley practically lives at the townhouse in New York."

Pandora wished she had a drink. "Harley has to be in New York. His father made him vice president of the bank."

"You must be proud of him; our husbands work so hard," Lillian gushed. She leaned forward conspiratorially. "I just came from Dr. Bancroft. We're going to have another baby. It's quite soon, Owen Jr. is only six months old." Lillian patted her stomach. She flashed a smile. "Owen and I love children, and I suppose this is what happens when we can't keep our hands off each other."

Pandora took Esme from Sally and greeted the other guests. Everyone cooed and aahed over Esme, and Pandora willed herself to enjoy the party. Willie arrived with a teddy bear almost as big as Esme. Adele never appeared. Pandora called Blythdale, and the maid told her that Mrs. Enright was lying down. Pandora tried not to think about how strange that was or how lonely she felt at the party without Adele or Harley.

Finally, the party was over, and the last guests drove away. Pandora was about to go upstairs when a car pulled into the driveway. It was Milton. Milton and Harley must have come together. Pandora was filled with relief. But only Milton was in the car; the passenger seat was empty.

"Pandora," Milton said, climbing the steps. "Can I come in?"

"Of course. You missed the party," she said. "The last guests just left."

"I'm terribly sorry." He followed her inside.

"Where's Harley? Did something happen?"

"Why don't we go into the living room," Milton suggested. "I wouldn't mind a brandy."

Pandora sat across from Milton on the sofa. Her father-in-law was usually so relaxed and confident. This afternoon, everything about him seemed out of character. He wore a business suit even though it was Saturday, and his tie was askew. His brow was creased into a frown, and there were deep lines around his mouth.

Milton poured two brandies and handed one to Pandora.

"You'll need one of these," he said. He took a deep breath and closed his eyes. "Harley was arrested last night. He's in jail in New York."

Pandora set the brandy on the side table and clutched the arm of the sofa to steady herself.

"Arrested!" She gasped.

"He was caught coming out of a bathhouse with another man." Milton's eyes darkened. "Porter Merrill, the politician. The police said they were drinking and engaged in lewd behavior. That's still a crime in a public space. They were both taken to jail and held overnight."

Pandora reached for the brandy. A sharp pain formed between her shoulders, and she found it hard to swallow. Milton must be mistaken. Harley wouldn't put himself in that kind of situation. He'd promised to remain faithful.

"Are you sure? Perhaps it was a group of young men, carrying on and having fun," she suggested. "A man like Porter Merrill must have a lot of friends."

Milton shook his head. "It was only Harley and Porter. There's no doubt what they were doing."

A sick feeling overtook Pandora, like a sudden fever at the beginning of the flu.

"Does Adele know?"

"Adele answered the phone when the police called Blythdale. The doctor came and gave her some pills. I'm sorry she missed Esme's birthday party."

"When did this happen?" Pandora asked.

"Last night. The police didn't get hold of me until this morning," Milton answered. "I drove straight to the jail to post bail, but Harley won't leave until Porter is released too. No one can get hold of Porter's wife, and his parents are out of the country."

"We have to get Harley released," Pandora insisted.

"I tried to convince him; he looks terrible." Milton sighed. "He's unshaven, and his eyes are bloodshot."

For a moment, Pandora's fear and misery were replaced by rage. It was bad enough to have lunch with Porter in a brownstone in Greenwich Village. But Harley and Porter had been on the street, in full view of anyone passing by. How could Harley risk his reputation, their marriage, and Esme's future for a smutty interlude?

Only last weekend Harley had taken Esme to see a pony at the stables in Annandale-on-Hudson. Pandora and Harley saw a play at the Poughkeepsie playhouse later that night. The next day, they ate lunch with his parents at Blythdale. Could the Harley who was so proud of his new loan programs at the bank, who couldn't stop boasting about Esme's growing vocabulary, be the same one who sat in a New York jail cell?

"How much did Harley have to drink?" Pandora inquired.

"I don't know. The police found a bottle of gin on Porter in the cell," Milton replied. "It was almost empty."

Pandora wanted to turn her anger on Porter. This was Porter's fault, he seduced Harley. But she knew that wasn't true. From the first time she had seen Porter at their wedding, she had known Harley was in love with him. She detected a hopelessness about Harley when anyone mentioned Porter—as if Harley could do nothing to control his feelings.

Her heart went out to Harley; she wished that everything had been different. That Harley had loved her as a woman, and she'd never made love with Archie. Their marriage would have been a closed circle with Esme at the center. Porter wouldn't have been allowed in, and none of this would have happened.

"How is Porter?"

"I didn't see him." Milton frowned. "There will be a terrible scandal. It's already on the front page of this afternoon's newspapers."

"It's in the newspapers already?" she asked.

Milton reached into his suit pocket; he handed her a folded-up newspaper.

"I didn't know if I should show it to you."

Harley's photo stared back at her. Porter's arm was draped around Harley's shoulder, and they both wore dazzling smiles. Pandora had never seen the photo before, perhaps it was taken at a political fundraiser. Underneath was another photo, one of Harley outside the jail. His hair was disheveled, and he had a cut on his cheek.

Pandora's stomach wrenched and she thought she might faint.

"Porter's opponent will make sure this stays in the news; that's the way politics works." Milton looked at Pandora. He seemed suddenly older. "Harley will be caught in the middle of it."

Porter and Doris were married now. Pandora and Harley had been invited to the wedding. They didn't go because they were in Palm Beach for Thanksgiving. Porter was running for senator. If he won, he and Doris would move to Albany, and Pandora wouldn't have to worry about him anymore. But now, with this scandal in the papers, that was unlikely to happen.

"A crowd formed in front of the jail," Milton said. "Somehow, Harley cut his cheek."

"A crowd?" Pandora repeated, puzzled.

Milton fiddled with his cuff links. "Of people who hate homosexuals."

Pandora looked at Milton in horror. Her cheeks burned and her throat was dry.

"I have to go down there; Harley could get hurt."

"It's not a good idea." Milton shook his head. "I've decided this needs to be handled privately. Anything we do will create more of a stir."

"What do you mean, 'privately'?" Pandora demanded.

"The bank can't risk losing its most important clients." Milton rubbed the rim of his glass. "Things are a bit precarious at the moment; the bank has overinvested. I can't afford a scandal."

"Harley can take a leave of absence," Pandora urged. "We'll take Esme to Palm Beach; Adele can come with us. In the summer, we'll go abroad . . ."

"Pandora." Milton stopped her. "It's not that easy."

Pandora sipped her brandy. Her eyes widened and she looked at Milton.

"What do you mean?"

"Homosexuality is an aberration. If I condone it in any way, everyone will turn against me," Milton continued. "The only way to save the bank is to make it clear that Harley isn't my son anymore."

"Harley is your son," she said fiercely. "Times have changed. Homosexuals have almost become accepted in New York. Virginia said that at the Cotton Club there are as many homosexuals in the audience as not."

"Harlem isn't the Yale Club, and it isn't Wall Street." Milton shook his head. "The bank's customers are old fashioned."

Something in Milton's voice frightened Pandora.

"We'll go to Europe," she offered. "Perhaps all Harley needs is a few months at a Swiss spa."

"If you appear to support him, it will ruin your reputation forever. Think what it will do to Esme. She won't have friends or be accepted into the right schools because her father went to jail for being a homosexual."

Pandora thought about her night with Archie. If anyone found out, it could ruin Esme forever. Harley had made a mistake, just like Pandora. She couldn't abandon him. This was the first test of their marriage. Pandora would insist that Harley never see Porter again. She would encourage him to take time off.

"Esme doesn't go to school for years; it will be forgotten long before that."

"The best thing is for Harley to go away for a while," Milton said as if she hadn't spoken. "I have a cousin in Massachusetts with a house on a lake. Harley will go there. I've already spoken to Annie in San Francisco. Adele will visit her. I suggest you take Esme and Sally to Europe. Just for a few months. I'll pay for it of course."

"I can't," she argued. She would have gone to Europe with Harley, but not by herself. "The opening of my boutique is next week."

Milton glanced at her kindly. He rubbed his brow, and his shoulders hunched over.

"Do you really think people will come to your opening while your husband's name is splashed across every newsstand? I'll continue to pay the rent; you can hold the opening when you return."

Milton was right. Anyone who knew about the scandal would avoid her boutique. The full weight of Harley's betrayal washed over her. All Pandora's dreams, everything she had envisioned for their future, would be lost.

A disturbing thought came to her. If Pandora took Esme to Europe without Harley, wasn't she behaving like her mother? Laura left when the doors to society closed to her, Pandora didn't want to do the same.

Yet she had to protect Esme. If she went to Europe, she and Esme would return to Harley, and they would be a family again.

Milton stood up and paced around the room.

"The RMS *Olympic* leaves for Southampton next week. You and Esme and Sally will be on it. Until then, stay inside and don't talk to reporters." He reached into his pocket. "Harley wrote you a letter; he wanted me to give it to you."

Milton walked to the door; Pandora followed him.

"Whatever Harley says in the letter, don't forget what he's done." Milton turned around. "It's a sickness, Pandora. Harley can't control his actions, and he's never going to change."

After Milton left, Pandora stuffed the letter into her purse. She had to get to Harley as soon as she could. No matter what Milton said, Harley was still her husband. She had to make sure he was all right.

~

The Yorkville Prison was in the basement of the courthouse on Fifty-Seventh Street at Lexington Avenue. Pandora was shocked to find it was on the same block as her boutique. She parked hurriedly and tried to make her way inside. But a crowd had gathered around the entrance. They carried signs pasted with the newspaper articles about Harley's and Porter's arrests.

Pandora scanned the words printed on the signs: "Protect our Children, Keep Homosexuals Locked Up and Throw Away the Key."

The blood rushed to her cheeks, and she had to stop herself from ripping the signs from the protestors' hands. Harley was a wonderful father. He would never hurt a child.

She managed to squeeze inside the courthouse and walked quickly to the desk.

"Can I help you?" a man asked. He wore a gray uniform and was poring over a black ledger.

"I need to see my husband, Harley Enright."

"I'm sorry, ma'am." He shook his head. "The jail cells are locked for the evening."

"It's urgent. I'll only be a minute," she pleaded.

"Those are the rules. You can come back on Monday."

Pandora took a deep breath. She couldn't leave without seeing Harley.

"Please," she said desperately. She opened her purse and took out her wallet. "I have enough money to get him released."

"The prisoner already refused bail." He closed the ledger. "Go home and take a bath; let him sleep off his hangover. Your husband will be happy to leave on Monday."

Two guards stood at the top of the basement steps; she couldn't sneak past them. She had to think of some way to get to him. She couldn't leave him here until Monday.

An acrid smell hit her as she walked outside. It reminded her of a pot that sat on the stove too long. She saw a flicker of orange and heard a loud popping sound. Flames erupted around her. She heard glass shattering and people shouting.

The crowd lurched forward, and then people scattered and ran. It all happened so quickly. The flames licked the windows of the jail, melting the glass and leaving the iron bars black and filthy. The buildings on each side of the jail caught fire, and more windows shattered from the heat.

Frantically, she turned back to the jail, but someone took her hand. He dragged her down the street, only stopping when they reached the corner.

The man's shirt was torn, and his hair was covered in ashes.

"I can't leave. My husband is in the jail." She wiped the soot and sweat from her forehead.

"You'll be killed if you go back there," he said in warning. "Soon, there won't be any of the courthouse left."

The fire continued to spread. People ran in all directions. Harley was in the basement; there were bars on the windows. He had no way to escape.

Suddenly, an explosion ripped one wall of the courthouse open. She heard sirens and people screaming. Pandora watched in horror as the building crumbled like some great prehistoric animal that was too tired to keep standing.

Pandora glanced down the street and gasped. The fire had already spread to her boutique. One window was broken, and orange flames filled the interior.

She tried to run to it, but the swell of people moving toward her made it impossible. She stood frozen and watched everything she had worked for, the racks of bright dresses, the elegant furniture, and the cases of cardigans and sweaters, become a mess of charred remains. The walls caved in like a house of cards.

When there was nothing left to see, Pandora started walking. She walked down Fifty-Seventh Street and turned onto Lexington Avenue. She walked past Bloomingdale's with its smart window displays, past apartment buildings with uniformed doormen, past a skyscraper under construction.

She walked until her calves ached, her head throbbed, and her back felt like it would break. Why had it all seemed so important? The money, the success, the social standing. Wasn't love the only important thing? But now he was gone. He couldn't possibly have survived. He had been trapped in the basement, and she had seen the explosion.

After she was too tired to walk anymore, she made her way back to her car and drove slowly back to Summerhill. Her hands clutched the steering wheel so tightly she could barely feel her fingers. She had to keep pushing away the tears to see the road.

Finally, she pulled into Summerhill's gates and dragged herself up the front steps. Harley's letter was still in her purse. She had forgotten about it! What had Harley written, and how could she bear to read it when he was surely dead?

First, she poured herself a shot of brandy from the decanter in the living room. Then she unfolded the paper.

My dearest Pandora,

If you are reading this, you know what I've done. It's all my fault, Pandora. I should never have married you in the first place. You've been the ideal wife. You supported me and you brought me such happiness: your love, our home, and our precious daughter. I could never be a good husband because only half of me wanted those things, the other half wanted something else. Something you could never give me.

I can't fight who I am, Pandora. It's as impossible as expecting the moon to turn into the sun. And I can't live without being the real me. To try and do so again would only cause more pain.

I have decided to take matters into my own hands and end things now. My parents have suffered enough. They would never recover from the ongoing shame of their son being a homosexual. What kind of life will Esme have with me as a father? And you deserve much more; I want you to be happy.

It's better if I'm remembered fondly, one of those people who float through the world for a while, before making his departure.

You and Esme will be provided for. I hope one day you can forgive me, Pandora. Nothing you could have said or done would have made things turn out differently.

Give Esme a kiss for me.

Yours,
Harley

The paper fluttered to the floor; a fresh wave of grief overcame her. Had Harley taken his own life, or had he died in the fire? If only she had arrived at the jail sooner, or if the guard had let her through. Perhaps it would have turned out differently.

At least she had Esme. Pandora would make sure Esme knew how much Harley loved her. It wasn't much, but for now, it was the only thing she could think of to do for Harley.

Chapter Sixteen

March 1929, Beaulieu-sur-Mer, France

The fire turned into one of the biggest in New York's recent history, and the scandal too. The newspapers stayed full of it. Even when Pandora boarded the RMS *Olympic* to Europe, Harley's and Porter's names remained plastered across the headlines: "State Senator Front-Runner Porter Merrill and Bank Vice President Harley Enright Caught in Lewd Behavior," "Fire Caused by Protestors outside Jail Destroys Three City Blocks," "Five People Killed and Dozens Injured."

She couldn't believe Harley was dead. Every day, she crisscrossed the ship's deck as if consumed by a fever, and wondered whether he killed himself or if the fire did it for him. She didn't know which was worse. If only she had reached him in time, maybe she could have saved him. Even though their marriage was not what she had expected, she and Harley had still loved each other, even if just as best friends.

No one had ever been so supportive of her career. She loved talking to him about the boutique. His enthusiasm and belief in her had meant so much. How would she create new designs without his gentle praise and support?

And he had been such a good father. When Harley was with Esme, she was his sole focus. He could read to her for hours, and she often heard him singing to Esme when she was supposed to be asleep. Even

Adele praised his devotion. Milton never had that kind of patience with his children.

Pandora missed him desperately.

She tried not to think about it, to concentrate on the crossing instead. But it was impossible. She yearned for him. She wanted him to be on the ship with her and Esme. To take Esme swimming in the swimming pool and read books in the library. She wanted to dine together in the *Olympic*'s two-story dining room and whisper when they saw the famous passengers, Mary Pickford and Douglas Fairbanks.

And she longed for her boutique. The entire shop had burned to the ground. The feeling wasn't anything like the pain of losing Harley, but it still tugged at her like a heavy weight. All the weeks and months of sitting at her sewing machine, all the glorious fabrics, the carefully chosen accessories, gone forever. She wondered if she would have the courage and strength to try again. For now, even thinking about finding a new space and hiring a new staff made her head ache.

She longed for Adele's company too. Adele was on her way to San Francisco. Pandora could still picture the way Adele looked when they said goodbye. In the space of a few days, Adele changed from a beautiful older woman to a pale ghost. Her eyes were rimmed with red, and when Pandora hugged her, she felt thinner.

Milton seemed to almost shrink overnight. He stood on the dock when the ship sailed, Esme waving her plump fist furiously from the deck, and Pandora could see the tears in his eyes.

Since Harley's death, Pandora wondered if she should free herself of her secret. But she couldn't do it. Adele needed to think she had something left of Harley. The revelation would bring Milton more shame when he was still reeling from the articles in the newspaper. And there was Esme to think about. If Archie didn't acknowledge Esme as his own and Esme ever found out, she would be devastated. It was better that she grow up hearing stories about Harley pushing her in her pram and taking her to meet the ponies.

She hadn't had time to see Virginia before she left. She tried writing letters to Willie and Virginia and Archie, but she didn't know what to say. Finally, she put away the writing paper. There would be time to write from the South of France. When she was sitting in the warm sun, gazing at the Mediterranean, she would feel better.

After disembarking in Southampton, they took the train and the ferry across the channel and finally a taxi from Nice to Beaulieu-sur-Mer where Suzanne Lenglen lived. Beaulieu-sur-Mer was a tiny village wrapped around the coast made popular by Queen Victoria at the end of the nineteenth century. There was a train station, along with more than a dozen hotels, facing the small harbor. The loveliest thing about it was the main square. The taxi driver insisted on stopping so Esme could have fresh lemonade. Citrus trees lined the sidewalk, and bougainvillea spilled out of window boxes. Vendors sold tomatoes and berries at the outdoor market, and in the middle of the square stood a wrought-iron music kiosk, where in the summer they held concerts.

After Esme drank her lemonade, the taxi climbed into the hills. From above, the Mediterranean became a turquoise blur edged with white like a piece of Wedgwood wedding china. Just when Pandora began to worry that Suzanne's villa was so high up that she wouldn't be able to walk to town, the car stopped in front of an orange stucco home with green shutters, surrounded by pine trees and a rubber tree whose gnarled roots dug into the dirt.

"Oh, it's breathtaking," Pandora said to Sally, as the taxi driver arranged their luggage on the steps.

Sally was a petite twenty-year-old from Queens. She had four younger siblings and was used to taking care of children. Esme adored her, and Pandora saw her almost as a friend, instead of merely a nanny.

"It's so big; how can it belong to one woman?" Sally wondered.

"Suzanne Lenglen is the biggest tennis star in Europe; she can afford anything she wants." Pandora smiled, breathing in the scent of pine needles. She felt a little better than she had on the ship. The warm sun and sea air calmed her nerves. "Why don't you take Esme to look at the view. I'll see if Suzanne is home."

The interior was dark and cool, with a stone floor and wooden ceiling fans. The furniture seemed scattered about rather than arranged: a dark brown sofa next to a floral armchair in the living room, a long oak table and mismatched chairs in the dining room, and a small room that Pandora guessed was a study but was filled with Suzanne's trophies.

She heard a voice and walked toward it through an arched doorway to the kitchen.

A man wearing an open-necked shirt and a striped apron hunched over the counter. He held a knife in one hand and a strange-looking vegetable in the other.

He resembled a French film star, with light brown hair and a small moustache. His eyes were hazel and he had tan, narrow cheekbones. He said something in French, but she shook her head and replied that she spoke only English.

"Come in, you have perfect timing," he said again in accented English. "My hands are oily, and I can't get a grip on this eggplant."

Pandora held the eggplant on the cutting board while he sliced it with the knife.

"Thank you, I would have wrestled with it for ages."

"Why didn't you wash your hands first?" Pandora wondered.

"I put the olive oil on my hands on purpose." He reached for a wooden bowl. "It's the best way to mix a salad. Butter lettuce and mesclun and eggplant. It's going to be delicious."

"You mix the salad with your hands?" she asked in astonishment.

The man laughed. Pandora guessed that he was about thirty. His teeth were white and straight, and he had a dimple on his cheek.

"You're American," he remarked. "In France, we use our hands when we cook. There's no better way to dress the salad."

"I'm looking for Suzanne," Pandora explained. "I'm Pandora. My daughter and I are staying with her."

"Maurice Flaubert." He nodded. "I'm not related to the writer, though I'm a fan of his work. Have you read *Madame Bovary*? It's one of my favorite books."

"I'm afraid I haven't." Pandora shook her head.

"Then I shall find you a copy," Maurice said decidedly. "I'd offer to shake your hand, but it would only get oily."

Pandora had never met anyone like him. Every word that came out of his mouth was somehow springy, like a slice of Esther's sponge cake. He carried himself with an easy confidence that she assumed must have to do with being French.

"Is Suzanne here?" Pandora asked.

Maurice shook his head. "She's at the tennis club. She trains harder than a horse before Prix de l'Arc de Triomphe at Longchamp's. She leaves for the club at sunrise and only stops for a quick lunch and practices again until dinner. Then she stays up after everyone goes to bed. Don't take a room facing the swimming pool, she splashes at night for hours."

"Is there a maid or housekeeper? My daughter, Esme, is only one, and soon she'll need her bottle and a nap."

"Suzanne never keeps a housekeeper for long. The last one left because the guests kept multiplying," he said with a grin. "We all pitch in. The others have gone to the beach, so I offered to prepare dinner. You can help; do you know how to bread a veal?"

Pandora felt like she didn't have a choice. Sally and Esme were sitting happily in the garden for now. It would be rude to let Maurice do all the work since she was a guest too.

"You can show me," she offered.

Maurice taught her how to coat veal cutlets with a mixture of egg whites and olive oil.

"The best part is the bread crumbs"—he gathered bread crumbs in his palm—"hot and golden, straight from the oven. Veal Milanese is one of my favorite dishes."

"That sounds Italian, and we're in France." She frowned.

"Italy is only a few miles away; the Italian Alps are right behind us." Pandora had no idea they were so close to Italy.

He noticed her puzzled expression. "You're in Europe now; you'll learn the geography," he said as he walked to the counter and picked up a bottle of wine. He poured two glasses and handed one to Pandora. "This is a petite rouge; the grapes are grown in the Italian Alps."

Pandora hardly ever drank wine and never during the day. In Hyde Park she drank the cocktails Harley prepared when he arrived home or the champagne served at dinner parties and weddings.

"You drink wine during the day?" she asked, horrified.

Maurice took a sip and shrugged. "Wine is one of the greatest pleasures in life. Why would I put off drinking it until evening?"

Pandora set the glass on the counter. It would only give her a headache.

"Americans are so rigid." Maurice took another sip. "Last month, we had a couple from Boston who dressed every night for dinner."

"It's good manners to dress for a dinner party," Pandora said stiffly. "Do you always say such unkind things about Americans?"

Maurice wiped his hands on his apron. He eyed her appreciatively.

"You're right, I apologize." He nodded. "Since the war, the Riviera is full of rich Americans. They crowd the cafés and get angry at the waiter if their eggs take too long to arrive."

He took her hand and led her to the window. Whitewashed villas with flowering gardens dotted the hills. Below them she could see the cobblestone streets and peaked roofs of the village.

He placed his hands on her shoulders. "Tell me, when you're looking at this, how could you be in a hurry?"

"You're right, it's beautiful," she agreed. "I could stare at it for hours."

"You see"—he turned her around triumphantly—"you're already thinking like a European." His eyes traveled over her blond hair held back by a clip, her traveling outfit of a pale blue blouse and pleated skirt. "You can shop for clothes in the village. By the end of the week, you'll be as sophisticated as any French woman." He paused, and his eyes returned to her face. "You already are as beautiful."

~

After they finished preparing the veal, Maurice bicycled into the village, and Pandora went upstairs to get settled. She felt awkward choosing their rooms. At the house parties she attended in Hyde Park, the hostess assigned the appropriate guest rooms. But Maurice assured her that's how it was done. She offered to squeeze into one room with Sally and Esme, but Maurice said because it was March, the villa was half empty.

In the late afternoon Pandora sat on a stone bench in the garden. Everything was different from Summerhill or Riverview. Even the gardens. At home, every inch of garden was designed by landscape architects and featured pergolas and manicured hedges. Suzanne's garden looked almost wild, with overgrown thorny rosebushes and a shed that leaned over so far Pandora was afraid it would fall.

The temperature was cooler than she had anticipated, so she wrapped herself in her coat. Suddenly she felt homesick; she wished she hadn't come. If she were at Summerhill, she could talk to her father or she could go into New York and see Virginia. Willie had been supportive of her going to Europe. The South of France was so healing, and Suzanne was a gracious hostess. But she missed him. Perhaps she would write to Milton and say it was a mistake, that she and Esme belonged in Hyde Park. She didn't want to stay in a house full of strangers so far from home.

A woman appeared at the gate. She wore a sleeveless white blouse and a skirt that stopped just below the knees. She had a cardigan wrapped around her waist, and she wore lace-up canvas shoes. At first Pandora didn't think it was Suzanne. No one dressed like that to play tennis. Women wore skirts with petticoats that covered their calves and ruffled blouses with little jackets. Then she recognized the headband tied around her dark, wavy hair. Suzanne was famous for *le bandeau*. Women all over Europe copied the look.

"Pandora!" Suzanne kissed her on both cheeks. "Look at you! The last time I saw you, you were a gangly teenager. Now you're a beautiful young woman and a mother. I don't know how you do it."

"The mothering part is easy," Pandora said, relieved that Suzanne had finally appeared. "Sally, the nanny, is a great help, and Esme is an easy child."

"I don't have the patience to be a mother." Suzanne sat beside her. "I can barely look after my goat."

"You have a goat?" Pandora's eyes widened.

"Most people on the Riviera keep farm animals." Suzanne shrugged. "Goats are playful, and they produce the tastiest cheese. You'll see; we'll have some at dinner."

Pandora realized she was hungry. She hadn't eaten anything since the taxi stopped in the square.

"It sounds delicious," Pandora said. "We traveled all day; I'm hungry."

"I should have sent someone to pick you up in Nice," Suzanne apologized. "You can help yourself to anything in the kitchen."

"I was already asked to help prepare dinner," Pandora said with a smile. "I breaded the veal."

"That must have been Maurice," Suzanne offered. "He's an excellent chef. He trained at the Cordon Bleu school in Paris, but he doesn't want anyone to know."

"Why not?" Pandora wondered.

"He's afraid he'll have to turn it into a proper job, and he doesn't like to be tied down." Suzanne's tone became gentle. "I want to talk about you. Your father wrote and told me about Harley. I hope you don't mind that he told me."

Tears stung Pandora's eyes, and she glanced down at her wedding ring. She hadn't taken it off.

"Of course not." She shook her head. "Everyone knows; it was in all the newspapers."

"I can't tell you how sorry I am. To lose your husband and Esme's father is unthinkable. You're too young and lovely to be a widow." Suzanne squeezed her hand. "The Riviera is the best place to heal; it's been healing people for ages. One can't walk on the beach or visit the casino in Monte Carlo or go shopping in Nice without being grateful to be alive."

Pandora felt her emotions well up like the rain in the gutter after a storm. She had promised herself she would be strong for Esme. There was nothing she could do about the past.

"I'm not ready for those sorts of things," Pandora replied. "I'm happy to just stay here and read and play with Esme."

"I know a little of what you're feeling." Suzanne tugged at her bandeau. "I lived in Paris until I was eleven. Then my younger brother, Marcel, became ill, and my parents moved us to the South of France. My brother died, and my father started taking me to the tennis club. From the moment I picked up a tennis racquet, I was happy," Suzanne finished. "Life has a way of surprising you."

"It's not just Harley," Pandora reflected, "though of course that's most of it. I was also about to open my own boutique. I don't know when I'll have the strength to do it again."

"You will," Suzanne assured her. "When the war began, Wimbledon and the French Open were canceled. All the young men were away fighting the Germans. After the war ended, I realized in a way it had been a blessing. I spent those four years practicing, and I met your father. Before him, I was a good player, and he made me great."

"I'm being a terrible guest," Pandora said guiltily. "I haven't thanked you. You're so good to take us in; I'm very grateful."

"I adore having company. When the villa is empty, it reveals all its flaws: the floors are slanted and the windows don't close and the plumbing is ancient," Suzanne responded. "When it's full, I only notice that the dining room is big enough to seat twelve people, and there are orange trees, so we can eat oranges. I do get preoccupied, though," Suzanne warned her. "Wimbledon is in July, so the whole month of June you won't see me except at dinner."

Pandora couldn't imagine staying until June. She would miss Summerhill and everyone at home too much.

"We'll be gone before June," Pandora assured her.

"You might think that now; wait until you've watched the sun set over the Mediterranean. Or until you've driven down the coast and gathered shells," Suzanne said with a knowing smile. "You'll want to stay on the French Riviera forever."

~

Before dinner, Pandora had taken a bath. Suzanne was right, the plumbing was ancient. The water took ages to heat up, and then it dripped out of the tap.

She didn't care what Maurice said, she was going to dress formally for dinner. Her daytime tea dresses weren't appropriate, and she believed in dressing up at night. It was only good manners.

She chose the white gown with butterfly sleeves that she wore for the Winthrops' Fourth of July party almost three years ago. How young and naive she had been! Everything about that weekend had thrilled her: the butler that welcomed them into the Winthrops' house; the grand salon with its frescoed walls and furniture upholstered in velvet that was almost pink and almost white, just like Virginia's lipstick; Virginia insisting that Pandora wear her diamond-and-sapphire necklace; and Pandora gazing in the mirror and feeling like a princess.

She took a brush to her hair and pulled it through. She was only twenty-three, what would she do with her future? Would she ever fall in love and get married again, and would there be more children? It wasn't the time to think about it. Everyone was downstairs; she didn't want to keep them waiting.

She had expected the evening to start with cocktails. But when she appeared, the guests were already seated at the dining room table. Suzanne sat at the head of the table, and Maurice sat in the middle. There were two other couples at the table and an older man dressed in navy pants and a shirt with a round collar and French cuffs. He had a lizard-skin watch strapped to his wrist, and he wore gold cuff links.

"Pandora, you must think it's terribly rude that we're already seated, but everyone is hungry," Suzanne said in apology. "Sit next to Maurice."

Maurice looked even more handsome than he had earlier that afternoon. He wore a lounge jacket over a white shirt that made his skin seem even darker. There was a sheen to his cheeks, and he had slicked back his light brown hair.

"I must introduce you to everyone," Suzanne said. "Armand and Marie are from Paris." She nodded at the older man and woman sitting opposite Maurice.

The other couple, Lionel and Jane, were British and in their thirties. Luckily for Pandora, they spoke little French, so the whole table spoke in English.

"And this is Jean Patou," Suzanne finished, pointing to the older man wearing the lizard-skin watch.

Pandora's mouth dropped open. Jean Patou was one of her idols. He was one of the most famous French fashion designers. After the war, he opened an atelier in Paris frequented by European royalty. His clothes were known for their modern aesthetic. He'd just invented a line of men's neckties using the same fabrics as his women's collection, instead of the traditional black or white.

"Jean designs my tennis dresses," Suzanne explained. "I'm so lucky; I wouldn't win a match without him."

"I'm the lucky one. Suzanne is la Divine; every woman in Europe wants to dress like her," Jean proclaimed in English. "The tennis attire women are forced to wear is absurd. How are they supposed to hit a ball wearing a dress that's so long they'll trip? Tennis is similar to ballet. Ballerinas don't take the stage in corsets; they wear costumes that let them move."

That explained Suzanne's outfit this afternoon. The sleeveless blouse and knee-length skirt.

"Are you traveling with your husband?" the British man, Lionel, asked. He had thinning blond hair and a sharp chin.

"My husband died recently. I'm traveling with my one-year-old daughter, Esme," Pandora replied, picking up her wine glass.

Maurice turned to Pandora with a somber expression.

"I'm very sorry; one never knows what the day will bring. The important thing is to enjoy oneself," Maurice remarked. "I'd rather my tombstone say that I got the most out of life than that I worked in an office copying letters or adding figures in long columns."

"Don't listen to Maurice," Suzanne said to Pandora. "Even in France, most of us enjoy our work. Only Maurice prefers to spend his days reading novels by the pool and playing in the kitchen."

Pandora didn't say anything. She had never met a man who didn't have some kind of profession.

The conversation turned in a different direction, and Maurice brought out a thick soup made with peas and carrots from Suzanne's garden. It was followed by the veal, and for dessert they had beignets from a patisserie in the village, dusted with sugar and accompanied by blueberries.

After dinner, everyone moved to the living room for brandy and games. Maurice asked her to help with the dishes. Pandora was tempted to refuse. She didn't like some of the things he had said about Americans. But no one else offered, and she couldn't let him do all the work.

"Why did you ask me to help?" Pandora demanded, when they both stood in the kitchen. Maurice had taken off his jacket and rolled up his sleeves. "You obviously don't like Americans."

Maurice tied the apron around his waist. He wiped his hands on his pants.

"On the contrary, I've met some fascinating Americans. Ernest Hemingway and I once spent hours at a café, talking about his time as an ambulance driver in Italy during the war. And I've always enjoyed seeing F. Scott Fitzgerald at parties. He lived in Antibes for two years. He's going to write a book about all of us on the French Riviera.

"Let me tell you a story," he continued. "My father is a famous surgeon in Paris. I was sent to medical school and expected to follow in his footsteps. One night I was studying my medical books, and I had terrible pain that turned out to be an ulcer. My stomach was on fire; I could barely swallow.

"My grandmother gave me a prescription: throw out the medical books and join her in the kitchen instead. Ever since I was a child, I loved helping her cook. It didn't matter what it was; beef bourguignon, duck confit, a chocolate gâteau. I abandoned medical school, and the ulcer disappeared." He paused. "I sense something similar in you. You're trying to do what's expected of you, but you really want something else."

The hair on the back of Pandora's neck bristled. How dare Maurice make assumptions. They had just met; he knew nothing about her. Even if what he said was true, she couldn't let him see it.

"Before my husband died, we were happy," she said sharply, trying to believe it herself. "We had each other, a beautiful home, and a child. My daughter, Esme, is the best thing that ever happened to me."

"You're too beautiful and spirited to devote yourself to raising a child." His eyes were probing. "You're a young woman in a butterfly-sleeve dress who is actually a butterfly waiting to spread her wings."

Pandora stepped away, taken aback. Maurice acted as if he knew her, yet they had just met.

"You're in the South of France now," he said, turning on the faucet. "All you have to do is breathe in the ocean air, and the rest will take care of itself."

~

It was almost midnight when Pandora retired to her room. After she helped Maurice in the kitchen, she joined the others in the living room for charades. Eventually everyone went to bed except Suzanne. Pandora could hear her splashing in the pool. She wondered how Suzanne stayed warm. The night air was chilly with a cold breeze.

As she sat at the dressing table, a knock sounded at the door. She peered into the hallway, but found only a book propped against the door.

It was a copy of *Madame Bovary* in English with a note tucked inside the cover.

To ma petite butterfly,
The first step in your education.

Chapter Seventeen

At the end of April, Pandora had been in the South of France for a month. The weather was unseasonably warm, and Esme and Sally spent most of their time at the beach. Esme blossomed more every day. She came back to the villa each afternoon, her round cheeks with a golden hue, white sand stuck to her feet.

She loved building sandcastles, and she and Sally spent hours searching for shells. She even picked up a smattering of French. Her small vocabulary included *"la plage"* for beach and *"une glacée"* for the ice cream she and Sally ate in the village square. Pandora took Esme to the barn to feed Suzanne's goat. They picked flowers together, and a few times Pandora borrowed Suzanne's car and they had picnics in the hills above Nice.

After a few weeks, letters arrived from Milton and Adele and Virginia. Milton only sent a check with a short note, but Adele sent three tightly written pages. She was in San Francisco with Annie and her family. Annie was pregnant with her third child, so Adele felt useful. But she missed Pandora and Esme and longed for the time when they would all be back in Hyde Park.

Adele hardly mentioned Harley's death. Pandora understood; it was still too raw. Pandora wondered if Adele had known about Harley before they got married. Even if she had told Pandora, it wouldn't have changed anything. Pandora had loved Harley. They believed their arrangement would work.

Virginia's letter was brimming with news about Riverview Press. Millie was working out wonderfully; Virginia couldn't imagine how she had survived without her. The *New Yorker* had reviewed their latest book, and Virginia was planning her first author tour. Pandora also received a loving letter from her father. Willie missed her terribly, but he knew from personal experience that there was no better place to heal than the French Riviera.

Archie wrote to her from London. Lucy was still in St. Louis with her father; the wedding would take place as soon as he recovered. Archie offered to visit Pandora, but she declined. She wasn't ready to see him. What if she slipped and told Archie that Esme was his daughter? Esme reminded her a little of Archie. They had the same very blond hair. She couldn't risk revealing her secret when it could hurt so many people.

Pandora planned to go shopping in the village. She wanted to buy gifts to send to Riverview: a French tea towel for Esther and a smart shirt for her father. She would also send presents to San Francisco: bars of wonderfully scented French soaps for Adele and a lace gown for the new baby.

There was a knock at the front door and Pandora ran down the stairs. The sun streamed into the living room, making patterns on the wood floor. Suzanne was still upstairs, and Maurice had taken the bicycle. The two other couples were on a day trip to Avignon, and Jean Patou had left for his own villa in Cap Ferrat to work on his new collection.

A woman in her late twenties stood on the doorstep. She was breathtakingly beautiful in the way only a French woman could be. Her hair was bluntly cut at the nape of her neck, and she had large aquamarine eyes. Her mouth formed a dark red pout, and she had a heart-shaped mole on her cheek.

"Can I help you?" Pandora asked in English.

"I'm looking for Maurice," the woman answered.

Pandora had hardly seen Maurice lately. In her first week at the villa, they had spent a lot of time together. He taught her to make bouillabaisse, and one afternoon they went swimming in the ocean. Afterward, Maurice spread out two towels and they lay on the hot sand. Then he went away for two weeks. Suzanne told her that he went to Montpellier to visit his grandmother.

Without Maurice to cook, the other guests ate at restaurants. Pandora usually had an early dinner with Sally and Esme in the kitchen.

He had returned a few days ago, but he was out on his bicycle. "Maurice isn't here, he took the bicycle somewhere," Pandora said. She opened the door wider. "You're welcome to wait."

The woman peered inside as if deciding whether it would be comfortable.

"I'll do some shopping and come back later." She shrugged. She pulled a gold cigarette case from her purse. "Perhaps you could give this to him; he left it at my flat."

Pandora watched her walk to a small red car. She wore a white sailor suit with a royal-blue jacket, and her skirt swayed when she walked. She reached into the passenger seat and put on a wide-brimmed hat.

Pandora closed the door and turned around.

"Who was at the door?" Suzanne appeared beside her.

"A woman for Maurice." She held up the cigarette case. "She wanted to return this."

"Ahh," Suzanne said knowingly. "It must have been Nanette."

"Who's Nanette?" Pandora wondered.

"Maurice and Nanette are engaged, or were engaged, I can't keep track." Suzanne carried her cup of coffee into the living room. "They're one of those couples that are so passionate, they either make each other dizzyingly happy or start throwing things. Nanette refused to get married unless Maurice found a job. Before he had time to agree, she ran off to Paris and became a model. Nanette is one of the reasons Maurice came to the Riviera."

Pandora didn't know why meeting Nanette bothered her. She had no interest in Maurice or any man. Still, she had enjoyed his company. She had even read *Madame Bovary*. At first it shocked her—Emma Bovary neglected her husband and child to have an affair that ended in tragedy—but the writing was so elegant, and the sensuous passages left her somehow breathless.

"I'm glad I never got married," Suzanne said from her spot curled up on the sofa. "I'd rather play tennis and have affairs instead."

It was Sunday, the day Suzanne took off from tennis. She didn't even get dressed on Sundays. She spent the whole day in a robe, drinking coffee and eating handfuls of raisins and nuts to give her energy.

"Have you thought more about opening a boutique?" Suzanne asked. "You could open one here in Beaulieu-sur-Mer. So many tourists are looking for dresses."

It was a good idea, but Pandora's heart wasn't in it. For the first time since she could remember, when she opened her notebook, the ideas for dresses didn't come. Every time she tried to draw, she pictured the dresses that had burned in the fire. At first, she told herself it was too soon, she needed rest. But she was beginning to panic. What if inspiration never came to her again?

"We can't stay here forever; at some point we have to go home," Pandora said. She didn't want to admit her fear to Suzanne that she had lost her creative drive. If she did, then it would feel more real.

"I don't want you to leave, but I can tell that you need to do something," Suzanne said thoughtfully. "You remind me of when I was about your age. I lost my spark for tennis. I was tired of practicing; I was even tired of winning. I wanted to take time off," she confided. "My tennis instructor looked at me sternly and said that before I knew it, I would be thirty, and it would be too late. If I wanted to be a tennis champion,

I couldn't stop playing. You're young and intelligent. Decide what you want, then go out and get it."

~

Later that day, Pandora stepped out of the men's shop on boulevard Marinoni and turned onto the square. At times like this, when the shops and cafés were filled with visitors enjoying the sunshine, she wished more than anything that Harley were beside her.

Harley would have loved Beaulieu-sur-Mer as much as she did. Her favorite place was the Hôtel Bristol. It was painted yellow with a white portico flanked by marble angels. Circular windows overlooked the bay, and a curved balcony had tables and chairs for visitors to sit and admire the view.

Pandora imagined exploring the village with Harley. They would have visited Église du Sacré-Coeur with its brick clock tower and stone facade, while Sally took Esme to play with other children in Parc Beaulieu. Afterward they would have all met for afternoon tea at the Hôtel Métropole. In the evenings, they would have left Esme with Sally and joined other couples for cocktails and lobster caught fresh the same day. It would have been so beautiful, and they would have been happy.

"Pandora." A male voice interrupted her thoughts. "Come join us."

The man stood up and waved. It was Maurice, at a table at an outdoor café with Nanette.

Pandora crossed the square and joined them.

"Are you sure?" she asked. "I don't want to interrupt your lunch."

"You're not interrupting, and we're only having coffee," Maurice replied companionably. He turned to Nanette. "Pandora is a guest at Suzanne's villa."

"We already met." Nanette nodded. She held a cigarette, and a pearl cigarette case lay open in front of her. "I gave Pandora your cigarette case." She looked pointedly at Maurice. "I was sure you wouldn't want to be without it."

Maurice motioned for Pandora to sit down.

"Nanette is a fit model for a couturier in Paris," Maurice said.

"It can be boring to have pins stuck in you all day." Nanette took a drag of her cigarette. "But it pays well, and I can borrow dresses whenever I like."

"You see, America isn't the only place where women are becoming independent." Maurice lit a cigarette and inhaled sharply. "Soon, women won't need men at all."

Nanette chose to ignore him. She turned to Pandora instead.

"Is your husband traveling with you?" she asked.

Pandora shook her head.

"I'm a widow. I'm with my daughter and nanny," she said vaguely.

"Pandora has a talent for fashion design." Maurice pointed to her handbag. "She keeps a notebook of her sketches."

Pandora had shown Maurice the sketchbook the first week she spent at the villa. But since she arrived she hadn't been able to draw any new dresses. Instead, she had filled the sketchbook with drawings of Esme at the beach and Suzanne playing tennis.

"Can I see?" Nanette leaned forward.

Pandora handed her the notebook, and Nanette flipped through the pages.

"These are wonderful," Nanette commented. "I saw Suzanne play at Wimbledon in 1925. It was unbearably hot; I almost fainted." She turned to the next sketch. "If only the spectators were allowed to dress the same as the players. British women dress for Wimbledon as if they're going to the theater. In stockings and gloves and felt caps. It's the same at the French Open. I'll never watch tennis again."

It was true. Since coming to the French Riviera, Pandora had spent long afternoons in the sun, watching Suzanne cross the tennis court in lightweight outfits that would have been considered scandalous in New

York, while Pandora herself wore stockings and one of her tea dresses that covered her ankles. It would be even more unbearable during the summer.

Pandora could feel the beginnings of a great idea growing in her head. She jumped up and grabbed the notebook from the table.

"I have to go," she announced. "I have a prior engagement."

Maurice glanced at her curiously.

"You haven't had your café au lait," Maurice offered.

Pandora was too excited to stay a minute longer. She nodded at Nanette. "It was a pleasure to meet you; I'm sure I'll see you again."

Pandora spent the rest of the afternoon at the dressing table in her room. For the first time since Harley died and her boutique burned in the fire, she couldn't draw fast enough. She filled page after page with dresses and cardigans and sweaters.

Up until now, her dress designs had been inspired by her favorite designers: Chanel, Jeanne Lanvin, Elsa Schiaparelli. They were all elegant and refined, dresses that society women would wear to weekend house parties and dances. Pandora's new designs were different, unlike anything any other designer had created. At five o'clock she was finished. She hadn't eaten all day and was tempted to find something to eat in the kitchen. But she was too excited. She wanted to share her idea now, to find out if she had something.

Pandora found Suzanne flopped on a sofa in the living room. She suspected Suzanne hadn't moved all day. A magazine lay open beside her, and a tray with half a sandwich sat on the coffee table.

"Where have you been?" Suzanne inquired. "Maurice is still out, but everyone else is swimming."

"I've been busy," Pandora replied. "Could I borrow your car? I'll be back in a few hours."

"Does it involve a man?" Suzanne raised her eyebrows.

Pandora smiled. "Not exactly. It's nothing really, I'll tell you when I return."

~

The villa where Jean Patou was staying perched high in the hills above Cap Ferrat. It was more elegant than Suzanne's villa, with marble arches and a red-tiled roof like a Moorish castle. Palm trees flanked the entrance, and a fountain murmured in the rose garden.

A maid answered the door. Pandora suddenly felt embarrassed. She should have called first. Jean Patou was a well-known designer; he wouldn't have time to see Pandora. But she had been afraid she'd lose her nerve. And it would have been difficult to explain over the phone. It was better to talk with him in person.

Jean appeared behind the maid dressed in a smoking jacket and open-necked shirt. His pants were black silk, and he wore gold slippers.

"Pandora, what a pleasant surprise," he said in greeting. "How is everyone at the villa?"

"I should have called," Pandora apologized. "I hope I'm not interrupting."

"A pretty young woman is never an interruption," Jean replied. "Let's sit in the small salon."

Pandora followed him into a room bathed in sunlight. It had high ceilings, and paintings of the Riviera hung on the walls. Sofas uphol-stered in seafoam green faced each other across a glass coffee table.

"Oh, it's beautiful," Pandora breathed.

"It would be if I didn't have my designs thrown everywhere." He gathered fabrics scattered over the sofas. "The maid is bringing coffee and biscuits. Please sit down and tell me why you're here."

Pandora sat opposite him and took out her notepads. She took a deep breath to calm her nerves.

"I've been designing my own dresses since I was fifteen," Pandora began. "I've always gotten my inspiration from other designers; I've never had an entirely new idea."

She paused, hoping she was making sense.

"This afternoon, I was thinking about the tennis dresses you made for Suzanne. You said you were designing clothes for golf and swimming. What if the spectators wore more casual clothing? If at a tennis match women in the stands could display their calves and shoulders"— she showed him the sketches—"it would be much cooler."

Jean flipped through the pages.

"These are quite good." He nodded. "It would depend on the fabric. Silk is too hot, even organza can feel confining. You'd have to get rid of the stockings; it's impossible to feel cool with something clinging to your legs."

Pandora had been wearing stockings since she was sixteen. But Jean was right. Even if the stockings were sheer, they were too hot to wear in the sun.

The maid set the tray on the table. Jean poured two cups of coffee and handed one to Pandora.

"Suzanne said you're on the Riviera on holiday," Jean said, puzzled. "Do you plan on opening a boutique in the South of France?"

She shook her head. "We won't stay here forever; soon we'll go back to New York."

Pandora stopped, suddenly self-conscious. What had she been thinking, bringing her designs to one of the most famous fashion designers in Europe? She had no experience in sportswear, and there were probably dozens of reasons why the clothes wouldn't work.

"What made you want to be a fashion designer?" Jean asked, sipping his coffee.

"I've never wanted to be anything else," Pandora reflected. "To me fashion is not just about beauty or even style, it's about expressing oneself. A woman's wardrobe should make her happy. The clothes she

221

wears throughout her day—a cotton day dress while she's at work, a velvet cocktail dress for drinks and dinner—should make her feel as if she's accompanied by her closest friends."

"How interesting," Jean mused. "I've never heard fashion described that way before."

"Every woman has pieces of clothing that are special to her: the dress she wore when she first fell in love, the shawl she used to cover herself when she nursed her baby. I want her to feel that way about all my designs so that she can't live without them." Pandora's cheeks flushed with excitement.

"During the war, I was a captain in the Zouaves, the French infantry," Jean recounted. "I wore the same uniform every day; it was covered in so much mud, I forgot its true color. I spent every moment dreaming of clothes I would design after the war: dresses with bright geometric shapes, ball gowns in colors no one had used before—beige verging on green, burnished silver like the inside of an oyster. It's what kept me alive.

"The fashion business is always challenging." He set down his cup. "My women's bathing suits are so scandalous the Paris department stores refuse to stock them." He smiled at Pandora. "Only two things are important: that you believe in yourself and that you want to succeed more than anything. Then you can't fail. I have an idea. Come and work at my atelier in Paris. I don't pay much, but you'll learn everything about running your own fashion house."

Pandora had never been to Paris! She dreamed of seeing Patou's atelier. But she missed Virginia and Adele and her father. And Esme needed to grow up in America. At some point she had to go home.

She thanked him. "It's a wonderful offer. I'll certainly think about it."

~

Suzanne was asleep in the living room when Pandora returned to the villa. Pandora was hungry and went to the kitchen to find something to eat. Maurice sat at the kitchen table. A tray held a bowl of soup and a large chunk of bread.

"Pandora." He looked up from his soup. "Where have you been? Everyone else went to the village for dinner."

"I was visiting," Pandora remarked. "I'm hungry; I haven't eaten all day."

"I made vichyssoise. It's served cold, with crusty bread." He pointed at the bowl. "I used a version of my grandmother's recipe. She believes that food is the best way to mend a broken heart. It really works."

"It sounds delicious." She sat down. "Is your heart broken?"

Maurice filled a bowl with soup. He placed it in front of Pandora.

"Perhaps only bruised, not broken," he assured her. "Suzanne told you that Nanette and I were engaged."

Pandora flushed slightly. She picked up her spoon.

"Suzanne shouldn't have mentioned it; it's none of my business."

"Nanette and I have been on and off for years," he said with a shrug. "She's like those Band-Aids you have in America. Whenever you try to peel one off, it makes the wound worse. Nanette feels the same about me. Nanette was staying in Montpellier, I went there to finish it for good."

"Why are you telling me?" she wondered.

Maurice placed his spoon on the table. He leaned forward and touched her hand.

"Because the first week you were here, all I wanted was to kiss you," he replied. "I couldn't even consider it unless I was free."

Pandora pulled her hand away. She tried to think if Maurice had given any clues that he was interested in her. There had been the day when they went swimming in the ocean. Afterward, he lay the towels down next to each other. He looked so handsome in his bathing suit, but she hadn't let herself think about him in that way.

And there was the attention he paid to her when they prepared meals together. He had stood so close when he showed her how to slice vegetables and mix a salad. She had thought he was simply teaching her the French way to cook.

"You should have asked me first. I'm a recent widow." Her voice was slow and careful. "I would have told you to stay with Nanette."

"I wouldn't have listened to you. Nanette and I were wrong for each other," Maurice rejoined. "Young widows can be lonely as well as beautiful."

"Well, you made a mistake," she said lightly. "I'm not interested in finding a man."

They ate the rest of the meal in a new silence. Maurice brought out a lamb cutlet, and they shared a pear from the garden for dessert. After Pandora helped with the dishes, she went upstairs. Esme was asleep in her crib; Sally dozed on the bed beside her.

She entered her room and sat at the dressing table. The moon was bright, and she could hear frogs in the garden. Suzanne said she should decide what she wanted and go out and get it. And Jean Patou said that as long as she believed in herself, she couldn't fail.

She took out her notebook and made a list of what she wanted.

She wanted not to rely on anyone—not Milton or Adele or even her father—for money or her well-being.

She wanted something of her own, something that she was passionate about.

And she wanted to make Esme proud of her.

Pandora stopped writing and gazed out the window. She had told Maurice that she wasn't interested in men. But Harley was dead, and nothing would bring him back. She couldn't help but think about the night she spent with Archie.

She picked up the pen and added one more line.

She wanted to experience the pleasures of being a woman.

~

The living room was empty when she went back downstairs. Maurice was still sitting at the kitchen table with a book and a glass of cognac.

"I thought you went to bed." He looked up from his book.

His eyes were a golden shade of hazel. And his hair looked soft under the kitchen's light.

"I did. I wanted to do something first." She walked over to him.

She reached down and kissed him. It was a tentative kiss, her lips gently touching his mouth. He pulled her close, and the kiss grew deeper. She leaned into him, crushing her breasts against his chest.

"Pandora, I want you so much," he breathed, kissing her neck. He ran his hands over her blouse and buried his face in her hair.

She pulled away and wiped her mouth on her palm. She wasn't ready to make love to another man. A kiss was all she wanted for now.

A bright, tingling feeling started at her toes and traveled through her body. "Not tonight; I hope you understand. Good night, Maurice. Thank you for the soup."

Chapter Eighteen

June 1929, Beaulieu-sur-Mer, France

Suzanne had told Pandora that June in Beaulieu-sur-Mer was the love-liest month of the year, and she was right.

On a day in late June, Pandora sat at a table in front of the Hôtel Métropole with Sally and Esme. Guests came in and out of the glass doors, holding small dogs and carrying boxes of resort wear bought at the boutiques. For lunch she ordered pâté followed by *moules marinières* (steamed mussels with white wine) and *plateau de fromage* (a plate of French cheeses)—Brie and Camembert—for dessert.

Pandora sipped her lemonade, and for the first time since Harley died, she felt happy. The last two months had passed in a blur. Mornings, she sat by the swimming pool and worked on her sportswear sketches followed by lunch with Sally and Esme. In the afternoons, she watched Suzanne play tennis or took long walks in the hills. The evenings were usually filled with lively dinners at Suzanne's dining room table.

And there was Maurice. Their relationship hadn't progressed past passionate sessions on afternoon picnics and long nights of kissing and embracing. Every time Pandora decided she wanted more, for Maurice's mouth to travel down her thighs instead of stopping at her breasts, for his hands to undress her instead of opening just a few buttons on her blouse, something stopped her.

It wasn't that she was waiting for a commitment or even for Maurice to tell her that he loved her. For the first time in her life, she was enjoying the anticipation of sex. There was no rush; it would happen soon.

One of her favorite days on the Riviera was the day Maurice surprised her with an excursion to Baroness Eugenie Rothschild's Villa Ephrussi in Cap Ferrat. They started by choosing picnic items at the outdoor market in place Marinoni. They bought tomatoes and Italian olive oil and the traditional socca, pancakes made with chickpeas. Maurice was never more animated than when he introduced her to new foods. He reminded Pandora of Archie when he had told her his dreams of becoming a professor at Princeton.

Archie hadn't written again. She hoped he was happy; she missed him. The more time that passed, the more she wondered if she should tell Archie that Esme was his daughter. Being with Maurice and enjoying the attentions of a man had shaken something loose in her. It was time to put the memories of her childhood aside and not base her actions on her mother. Just because Laura had abandoned Pandora didn't mean that Archie would do the same to Esme. Laura hadn't wanted the lifestyle that Willie could afford, and she was willing to leave Pandora because of it. But Archie's situation was completely different. And Archie could teach Esme so much about life.

Every night, she composed a letter to Archie and then tore it up. It wasn't the kind of thing that one could reveal in a letter; she had to tell Archie in person.

After Maurice completed their purchases, they drove Suzanne's little car to Cap Ferrat. Maurice was a terrible driver. Pandora clutched the dashboard and prayed they wouldn't run into a farmer's truck on the narrow road or slam into a flock of sheep and be sent off the cliff.

When they arrived, Pandora saw that the harrowing drive had been worth it. Villa Ephrussi resembled a Venetian palazzo, with a view more glorious than any of the estates on the Hudson. The hills behind the villa were dotted with fruit trees and covered with pine forests so tall they touched the sky. From the front, the Mediterranean looked a deeper blue than any precious jewel, filled with sailboats and fishing boats and jaunty yachts.

"What are we doing here?" Pandora asked when the car pulled inside the gate.

"We're having a picnic." Maurice opened Pandora's door.

"But it's private property," Pandora said uncomfortably.

She noticed a group of gardeners carrying buckets. They were dressed strangely in striped shirts, with berets and red pom-poms.

"Baroness Rothschild is a friend of Suzanne's." Maurice gathered the picnic basket. "The baroness isn't home today, but she offered the use of her grounds," he said with a mischievous smile. "There are four separate gardens. I'm sure we can find a pleasant spot for our picnic."

Baroness Rothschild was part of the Rothschild banking family, the wealthiest family in France. She had married at the age of nineteen, but her husband was a drunk and a gambler. Eventually she divorced him, and instead of going into hiding and living quietly, she bought a seventeen-acre plot on the most glorious spot in Cap Ferrat.

They set up their picnic under the horseshoe-shaped staircase in the Florentine garden. At the top of the staircase a marble angel overlooked the philodendrons and water hyacinths.

"What are you thinking about?" Maurice asked when he had opened a bottle of wine and laid out the bread and tomatoes and cheese.

"That we haven't known each other long, but you seem to know me so well," Pandora mused, sipping her wine. Maurice had been right; a good wine was one of life's pleasures. There was no reason to always wait until evening to drink it. "I can't think of any place I'd rather be."

"You remind me of Baroness Rothschild," Maurice reflected. "You could have hidden yourself away after your husband died. Instead, you found your way to the most beautiful place in the world. Now you're designing sportswear; someday you'll be very successful."

Pandora's eyes welled up with tears. Sometimes she worried that Maurice only saw her as another rich American tourist, an interesting distraction. But he really understood her.

She recalled when she met Lillian at the Winthrops' Fourth of July party. Lillian boasted about traveling to France and Italy. Pandora had been embarrassed; she'd never been farther than New York. Here she was now, sitting in a garden whose design inspired the estates of the Astors and Vanderbilts.

Perhaps when Esme married, Esme would continue living at Summerhill, and Pandora would build her own villa. It wouldn't be the size or scope of the baroness's villa, but it would have the same beauty and attention to detail.

Maurice took the glass out of her hand. He wrapped his arms around her and drew her close.

"For now, let's not talk about Baroness Rothschild and concentrate on more important things," he said, kissing her. "There is nothing more valuable than exploring the physical senses."

～

The next day, Pandora sat across from Sally and Esme at the Hôtel Métropole, thinking about the picnic. It was only the presence of the gardeners that had stopped their kisses from progressing further. She was confident that she and Maurice would make love soon.

"I've never seen a child love pâté," Sally said, interrupting her thoughts. She watched Esme lick pâté from her chin. "Esme is becoming so French. When we go back to America, she'll want crepes for lunch instead of peanut butter sandwiches."

Pandora knew what Sally was getting at. In the last few weeks, Sally had begun making small comments about when they would go home. She had a beau named Tommy waiting for her. Pandora knew they had to return to Hyde Park sometime. She missed Summerhill, but she worried that the inspiration for her sportswear designs might disappear if she returned to New York. The French Riviera had provided a safe cocoon for the past four months, and she wasn't ready to leave.

"I'll stop by the shipping office this afternoon. We could book a passage for August or September. We'll be home to see the leaves change color," Pandora suggested.

That would give her time to complete her sketches. When they arrived home, she'd start looking for spaces for her boutique. Everyone would have forgotten the scandal. It was time to move forward.

Sally was about to answer when a couple approached their table.

"Pandora!" the woman exclaimed, taking off her hat. "Mabel mentioned you were in Beaulieu-sur-Mer. How nice to run into you."

It was Lillian and Owen. Lillian's light brown hair was cut short to her chin, and Pandora could see that her stomach was rounded underneath her chiffon dress.

"Do you mind if we join you?" Lillian asked. "I forgot how hot it gets on the Riviera." She patted her stomach. "Especially in my condition. I'm six months along."

"Of course." Pandora motioned to the chairs. "This is my nanny, Sally."

Lillian nodded dismissively at Sally. "I had my hair cut in Paris," she chirped. "Owen thinks I look incredibly French."

"I haven't been to Paris," Pandora commented. "We've only seen the Riviera."

"It is pretty here," Lillian agreed, turning her gaze to the harbor. "We almost didn't come to Europe this summer. Owen's been working so hard, I insisted." She looked at Pandora archly. "I can't imagine traveling by myself with only the nanny and the children. It would be half as much fun; one may as well stay at home."

Owen adjusted his panama hat. He shifted uncomfortably in his chair.

Pandora didn't know how to answer. She wasn't going to give Lillian the satisfaction of bringing up Harley.

"I'm so sorry about Harley," Lillian said as if she could read Pandora's mind. "When Owen and I heard the news, neither of us could believe it. We sent a huge flower arrangement to Blythdale. You must be devastated. You were clever to get away. It was still in the newspapers when we left."

Pandora gripped the edge of the table. She picked up a knife and cut a slice of Camembert. She didn't want to talk about the scandal or about how she still missed Harley. It was better to change the subject. She remembered how much Lillian admired Suzanne.

"Harley and I had planned on coming to the French Riviera anyway," Pandora replied. "I didn't want to disappoint Suzanne."

"I heard that Suzanne is favored to win Wimbledon next month." Lillian ran her fingers over her water glass. "Owen and I would love to meet her. We're staying at Grand-Hôtel du Cap-Ferrat. You and Suzanne should come for dinner tonight."

Pandora would love to dine at the hotel, which was supposed to be beautiful, but she couldn't give Lillian the pleasure of being able to say she had dinner with la Divine.

"Suzanne doesn't dine at restaurants, too many people clamor for her autograph," she answered. "And I have plans tonight. Perhaps another time."

Lillian and Owen ordered crepes and glasses of Beaujolais. Pandora tried to draw Owen and Sally into the conversation. But Owen just sipped his wine and let Lillian talk.

"Owen and I finally bought an estate," Lillian said when the waiter set down the check. "It's called Periwinkle. I hired Elsie de Wolfe to furnish it." She glanced at Pandora innocently. "You'll have to come for afternoon tea when you're back in Hyde Park. It's quite near Summerhill."

"I'd love to, but I don't know when we're going home," she said. "I'm happy here, and Suzanne loves having us. It will be hard to leave."

Seeing Lillian was disconcerting. Pandora wasn't ready to go home. What if people were still talking about Harley? How could she possibly have afternoon tea at Lillian's new house, knowing that she was only invited so the women could gossip about her after she left.

When they took leave of Lillian and Owen, Pandora let Sally take Esme back to the villa while she ran some errands. It was almost dinnertime when Pandora arrived back at Suzanne's villa. She set her hat on the table and walked upstairs to Sally's room. Esme cooed happily in her crib, turning the pages of a picture book.

"We just finished Esme's bath," Sally said, folding the bath towel over a chair. "We stopped at the beach on the way home. You wouldn't guess that a little while ago Esme's hair was full of sand, and she was shouting at a little boy for ruining her sandcastle."

"It sounds like he deserved it." Pandora laughed, sitting on the bed. "I've been to see Jean Patou. He offered to let me work at his atelier in Paris. I wouldn't be paid much, but I'll learn everything about running a fashion house."

Meeting with Jean Patou and showing him her sportswear designs had helped Pandora decide that she didn't want to open a boutique in either Hyde Park or New York. Harley's scandal would trail after her like a dog on its leash. Instead, she wanted to start a company that designed and manufactured sportswear. If she was successful, her collection would be sold in many stores. No one had attempted to create sportswear for spectators before, and she could offer women something brand new.

The realization of her new goal surprised her; she had wanted to create dresses since she was fifteen. For a while, she had put Jean Patou's offer to teach her about running a fashion house out of her mind. But the more she thought about designing sportswear, the more it all felt right. The great designers didn't limit themselves. Coco Chanel designed costumes for the Ballets Russes, and she had a line of perfumes. Jean Patou had a successful bathing suit line, and Elsa Schiaparelli had recently launched a collection of knitwear.

She would learn so much working at the atelier in Paris.

Pandora took an envelope from her purse. "I can tell you're homesick, and I don't expect you to stay. I bought your ticket for an August passage."

Sally arranged the blankets in Esme's crib.

"I miss my family. But I can't let some French nanny teach Esme her alphabet, and it will do Tommy good to miss me. I'll stay as long as you need me."

Pandora hugged Sally. "I'm glad. Esme and I would be lost without you."

Sally hugged her back, and a smile lit up her features. "I'll return the ticket in the morning. I have an intuition about this kind of thing. One day, you're going to be a famous sportswear designer. Esme will be so proud of you."

~

Maurice wasn't at dinner. Pandora found him afterward, in the room that served as a library and writing room. Novels were crammed next to a row of encyclopedias on the bookshelf, and there was a walnut desk with an old-fashioned inkwell.

Maurice glanced up from the desk. His eyes were hooded, and his brow creased in a frown. Pandora rarely saw Maurice in a dark mood. He was always humming while mixing a salad in the kitchen or singing as he rode off on his bicycle.

"I've been rereading Stendhal," he said, taking a book from the small pile on the desk. "*The Red and the Black* is one of the finest examples of French literature. It's about one man's bravery during the Napoleonic wars."

"I haven't read him," Pandora commented, sitting in a chair opposite him. "There never seems time to read. The days fly by."

"I saw you going into the shipping office this afternoon." He returned the book to the pile. "I thought these last two months were leading to something. Apparently, I was wrong."

Pandora's heart thudded in her chest. She and Maurice had never discussed a future. Still, she couldn't deny that she was attracted to him. He was charming and sophisticated; she found those hazel eyes and the dimple on his cheek irresistible.

"I'm not going to America," Pandora announced. "Jean Patou offered to let me train at his atelier in Paris. Sally, Esme, and I leave for Paris next month."

"Paris can be humid in the summer, and the American tourists are unbearable," Maurice said thoughtfully. "They think the only two places to see are the Eiffel Tower and the Louvre. Other sections of Paris during the summer are charming. The cafés in Montmartre are full of artists, and the outdoor markets sell peaches and apricots. I'll visit; we'll have picnics in the countryside."

Something moved inside Pandora. She didn't know if it was the way Maurice looked at her, the frown replaced by an eager smile, or how he seemed relieved that she wasn't going to America. She stood up and walked around the desk.

"We still have a month," she reminded him. "I don't want to wait any longer."

Maurice's voice was thick. "What are you saying?"

Pandora didn't answer. Instead, she leaned down and kissed him. His mouth tasted of cigarettes and brandy. She kissed him harder, and he stood up and wrapped his arms around her.

"Pandora, I want you so much." He groaned when she pulled away to catch her breath.

"I want you too." She nodded. "Now, tonight."

Maurice kissed her again, pinning her against the desk. Her body leaned into his, her heart beating so fast, she thought it might burst.

"Not here, not like this," he whispered into her hair. He took her hand, and together they climbed the staircase. Maurice's guest room was in the back, facing the garden. He pushed open the door and drew her inside. She started fumbling with her blouse, but he stopped her.

"We must take it slowly," he instructed.

He pulled out a chair and motioned for her to sit down. His fingers reached under her skirt and traveled down her thighs. A low, guttural sound escaped her mouth, and she bit her lip, embarrassed. Maurice stopped long enough to kiss her. Then his hands resumed their journey, rolling down her stockings and leaving them pooled at her ankles. She tried to drag him up so he would kiss her again. Instead, he buried his head between her thighs. Suddenly, hot waves came over her, and she gripped the sides of the chair. It was only when the shuddering subsided, and she again became aware of her surroundings, that she dared to meet Maurice's eyes.

"Come." He took her hand. "Now we move to the bed."

He undressed her first, unbuttoning her blouse and stopping to caress her breasts. Her nipples were hard against his fingers, and she found herself thrusting them forward, desperate for him to take them in his mouth. He kissed each breast separately and then unhooked her skirt.

She sat on the bed, watching him take off his shirt. His chest was a deep, dark tan, the color of almonds. Dark hair grew over his stomach. His thighs, when he took off his pants, reminded her of a drawing she once saw of Michelangelo's *David*.

"Lie down," he said, pushing away the pillows. "Stay perfectly still."

Pandora did as he instructed. She waited for him to climb on top of her the way Harley had, but instead he lay beside her. With one hand, he stroked her thighs, with the other, he made small circles around her breasts. Every time the pleasure grew too great and she squirmed away, he whispered in her ear and begged her not to move.

The waves started again, and her body arched toward his. This time, he rolled on top of her. Her legs parted, and then he was inside her, and everything she had experienced before was forgotten. Her body rose with Maurice's. Together they climbed and dipped, until they were both shaking and covered with sweat, and collapsed on the bed.

Pandora returned to her room at midnight. She sat at her dressing table, watching the silver light of the moon reflecting on the swimming pool. She had never felt like this before. Bright and alive and aware of all her senses.

Chapter Nineteen

February 1930, Hyde Park, New York

Pandora stood on the deck of the *Île de France* and watched the New York skyline come into view. It was the last day on the ship from Le Havre. In a little while, they would dock in New York Harbor.

Esme would turn two in a week; it had been a year since they left New York. Pandora felt guilty that she hadn't returned home sooner.

And she felt even guiltier about Archie. Archie was still in London. Pandora had finally written to him and suggested he visit her in Paris. But he never replied. She still wrestled with whether she should have told Archie that he had a daughter before he left for England.

It had all been so new and fragile. Harley was still alive, and she was determined to make her marriage work. Archie was newly engaged to Lucy. All she would have done was cause heartache and pain for everyone. Things were different now, though. Esme was a precocious toddler, and one day she'd grow up to be a beautiful young woman. Esme would gain so much from a relationship with Archie, and Archie would adore her. It would be up to Archie whether he told Lucy, but at least he would have a choice.

Pandora had become preoccupied with telling him the truth when she was living in Paris. She even considered showing up at his address in London, but she feared he would be furious and send her away. She couldn't bear the thought of Archie being angry with her.

Once, she imagined she saw Archie in Paris. She was having coffee with Maurice and noticed someone who looked like Archie through the café window. But it couldn't have been Archie. It was just another man with Archie's strong physique and floppy blond hair.

Every day she told herself she'd write to him again and tell him she urgently needed to talk to him. It couldn't wait until they both returned to America. But he hadn't responded to her first letter, and she lost her nerve.

She didn't know what to expect at home. She hadn't taken much notice of the ups and downs of the stock market last autumn. The letters from Adele, who had returned to Hyde Park from San Francisco, and from her father and Virginia were upbeat and optimistic.

It was only the day after the stock market crashed, when an American client burst into tears in Jean Patou's atelier because she had received a telegram saying her husband had lost everything and shot himself, that Pandora started reading the American newspapers.

As late as last September, the stock market was still on a dizzying high. It was in mid-October that the banks began to falter. Milton and the other influential bankers in New York tried to stop the panic. But nothing worked. The market plunged, and Black Tuesday ended everything.

After that, Pandora read everything she could about the market. Production slowed in factories, and four million Americans were out of work. Bread lines and soup kitchens formed in the major cities. Banks foreclosed on houses, leaving people homeless everywhere, and farmers couldn't afford to harvest their crops.

Pandora tried to find out how bad things were for the Van Luyens, and for Milton and Adele, but the letters she received were vague. Virginia's last letter only said that Virginia's father had a small heart attack and refused to take the castor oil prescribed by his doctor. Adele mentioned she was glad to be back in Hyde Park because, without client dinners to attend, Milton often forgot to eat and was becoming terribly thin.

Pandora guessed that even in their social circles, things were worse than Virginia and Adele let on. Before October, Jean Patou's atelier had been filled with American mothers and daughters ordering steamer trunks full of dresses. Pandora couldn't count the number of times a woman sporting a chic new haircut and a large diamond ring would confide that she was glad her husband wouldn't see the charges until she arrived home. In the months before she left, the saleswomen scratched a minimum of orders, and the atelier stayed in business by selling Jean's line of perfumes. Women who couldn't afford silk evening gowns could still feel beautiful by rubbing Amour Amour on their wrists.

Pandora pulled her coat tighter against the cold. The navy coat with gold buttons had been a parting gift from Jean, along with two dresses from his latest collection. Pandora would miss Jean so much. She would miss everything about Paris. She hadn't even minded the dreary weather in December and January. She found something soothing about the rain when she was warm and busy in the atelier, and there was always the promise of spring. Spring in Paris meant pink cherry blossoms on the Champs-Élysées and daffodils in Palais Royal Gardens. It meant long walks along the Seine and leisurely meals at neighborhood cafés.

When Pandora and Sally and Esme first arrived in Paris, Pandora used her monthly allowance from Milton to rent an apartment near the Luxembourg Garden. She could walk to work, and on weekends, she took Esme to ride the carousel or see a puppet show.

Esme was now a self-assured two-year-old who spoke French and English and never stopped moving. Pandora bought a little dog to tire Esme out. The toy poodle, Picasso, had become a much-loved addition to the household and traveled with them to New York.

Pandora had learned so much working in the atelier. She learned about yarn and fabrics and cut. Jean taught her how to haggle with vendors, how having Debussy play on the phonograph encouraged customers to order more expensive dresses. During her free time, Pandora worked on her designs. She had a suitcase full of sportswear to show dress shops in Hyde Park: sleeveless blouses with Peter Pan collars and matching pleated skirts worn just below the knees, dresses made out of jersey, knit cardigans for cool summer nights.

She would miss Maurice. Maurice had visited Paris at least once a month. He brought steaks and bottles of wine. They enjoyed romantic dinners and then retired to her bedroom. Pandora almost didn't recognize herself in bed with Maurice. She often led their lovemaking. Afterward when they were both spent and exhausted, Maurice would ask what she was smiling about. Pandora would kiss him and reply that she was glad Esme's bedroom was on the other side of the apartment.

But she wasn't sad to leave Maurice. She couldn't imagine living in Paris forever, and Maurice had made it clear he would never move to America. It was better to part now, while they still had warm feelings for each other, than for the relationship to grow morose and bitter.

"Are you sure you don't mind if I stop in New York and see my family?" Sally asked Pandora after the ship had docked and they were waiting with their luggage.

"Of course not! You haven't seen them in a year," Pandora said with a smile. "Plus, you have to show off your French cooking skills. Your mother and sisters will love your eggs in cocotte."

"It will be hard to make baked eggs with whipping cream if we can't afford the ingredients," Sally answered darkly. After the stock market crash, Sally's mother had been laid off from her factory job. Sally doubled the amount of money she sent every month, but it didn't stretch far with four younger siblings at home.

Pandora squeezed Sally's hand. "Things will improve. It can't stay this way forever."

At that moment, a redheaded young man approached them. He picked Sally up and twirled her around.

"I'm Tommy Sharpe," he said, introducing himself to Pandora. "Sally probably told you all about me."

Pandora giggled, recalling the way Sally sniffed whenever she said Tommy's name. There was obviously something serious between them. Sally's cheeks turned pink, and her eyes sparkled.

"I promise I'll be on the train to Hyde Park tomorrow," Sally said when Tommy was out of earshot. She looked at Pandora worriedly. "Will you be all right?"

"You mean how will I handle the women in Hyde Park now that I'm a widow with a two-year-old daughter?" Pandora asked, reaching for Esme's hand. Esme wore her new pink traveling coat and held the matching pink umbrella Pandora had bought as an early birthday present. "Don't worry about me, I'll be fine."

"If anyone gives you trouble, tell Esme to poke them with her umbrella." Sally grinned.

Sally and Tommy walked away, and Pandora began looking around for Adele. Suddenly she saw her. Adele's shoulders were thinner, and she had new lines around her mouth, but otherwise she looked the same.

"There you are! I thought I'd never find you in this crowd," Adele exclaimed. She reached down and gave Esme a hug. "Let's get out of here. I refuse to cry in front of so many people, and it's too noisy to talk."

Pandora found a porter to carry their bags. Once they got in the car, Pandora asked Adele how she and Milton were doing.

"Milton had to sell the Rolls-Royce Phantom, and he gave up the chauffeur." Adele sighed, maneuvering the car onto the street. She turned to Pandora, and her expression brightened. "I don't want to talk about any of that at the moment. First, I want to hear about Paris. You have a new hairstyle! And your clothes. You're right out of a fashion book."

They didn't talk about the stock market crash again until they were seated in the morning room at Blythdale. The house felt cold and empty. The fires in the living room and dining room weren't lit, and the drapes were closed in the library.

"I let the staff go except for the cook and the maid," Adele said, setting a tray with coffee and cream on the coffee table.

"I want to hear everything," Pandora said, accepting the cup that Adele handed her.

The smile that Adele seemed to be wearing like a mask faltered.

"Milton has aged more in the last four months than in thirty years," Adele admitted. "It's worse than when Alistair and Frank were killed during the war. Milton blames himself for his customers' losses." She stirred cream into her coffee. "Nothing I can say or do makes him see it differently."

"Milton must have money." Pandora frowned. "He sends a check every month."

Adele looked at Pandora guiltily. "I send the checks from my personal account. Milton would, but there isn't anything to send. And Harley's money is gone."

Adele told her that Summerhill was gone too. It hadn't been on the market. While Pandora was on the ship, they received an offer they couldn't refuse. Pandora almost couldn't bear the thought. Summerhill had been Esme's home. She couldn't keep accepting Milton and Adele's charity and live at Blythdale. She decided they would live at the cottage with Willie.

Pandora guessed that Willie didn't have any savings. What if she couldn't get her designs into a boutique and she ran out of money? After paying for the Atlantic crossing and Sally's salary, she barely had any left.

She would visit the dress shops in Hyde Park that afternoon.

Pandora gave Adele the presents she bought in Paris. A velvet cape for Adele and a selection of ties for Milton; then they drove to Riverview. Pandora was about to take her suitcases around to the kitchen when Virginia appeared.

"There you are." Virginia beamed. "I was getting impatient; I was going to come to Blythdale and kidnap you."

"I thought you'd be in New York." Pandora hugged her. She had missed Virginia so much. "How did you know I was here?"

"Adele told me. We practically fought each other to pick you up." Virginia grinned. "Adele only won because your luggage wouldn't fit in my car. Your father had to run some errands; Esther is waiting in the kitchen with an upside-down cake for Esme."

Virginia looked modern and sophisticated. Her hair was still cut in a bob, and she wore red lipstick. She was dressed in a pleated skirt and matching jacket and carried a smart handbag.

"You look more like Louise Brooks than when I left," Pandora said admiringly.

"I have to maintain a certain professional style," Virginia replied, crossing her hands in her lap. "I've just come from lunch with the owner of the Strand bookstore. He ordered fifty copies of the biography of Harriet Jacobs."

"I'm so proud of you," Pandora gushed. "I worried that after the crash, Riverview Press might not survive."

"Wolfgang and I took a pay cut, and we work long hours." Virginia shrugged. "Millie is a godsend. She's taken on the accounting. If any vendor tries to cheat us, we never work with him again."

Pandora beamed with pleasure. She couldn't wait to take Millie to lunch and hear all about it.

"What about Wolfgang? You never talk about other men, but you never talk about Wolfgang romantically."

"Wolfgang is like my second skin," Virginia said carefully. "But we're not getting married. A husband might try to control me; Wolfgang and I work better side by side."

Pandora nodded but thought to herself that she disagreed. She still believed in marriage. The point of love was to blend two lives and create a richer whole. She wondered whether she would ever trust a man enough to fall in love again.

Virginia told Pandora about Lillian and Owen. Lillian's father lost everything and jumped from his office window. Lillian and Owen moved back to Rosecliff with the children, and Vivian was living upstate. Pandora would send her a card; Vivian had always been so kind to her.

"Tell me about Archie," Pandora said.

"Lucy's father is better, and Lucy is back in Hyde Park. The wedding is going to be this summer. Lucy didn't want to wait until Christmas, and Louise Vanderbilt decided that having the wedding at Biltmore with its 250 rooms is too ostentatious." Virginia rolled her eyes. "It will be at their estate in Hyde Park instead."

"And Archie?" Pandora asked.

"Archie will come home from London in a couple of months. He's going to run my father's company."

"But your father only had a small heart attack." Pandora frowned.

"The first one was small, then he had another," Virginia admitted. "He only goes into New York once a week, and his doctor doesn't even approve of that."

"I'm sorry, I had no idea."

Virginia changed the subject to talk about all the books she planned to publish that season, but Pandora couldn't stop thinking about Archie. She had to tell him the truth about Esme. The secret had been weighing on her conscience for too long.

After they finished talking, Pandora borrowed Virginia's car and drove into Hyde Park. She had quickly calculated how long her savings would last. Even if she was frugal, it wouldn't last more than a few months. She refused to borrow money from Adele or Virginia. The sooner she got her designs into a dress shop in Hyde Park, the sooner she'd be able to support herself and Esme.

The first dress shop she visited on Main Street was closed. The mannequins were gone from the windows and a "For Rent" sign flapped on the door. She walked farther along the street to a shop with gold awnings. "Annalise's Fine Dresses" was written in cursive, and there was a red ball gown with a satin sash in the window.

"Good afternoon." Pandora addressed the salesgirl. "I'd like to speak to Annalise."

An older woman appeared from the back room. She wore a blue dress with a silk scarf. Her face was finely lined, and she wore her dark hair in a bun.

"I'm Annalise. May I help you?"

Pandora told her about training under Jean Patou in Paris. She described her sportswear and showed her a few pieces.

"This is wonderful." Annalise admired a blue-and-yellow-patterned knit dress. Jean had encouraged her to use fabrics with bold geometric shapes, and the dress was one of Pandora's favorites. "But I'm afraid I can't stock it."

"You can't?" Pandora questioned.

"The price point would be too high; customers couldn't afford it."

"All your dresses are high priced." Pandora frowned.

"They were." Annalise nodded. She pointed to a rack in the back. "Now the only ones that sell are discounted."

"Women must still buy clothes," Pandora said desperately. There weren't any other dress shops in Hyde Park; the closest department store was in Kingston. "What about the gown in the window. That must cost a fortune."

"Women can still dream about buying ball gowns," Annalise reflected. "I'm lucky to sell gloves and stockings. No one gives parties these days. If they do, women wear whatever is in their closets." Her brow furrowed. "The worst part is when clients try to sell me gowns they bought years ago."

Pandora left the shop disappointed. At least she wasn't trying to open her own boutique.

It was late and she was hungry.

She had been so sure that a local dress shop would stock her sportswear. She had to find someone who would take them.

Her and Esme's future depended on it.

Chapter Twenty

Pandora flipped through a magazine and tried not to appear anxious as she sat in the reception room at Lord & Taylor waiting to meet with Dorothy Shaver, the head buyer. Dorothy Shaver was one of the most powerful women in the fashion industry, and Pandora had been lucky to get an appointment with her.

Pandora had spent the last month redoing her designs. If wealthy women weren't buying dresses, she had to focus on working women instead. Knit dresses they could wear for casual evenings at home after a long day at the office or the factory. Practical sweaters and cardigans to wear on the weekends, on a date, or with their families.

"Miss Shaver will see you now," the secretary announced. She glanced at Pandora haughtily. "She's very busy; you have thirty minutes."

Dorothy Shaver's office was on the seventh floor overlooking Fifth Avenue. She sat at a maple desk next to a large potted plant. Modern art covered the walls, and a small dog was curled up in the corner.

"Good morning, Miss Carmichael." Dorothy shook Pandora's hand. Pandora had decided to use her maiden name in business. It felt more familiar, and she wouldn't be associated with Harley.

Dorothy was in her midthirties, with dark hair and close-set dark eyes. She wore a severe-looking navy dress and bright red lipstick. A triple strand of pearls hung around her neck, and she wore high-heeled leather pumps.

"Please call me Pandora."

"I don't often meet with first-time designers," Dorothy began. "You came highly recommended by Adele Enright. Adele is a loyal customer, and she has the best taste."

"Thank you so much for taking the time to meet with me." Pandora set her design book on the desk. She hoped her voice didn't betray her nervousness. "At first, I planned to design clothes for women to wear to sporting events, then I realized women should be comfortable all the time. Fabrics these days make it so easy to move. The best part about my designs is that the pieces mix and match. A woman can wear the same lightweight jacket with a few different skirts and have a new look each time."

Dorothy put on a pair of reading glasses. She motioned for Pandora to sit down.

"These are quite good." She flipped through the sketches. "I love the bold colors and shapes. A few other female designers are also creating sportswear: Clare Potter and Lilly Daché. I'm putting together a promotion called the American Look. Some of your pieces would be perfect for it."

Pandora almost couldn't believe her ears. She gaped at Dorothy.

"So you'll take them?" she said hesitantly.

"I'll make a list of what I want," Dorothy answered. "I'll need them soon and in large quantities."

"What kind of quantities?" Pandora asked.

Dorothy studied Pandora over her glasses. "When Lord & Taylor puts money into marketing and advertising, it doesn't expect to sell just a few sweaters and skirts." She paused. "Will that be a problem?"

Where would Pandora find the money to buy enough fabric?

"I'm not sure," Pandora said honestly.

Dorothy removed her glasses.

"Why don't you call me later when you sort it out." She picked up her phone. "My secretary will see you out."

~

Pandora stood on the sidewalk and wondered what to do. She could go to Enright's Bank and ask for a business loan. But Adele would hear about it and insist on lending Pandora the money herself. Pandora had taken enough from Milton and Adele; she had to do this without their financial help.

She marched down Fifth Avenue and entered J.P. Morgan & Co. The bank was almost empty, and it was easier to get an appointment with a loan officer than she had expected. A little man with owl-shaped glasses sat across from her, listening to Pandora's pitch. When she finished, he leaned back in his chair and gazed at her admiringly.

"This is splendid," he said enthusiastically.

"Then you'll loan me the money?" Pandora asked, relief flooding through her. She couldn't wait to tell Virginia.

"I'm afraid not." He closed Pandora's design book.

"You said it was a splendid plan." Pandora frowned.

"It is, but you'll need to borrow a large amount." He folded his arms. "What happens if after a few months you give up the business to stay home and raise children?"

"That's not going to happen." Pandora felt the heat rising inside her. "I'm a widow, and I already have a daughter and nanny."

The man stood up. He rubbed his glasses and held out his hand.

"I'm afraid J.P. Morgan and Company doesn't lend to women," he said amicably. "If you get married again, come see me. We'd be happy to lend the money to your husband."

Pandora tried Central Savings Bank and Public National Bank of New York but was told the same thing. No one would lend money to a woman. She was tired and frustrated. Suddenly she had an idea. She put her arm out and hailed a taxi.

"Levi Dresses on Broadway, please," she said to the driver.

Levi Dresses looked almost the same as it had when she visited a few years before, but even more dresses were crammed on the silver racks. Glass cases overflowed with purses, and the store now boasted a small shoe department.

Pandora approached a salesgirl wearing a black dress.

"I'm looking for the owner, Levi Rosen."

The salesgirl disappeared into the back and returned with Levi. He looked the same as Pandora remembered. His thinning hair was pushed across his forehead, and he wore a pin-striped suit with a vest.

"Do you remember me? I'm Pandora Carmichael." Pandora held out her hand. "You let my friend Millie Grimes buy a dress on credit a few years ago."

"Of course." He shook her hand. "Mrs. Grimes still buys her dresses here. She's a good customer."

Pandora felt happy that Millie was earning enough to buy more than one dress.

"Is there somewhere we could talk?" Pandora inquired.

He led her to a small office with a desk and two chairs. A window overlooked the factory floor. Rolls of fabric leaned against the wall in the corner, and a water pitcher sat on a table.

"I'm afraid I can't offer you more than water," he said pleasantly, pouring two glasses and handing her one. "I don't often have glamorous young women as visitors."

Pandora explained that the buyer at Lord & Taylor wanted to purchase her sportswear, but none of the banks would lend her money for the fabric.

"You knit your own fabric at Levi Dresses." Pandora pointed through the window. "I hoped you could advance me fabric on credit. I'd pay you back soon."

Levi's brow knotted together. He rubbed his chin.

"I'd like to help, but it's too risky," he apologized. "Lord & Taylor could pull their order, or you might not be able to deliver."

Pandora took a deep breath. She had to get the fabric. She had tried twice before to launch her career and failed. This was her only chance, and nothing was going to stop her.

She still wore her diamond engagement ring. She pulled it off and held it out to Levi.

"Do you remember I gave you my gold earrings as collateral for Millie's dress? This time, you can have my engagement ring. I have a whole drawer of jewelry at home. Diamond earrings and pendants and bracelets."

Pandora had planned on giving her jewelry to Esme; it would be a link between Esme and Harley. But this way she would give Esme something better. She'd build a successful business and show Esme that sometimes one needed to sacrifice to achieve one's goals.

"No one is buying jewelry; I don't know what I'd do with it." Levi shrugged.

"Keep it for a while; I'm certain I can pay you back," Pandora urged. "If for some reason I can't, it won't be difficult to find a buyer."

She'd read in the newspapers about men who were making money despite the downturn. There would always be someone who would buy precious jewelry at a good price.

"What will your husband say?"

"I'm a widow. It's up to me to provide for our daughter." She looked evenly at Levi. "I'm all she has. I can't let her down."

Levi held out his hand. "Miss Carmichael, you have a deal."

She shook his hand gratefully. Her eyes were as bright as the diamond on her engagement ring.

"You won't be sorry."

Pandora drove straight to Riverview. She couldn't wait to call Dorothy Shaver.

~

As soon as she arrived home, she ran into the cottage and dialed the number on the card.

"Dorothy Shaver, please," she said to the secretary. "This is Pandora Carmichael."

"Miss Carmichael." Dorothy Shaver's clipped tone came over the line. "How can I help you?"

"I wanted to confirm your order today." Pandora clutched the receiver. "Would a three-week turnaround suit you?"

Pandora heard Dorothy riffling through some pages.

"That would be the second week of April," Dorothy said, sounding impressed. "Yes, that would suit me perfectly." She paused. "Oh, one more thing. Does your company have a name?"

Pandora hadn't considered a name; she hadn't thought of her sportswear designs as a real company until that moment.

"It's Esme Sportswear, after my daughter."

"What a lovely name." Dorothy's voice softened for the first time. "I'm sure your daughter will be proud of you."

Chapter Twenty-One

Pandora delivered her first order to Lord & Taylor in April; it was an immediate success. Seeing her clothes in the department store window with "America's New Look" scrawled in red, white, and blue letters above them was better than anything she'd experienced besides Esme's birth.

Virginia insisted they celebrate with caviar and champagne at the Roof Ballroom of the St. Regis. Pandora didn't like caviar, and after working so hard she was exhausted, and the champagne gave her a headache. But she still felt giddy, gazing down at the bustling New York streets and knowing she was part of it.

Lord & Taylor had ordered enough pieces for one year, and one whole window at Macy's new store on Seventh Avenue was devoted to Pandora's knit dresses. Pandora received her first order from Saks and was in meetings with Woolworth's. With Suzanne's approval, Pandora added a headband called the Lenglen Bandeau to her summer collection. It was so popular that stores couldn't keep them in stock. Esme Sportswear continued to steadily grow and prosper.

Pandora paid Levi Rosen back what she owed him; she didn't need him to supply her fabric on credit anymore. Esme Sportswear had its own bank account at Public National Bank of New York, and Pandora was toying with the idea of creating a board of directors.

Next year, Pandora wanted to start a training program for young women interested in fashion design but who couldn't afford to attend college. There would be lectures by the new wave of female designers like Claire McCardell. Pandora would hire her own assistants from the program's graduates.

Today, Archie would finally arrive home. His trip had been delayed twice. So many wealthy Americans who had ventured abroad before the stock market crash wanted to return home that there weren't enough ships to carry them all. Pandora decided to meet his boat in New York.

The past few months, watching Esme scamper on the lawn with Picasso, her cornflower-blue eyes alight with pleasure, her blond curls tumbling to her shoulders, made Pandora feel even guiltier than she had before. She didn't have a moment's peace.

Even if she kept her secret from everyone else forever, she had to tell Archie. Esme needed a father, and Archie deserved to know he had a wonderful daughter. She couldn't wait to see him. She had missed him, their easy banter, their long chats over glasses of lemonade in the kitchen.

After she dropped Esme at Blythdale with Adele, she hurried back to Riverview to get dressed. As she was getting ready to go, a car pulled into the driveway, and Archie appeared in the entry. He had a green scarf knotted around his neck, and he wore driving gloves.

Pandora's mouth dropped open. She had forgotten how just seeing Archie made her happy. He looked more mature than when he'd left for England. He no longer wore his hair flopping over his forehead; instead, he had cut it short. The sloppy vests and baggy trousers he used to wear had been replaced by a pullover sweater and pleated pants. But the boyish smile when he saw her and the twinkle in his blue-gray eyes were the same.

He picked her up and twirled her around.

"What are you doing here?" She gasped when he put her down. "I was going to come to the dock to meet you."

"My ship docked early," he grumbled. "I was one of the few passengers who had no one to greet them. All the women standing on the ship's deck felt sorry for me."

"They probably thought no one was there to pick you up because you broke the hearts of all the girls you left behind," she teased.

"I was very well behaved on the ship," he protested with a grin. "Though there was an Italian countess who tried to coax me into her cabin. I told her I was engaged, and she said Americans are so puritan."

"How is Lucy?" Pandora inquired.

"I haven't seen her yet." Archie shrugged. "Lucy and her aunt spent a lot of time in London before Lucy's father grew ill, but we haven't seen each other in a while."

His eyes traveled over Pandora's navy-and-white dress from Jean Patou's collection.

"I want to hear about you. Look at you, with that chic French haircut and those elegant clothes. You're not the Pandora Carmichael I remember."

"If you had come to Paris, you would have seen my haircut for yourself." She touched her hair.

"You could have come to London," he shot back. "I sent half a dozen letters to the French Riviera, but you never replied. I even offered to visit; I thought you didn't want to see me."

"I never received them," Pandora said in surprise. "Suzanne receives so much fan mail and letters from people wanting something, she often dumps the whole lot in the garbage."

Pandora felt a small jolt of happiness. Archie had written to her.

"I always want to see you," she added.

She had a lump in her throat, and she felt like she had as a child, arriving at Riverview for the first time. Archie had been sitting in the kitchen then, and he'd immediately cut another slice of Esther's chocolate cake for her. They ate companionably at the table while Archie told her about Virginia and his dog, Speckles, and his favorite tree for climbing.

What would have happened if he had come to Paris? What would Archie have thought of Maurice, and would he have noticed how Pandora had changed? None of that mattered now; they were both home.

"I want to hear all about England," she said happily.

He took her arm and led her into the kitchen. He told her about his time in London, and Pandora told him about Paris and the orders from Lord & Taylor and all the other department stores.

"Lord & Taylor is lucky to have you," he said. "I'll drive to New York to see the window display. And I'll buy one of every item they sell."

Pandora smiled. Archie had always been so supportive.

"I can't wait to meet Esme. I brought her something; I'll go get it."

Archie disappeared, and Pandora sipped her cup of tea. It was so easy being with Archie. She had missed him more than she thought. She had to tell him about Esme. There was no reason to put it off. Even if Archie got angry with her, this wasn't about Pandora. It was about being honest with the two people who were so important to her.

"It's a musical bear." Archie set the teddy bear on the counter. "You wind it up and it plays 'Teddy Bears' Picnic.' It's all the rage in London."

"Esme will love it." Pandora smiled at the bear. "There's something I want to talk about, something you should know."

Pandora took a deep breath, and then told Archie how Harley admitted that he was homosexual days before the wedding, how they came to an agreement and decided to still get married. Pandora would have the money and social status to open her boutique, and in return, Harley would have a life protected from scandal.

"Harley and I loved each other, we both wanted to make it work." She fiddled with her teacup. "But it was still a shock. I never meant for our night together to happen. Then I found you in the study, and just once I wanted to make love with someone who desired me." She glanced at Archie to see his reaction. "Then I went to see Dr. Bancroft and found out I was pregnant with Esme."

Archie's brow was furrowed, and his eyes were darker than she'd ever seen them.

"What did Harley believe about Esme?"

"There was a night on the honeymoon when he'd been drinking," she said evasively. "Harley thought we conceived Esme then, but the marriage wasn't actually consummated."

Archie clenched his hands into fists. He paced around the kitchen.

"Why did you choose me? Did you ever think about my feelings?" he barked. "And why didn't you tell me that you were pregnant?"

"I wanted to, but it didn't seem right. You had just gotten engaged to Lucy, and I was determined to stay married."

Archie set his plate in the sink.

"This has been very enlightening." He turned to Pandora. "If you'll excuse me, I have to go."

"Where are you going?"

He wrapped his scarf around his neck.

"You're not the only one with commitments. I'm going to see Lucy, and then I'm going to sleep at the townhouse in New York." Without another word, he strode out the door.

After Archie left, Pandora went out to the cottage. She had never seen Archie so hurt and angry. She had tried to explain why she'd kept Esme's parentage a secret from him. She wondered if there could be another reason that he was so hurt. Could Archie have feelings for her? That was impossible. Ever since Pandora had arrived at Riverview as a child, she and Archie and Virginia had been inseparable. She remembered the leaves she and Archie used to collect. The ones they had written wishes on and kept in an old shoe box. But the wishes had been childish and innocent.

Pandora had done what she had to do. Even if Archie never spoke to her again, she had done the right thing by telling the truth. She told herself she felt better, but she was lying. She had an odd feeling in her chest. As if someone had cut out her heart with a pair of scissors.

Her sketchbook was lying on the coffee table. She flipped it open and picked up a pencil.

The best thing to do was focus on some new designs. Sitting in front of her sketchbook always made her feel better. She hoped it would work this time too.

~

For the next two weeks, Archie avoided her. If he was in the kitchen when she appeared in the morning, he picked up his bowl of oatmeal and piece of toast and went out to the terrace. When she came across him talking to his mother or reading in the study, he gave a curt nod and returned to what he was doing. Esme was usually in the nursery with Sally or playing on the lawn. A few times, Archie joined them.

Most of the week he spent in New York at the real estate firm. He spent the weekends with Lucy. It made sense; the wedding was in a little more than two months. But Pandora felt his absence as strongly as a wound that refused to heal. If only she could talk to him, make him see that she'd had no other choice. But she had already explained her reasoning, and he was furious. There was nothing she could do but wait and hope that eventually he would come around.

She missed him so much. More than when they had both been in Europe. Knowing that he was so close but refused to talk to her made her curl up inside.

She longed to share her successes with him and hear everything about running his father's firm. And she longed to see him with Esme. They had so much to give each other.

On Friday afternoon, Pandora sat in the living room at Blythdale, waiting for Adele to appear with Esme. Adele loved playing with Esme, and Esme adored spending time with Adele.

Adele entered the living room and gave Pandora a long look. "Esme is washing up; she was playing on the lawn. It wouldn't hurt you to take some time off and enjoy the outdoors." Adele studied Pandora's pale cheeks and narrow waist. "You've been working so hard all summer. You're thin as a bird."

"I can't stop working." Pandora shook her head. "As soon as I finish the winter collection, I have to start on designs for next spring. The fashion world is six months ahead."

"You have to make time for your personal life," Adele said. "I've decided to have a party. Not an entire weekend, just a garden party at the end of August. We'll have swimming and games on the lawn."

Pandora recalled the house party where she first met Harley. She remembered walking past the library, hearing Harley and Preston rehearsing. Harley pulling her inside and asking her to join them. The tentative feeling of starting something new and exciting.

She had tried so hard to make Harley happy, to build a good life. And it had ended in tragedy. She couldn't go through that again; it was better not to try.

Esme bounded into the room and threw herself into Pandora's arms. She smelled of hand soap and peanut butter. Seeing her daughter reminded Pandora that marrying Harley had given her Esme, which was the best thing she had ever done.

Maybe it wouldn't hurt to attend Adele's party after all.

"Perhaps you can give me suggestions on whom to invite." Adele interrupted her thoughts. "Owen and Lillian, Virginia and Wolfgang, and Archie. Though it might be awkward with Lucy."

"What do you mean?" Pandora inquired.

Archie and Lucy's wedding was scheduled for the first weekend in September. The ceremony would be held in the Vanderbilts' rose garden followed by a reception in the ballroom.

"The wedding has been called off," Adele said. "Apparently, Lucy rekindled an old romance when she was in St. Louis. The young man, Charles, is arriving in Hyde Park next week."

Pandora wondered why no one had told her. But none of the family was at Riverview. She would have to call Virginia.

"I didn't know," Pandora replied.

"It only happened a few days ago," Adele said. "Louise was upset at first, but Charles is a member of the Busch family, and they're very influential. I'm sure it won't take long for Archie to meet someone new." She smiled at Pandora. "He's always been so good looking, and now he's quite successful."

In the short time he'd been back, Archie was already doing a wonderful job at his father's real estate firm. He had saved it from the brink of bankruptcy and had bright ideas for the future. Pandora didn't know how Archie managed the reversal, but Virginia said Maude and Robert Van Luyen were very pleased.

A strange feeling came over Pandora. A flash of heat, followed by a sudden chill. She wondered if she was coming down with a summer cold.

"Are you all right?" Adele said, frowning. "Your forehead is shiny."

Pandora stood up. She walked uncertainly to the doorway.

"I probably picked up something from Esme. All I need is a bath and some aspirin."

Later that afternoon, sitting in the cottage and watching Esme play with Sally on the lawn, Pandora went over the conversation with Adele. She didn't need aspirin and she didn't feel like running a bath. She knew what was wrong with her. She was in love with Archie.

The realization had come to her as she was driving home from Blythdale. By the time she pulled into Riverview's gates, past the willow tree where Pandora and Archie and Virginia had built a swing, past the pond where they used to feed the ducks, she couldn't get it out of her mind.

In some ways, she had been in love with Archie ever since she could remember. She just hadn't recognized it. When she was young, he made her feel safe. Her mother had left, and everything about Riverview was new and strange. From there, it grew into a mutual admiration. They loved picking apples and doing homework together. Archie had always been there, with his blond good looks and devilish charm. He was as much a part of Pandora's life as her schoolbooks. Then Pandora fell for Owen and then Harley.

Had Archie had feelings for her too? The night they spent together before her wedding, he had been so caring after they made love. It seemed as if he wanted something more than Pandora could give. And he was so angry when she told him that Esme was his daughter. Pandora wondered if it was about more than Esme, that maybe he was hurt because Pandora had chosen Harley over Archie all those years ago.

Had she been in love with Archie even then? Is that why she had wanted to kiss him when she found him in the study two days before the wedding?

She wanted to talk to him, but she couldn't; she feared he would only send her away. Perhaps she'd see him at Adele's party, but that wasn't for a month. Maude Van Luyen would probably have introduced him to someone new by then, a member of the Dinsmore family or one of J. P. Morgan's granddaughters.

When she looked back on the last three years, she realized that one thing love had taught her was to be brave. She had found the courage to travel to Europe with Esme after Harley's death. She had put herself forward with Maurice so she could learn what it felt like to desire and be desired. And she hadn't taken no for an answer when she started her sportswear company.

Surely, she could find the courage to tell Archie how she felt about him.

She brushed her hair and applied lipstick and powder. Then she grabbed her purse and ran out to the car.

Archie's office was located in an elegant building on Park Avenue. Pandora climbed the staircase to the third floor. She felt even more nervous than when she'd waited at Lord & Taylor. Archie's secretary announced her, and Archie appeared in the doorway. He looked almost foreign to her in a three-piece suit and two-toned oxfords.

"Pandora, what are you doing here?" he asked in surprise.

Her courage deserted her, and she had to force herself not to bolt to the stairs.

"I want to talk to you about something; it's important."

Archie paused, as if debating whether he wanted to see her.

"We can go into my office."

Pandora shook her head. She wanted to go somewhere romantic to talk to him.

"Let's go somewhere we can get a drink or at least an ice cream," she suggested. "It's July in New York; it's terribly hot."

She took him to P.J. Clarke's on Fifty-Fifth Street. It was one of Virginia's favorite places. The owner, P. J. Clarke, lived in rooms above the restaurant. Since prohibition started, he'd made his own gin in the bathtub and served it secretly to the customers.

Archie ordered hot brown sandwiches for both of them. Pandora asked the waiter for a mint julep. She didn't usually drink cocktails during the day, but she needed it for what she had to say. At least Archie had agreed to come, but he was more aloof than she had ever seen him.

"Lucy introduced me to hot brown sandwiches," Archie said when the waiter brought ham and cheese on toasted bread, covered in Worcestershire sauce. "It's one of her favorite items on the menu of the Mayfair Hotel in St. Louis. I suppose now I'll never go there and try one."

"Adele told me about you and Lucy. I'm very sorry."

Archie took a bite of his sandwich.

"It didn't happen exactly as Lucy said," Archie replied. "I called it off with Lucy, but I know she's glad. She can marry Charles without Louise being angry. Apparently, Lucy is in love with him."

"Why did you break it off?" Pandora asked.

Archie wiped his mouth with a napkin. He took a moment to answer.

"I had to stand up to my parents eventually. I don't mind running the real estate company. In fact, I enjoy it. It's not only about building bigger penthouses for the wealthy; it's a way to help others. People like the Vanderbilts and the Fricks are selling their mansions on Fifth Avenue, and New York's commercial district is moving uptown. I've been buying the land to build skyscrapers and office buildings. When the economy turns around, that will create more jobs," Archie said excitedly. "Thousands of secretaries tapping on typewriters at the same time, tourists spending money at high-rise hotels. And I'm going to build neighborhood schools so that all the children in New York can get an education."

Archie was right. The blocks around Lexington Avenue where Pandora's boutique burned in the fire were now full of elegant shops. Elizabeth Arden and Helena Rubinstein opened flagship stores near Bergdorf Goodman's, and a Gimbels department store had opened close by.

"I realized that my parents need me more than I need them," Archie continued. "And I can't compromise when it comes to love. Lucy and I spent a lot of time together in London." He grimaced.

"What did your parents say?" Pandora inquired. Archie had never defied his parents before.

"My mother was devastated, but she'll recover." Archie shrugged. He looked at Pandora. "I'm older. I can't live my life for someone else, and I can't live a lie."

Pandora knew Archie was referring to her marriage to Harley. She had to tell him her feelings, but she didn't know where to start.

"I came to tell you something. Something about us."

"You already did." He cut her off. "You made your choices, Pandora. Neither of us can change what happened. You can't know what it's like to simply be told that you have a daughter. But Esme is lovely; I hope to build a relationship with her."

"It's not about our night together or even about Esme," she pushed forward. "You see, I realized something today. I should have seen it long ago." She sipped her cocktail. "I have feelings for you. I've had feelings for you forever."

"What do you mean?"

"It's difficult to describe," she said pensively. "It's not the girlish infatuation I felt for Owen or the friendship I had with Harley. I loved Harley, but there was always something missing. With you, it's everything at the same time."

Pandora realized she was talking to Archie as if he was a confidant as well as a lover.

"Why didn't you say anything before?" Archie said in shock.

"I don't know. You were always there for me. I was blind to my feelings, and you never said anything either. I'm telling you now and wondering if you feel the same."

Archie was silent for so long that Pandora's hands trembled, and she felt slightly ill.

"I can't answer right now," Archie said finally. He glanced at his watch. "I have to be somewhere, and I can't put it off. Can we talk later?"

Pandora was shocked. She had poured her heart out to him. He had to say something.

"Yes, of course." She nodded. She wouldn't show him how upset she was. "I have to go anyway; Sally is expecting me at Riverview."

Pandora watched him walk out of the restaurant and wondered if he would ever come back to her.

Chapter Twenty-Two

July 1930, Hyde Park, New York

Later the same evening, Pandora sat on the porch in front of the cottage and thought about Archie. Esme was asleep, and Willie was reading in the living room.

She had told Archie everything, and he hadn't responded. There was nothing else she could do. Her heart felt so heavy.

She was about to go inside when Archie appeared on the lawn. He was still wearing his suit, and he carried a rectangular box. Her chest tightened; she wondered what he was doing there.

"There you are," he declared. "I brought you something."

It was the shoe box that they had used to collect leaves. Pandora hadn't seen it since they were teenagers.

"Open it," Archie urged.

Pandora pried it open. She recognized her own handwriting on some of the leaves. There were other leaves she hadn't seen before. Archie must have collected them. She gathered them and read the wishes out loud.

"I wish Pandora has her dream wedding. I wish Pandora's boutique is successful. I wish Pandora is safe and happy on the French Riviera." Pandora gulped.

"I don't understand," she stammered. "We stopped collecting leaves years ago."

Archie's eyes shone pale blue under the porch light. He had never looked so handsome.

"We stopped collecting them together, but I kept up the tradition," he corrected her. "I was always thinking about you, Pandora. I only wanted you to be happy." He waved at the box. "Read the last leaf."

Pandora turned it over. "I wish Pandora loved me back."

Her eyes filled with tears, and her heart seemed to beat too fast.

"Why did you wait until now to show me?"

"I dug the box out the day I broke up with Lucy." Archie took her hand. "It's always been you, Pandora. There's never been anyone else, there never will be. But you fell in love with Owen. After Owen proposed to Lillian, I was going to say something. Then you and Harley fell in love. Harley was my close friend, so I stepped aside."

"You never said anything, even the night we made love," Pandora said, almost to herself.

"I did say it that night, but you didn't seem to hear it. Why do you think I agreed to go to England? I couldn't bear to be around your marriage. I thought about you the whole time I was there. After you didn't respond to my letters, I even went to Paris." His eyes darkened. "But I saw you sitting in a café with a man, so I turned around and took the first train back to London."

It really had been Archie she'd seen outside the café window in Paris! If only he had come inside, or if she'd realized it was him and ran after him, they might have been together sooner.

Archie kept talking. "I couldn't defy my parents, and I couldn't break up with Lucy. It was only when I came home and saw you again, so sure of yourself and looking so lovely with that French haircut, that I had to act."

Pandora felt almost dizzy with happiness and relief.

"You were so angry with me. I thought you'd never speak to me again."

"I was angry at you, and I had my pride," Archie agreed. "But what good would my anger do if it meant living without you."

Pandora couldn't help but smile.

"So you do have feelings for me?" Pandora had to hear him say it again.

Archie pulled her close. He touched her mouth.

"If you don't believe me, I'll have to show you."

Archie's kiss was long and deep; Pandora thought she'd never breathe again.

They pulled apart and Pandora laughed.

"I believe you, but you might have to keep showing me." She reached up and kissed Archie again. "We have years of kissing to catch up on."

~

The next morning, Pandora sat in the cottage's living room, sipping a cup of coffee.

Virginia appeared in the doorway. She wore one of Pandora's own designs, a yellow pleated skirt and sleeveless yellow blouse. She had a Lenglen Bandeau wrapped around her forehead.

"I didn't know you were home," Pandora said in greeting.

"I just arrived." Virginia sat down opposite her. "I saw Esme playing on the lawn."

Esme and Picasso were spending the morning chasing each other in the garden while Pandora caught up on some paperwork.

Pandora handed the shoe box to Virginia.

"I recognize this," Virginia responded, puzzled. "It's from a pair of mother's old Stead and Simpson pumps."

"I have something to tell you. It's about me and Archie." Pandora sat back against the cushions.

Virginia glanced at Pandora questioningly, and Pandora let it all tumble out. That she realized she had always been in love with Archie. She told her of driving into New York to tell him her feelings and hoping he felt the same. Their meeting at P.J. Clarke's and then Archie appearing at Riverview with the shoe box and telling Pandora he was in love with her too.

The only part she left out was her secret about Esme. She would never share that with anyone but Archie.

"I always knew you would end up together," Virginia said when Pandora finished.

"You never said anything."

"We were so young; you were hardly going to get married at fifteen," Virginia reflected.

It seemed so obvious to Pandora now. The way Archie always tried to protect her, how there was a skip to her step when he was around. Whenever they were apart, she felt like a piece of her was missing.

Perhaps it had taken this long for a reason. They both had so much growing up to do.

"You don't believe in love and marriage," Pandora said.

"I don't believe in marriage for myself," Virginia answered. "But I publish books for a living." She smiled. "Literature isn't anything without love."

Chapter Twenty-Three

The afternoon of Adele's party, Pandora got ready in the cottage at Riverview. She stood in front of the small closet and wondered how her life would have turned out if Harley's scandal had never happened and the stock market hadn't crashed.

She would be in her dressing room at Summerhill, putting the finishing touches on her makeup. Her closet would be filled with expensive dresses from Paris and Palm Beach, and from her bedroom window, she would look out on Summerhill's manicured hedges and the tiered garden that led down to the Hudson. Harley would appear, boyish and handsome in a white vest and straw hat, his cheeks tan and his hair golden from a summer of house parties. Esme would join them in a pretty pink dress, her doll trailing beside her, and they'd drive to Blythdale together.

Sometimes it still made Pandora so angry. Harley had risked everything to be with Porter. Harley wouldn't be there when Esme graduated from high school, when she started college, or when she got married. And Milton and Adele would never recover from the loss. They had Annie and her children, and Esme, but it wasn't enough. The burden of losing three sons would stay with them forever.

At other times, she felt sorry for Harley and even blamed herself. She should never have agreed to marry him, and she shouldn't have insisted that he remain faithful. Harley couldn't help being homosexual. If only she had been able to tell him that nothing was worth taking his own life. And she would never know if he killed himself or if he died in the fire.

She hoped that one day the world would be different. That men like Harley could live their lives in the open. What kind of life was it for those men? To be denied your goals or dreams because the one thing you wanted, to love and be loved for who you were, wasn't possible.

As Pandora looked over the partygoers on the lawn at Blythdale, she knew she was lucky. She had Esme, her friends and family, and now she had Archie. Pandora saw Archie standing on the terrace. He looked incredibly handsome in a white polo sweater and white shorts. His blond hair had grown longer again, and his face was tan from weekends in the sun.

"There you are," he said as he joined her. He kissed her gently. "I'm sorry I'm late; I stopped at Riverview to talk to your father."

"To talk to my father?" Pandora repeated.

Pandora hoped Archie wasn't going to propose. She wasn't ready to get married.

For the first time in her life, she was really enjoying herself. She wasn't worried that Archie didn't share her feelings, the way she had worried with Owen. And she wasn't nervous that something fierce and irreversible would happen to shatter their happiness, like when she was married to Harley. And their relationship wasn't simply the sexual desire she experienced with Maurice. Being with Archie was everything she wanted at the same time. For now, she didn't need anything more.

Archie noticed Pandora's expression. He grinned.

"Don't worry, I'm not going to drop down on my knee like Owen with Lillian in front of all these people." He chuckled. "I told Willie what I thought he should know." He took Pandora's hand. "That from now on, I'll put your and Esme's happiness before my own. I'd never do anything to hurt you."

Pandora reached her hand up to his face and kissed him.

Archie went to talk to Virginia and Wolfgang, and Pandora walked down to the river. The sun glinted on the water, and the maple trees were just starting to turn the gold and orange of early autumn.

There was nothing more beautiful than the grand estates along the Hudson. The gracious mansions and rolling, green lawns. Blythdale's marble pergola and manicured clock garden, the Vanderbilts' acres of farmland, Riverview's tennis court and swimming pool. Pandora had lived more than half her life in Hyde Park; she never wanted that to change. Yet at the same time she was ready for something more. For Esme Sportswear to be in department stores across the country, instead of only in New York. To one day travel to Europe with Archie and go to all the places she had never been.

Pandora had gone through so much. The joy of Esme's birth, followed so soon by the pain of Harley's scandal and death. The satisfaction of starting her own sportswear company and now the giddy happiness of being with Archie.

If she had learned anything, it was how much she valued the people in her life. People she loved, and who loved her for who she was. Willie, who only wanted her to be happy, and Virginia, who was like a sister, and Adele, whom Pandora admired for her kindness and courage. Esme had those people in her life too. Now she had Archie, and perhaps one day, a brother or sister. More people to love her, to teach her about the world.

Pandora couldn't think of anything better to give her daughter than that.

Epilogue

The last weekend in June, Pandora sat in her dressing room of the villa in Rhinecliff.

Today she and Archie were getting married, and they'd spend their first night together in their new home.

The villa was called Villa Beaulieu, in honor of Baroness Rothschild's villa in Cap Ferrat. It was farther up the Hudson than Riverview and Blythdale, in the hamlet of Rhinecliff.

The house had one wing completed, and the rest of the grounds were still piles of dirt. Pandora had bought the land last autumn and designed the house herself. She painted the exterior the same ochre color as the baroness's villa, and she put in a French garden shaped like a rowboat. Esme loved to skip stones in the lily pond and listen to the musical fountain.

Archie had proposed on Christmas Eve, after midnight services. A horse-drawn sleigh was waiting when they emerged from the church. Archie got down on one knee, took a velvet box from his pocket, and gave her a diamond-and-emerald ring that had been in the Van Luyen family for two generations.

They decided on a small wedding at Villa Beaulieu.

The day would be important not just because she was marrying Archie. Pandora was finally going to put her secret to rest. Before they left on their honeymoon, she was going to tell Adele and Milton and Virginia and Willie that Archie was Esme's father.

She had come to her decision gradually over the last year. Seeing Archie and Esme play together made her realize how much Archie contributed to Esme's life. They were developing a bond that Esme would never share with anyone else. Esme needed to know that Archie was her father.

Pandora was confident that Adele and Milton's love for Esme wouldn't change. Families were formed in different ways. Virginia would be shocked, but she would adore being Esme's aunt as well as her godmother. And Willie would understand. He had taught Pandora the importance of love in a marriage.

She wouldn't worry what people like Lillian would say if they found out. She had to do what was best for Esme, and she was determined to teach her that social standing and wealth were nothing without love and integrity and honesty.

Adele poked her head in the door. She wore a green chemise dress with a white sash. A pearl necklace hung around her neck, and she carried white gloves.

"You look beautiful," Adele breathed.

Pandora had designed her own wedding gown. She had decorated the fitted silk bodice with rose appliqués. The tiered chiffon skirt had more layers than Pandora originally intended, but Esme loved watching Pandora twirl in front of the mirror.

"You and Archie look so happy together," Adele reflected. "And Esme is lucky to grow up with Archie as a stepfather. Anyone can see how much he loves her."

Pandora was tempted to share her secret then. But she and Archie had decided they would do it together after the reception.

Adele left, and there was a knock. Pandora thought it would be Willie, but it was Archie. He looked incredibly handsome in a black topcoat and tails. His hand covered his eyes, and he carried a top hat.

Pandora gasped. "What are you doing here? The groom can't see the bride before the wedding."

"I'm not going to look," Archie promised. "I need you to settle a dilemma. Esme says Picasso is part of our family, so he should be at the wedding."

Pandora let out a laugh. She often thought Esme would grow up to be a lawyer. Already at the age of three, Esme delighted in nothing more than arguing her point of view.

Pandora compromised. "He can be at the ceremony but not at the dinner."

"Are you sure I can't peek at the bride before I go?" Archie teased.

"Certainly not," Pandora said, horrified. "Wedding traditions are important."

Pandora turned back to the mirror and put the finishing touches to her makeup. She had just applied lipstick when her father appeared. A yellow handkerchief stuck out of his jacket pocket, and he wore suspenders and black leather shoes.

"You look even more handsome than the first time we did this," Pandora joked, adjusting the boutonniere in Willie's buttonhole.

Tears formed in his eyes, and he blinked them away.

"And you're even more radiant."

Pandora slipped on long white gloves and took Willie's arm. The lawn looked glorious in the late-afternoon sunlight. The aisle was scattered with pink rose petals, and great urns held white orchids. More roses formed an arch where the minister stood, and behind it, the Hudson shimmered like a magic carpet.

Esme walked down the aisle first, in a white organza dress and satin slippers. A wreath of pink roses encircled her blond ringlets, and she moved with the poise and confidence of a tiny ballerina.

Virginia came next, regal and elegant in an indigo-colored drop-waisted gown and beaded headdress.

Archie waited under the arch. Even though Pandora had seen him moments earlier, her heart still beat rapidly in her chest. He looked so proud and happy in front of the guests, as if he had won the greatest prize.

"Are you ready to give away the bride?" Pandora whispered to Willie.

Willie held out his arm. He turned to Pandora.

"You're not the kind of woman who is given to a man," he whispered back. "You are becoming Mrs. Archie Van Luyen, and you are also Esme's mother. But you will always be Pandora Carmichael, a modern woman."

Pandora took her father's arm. She stepped onto the lawn and smiled.

"I wouldn't want to be anyone else."

ACKNOWLEDGMENTS

Thank you to my agent, Johanna Castillo, for taking such good care of me and my books. Thank you to my editor Alicia Clancy; I'm so glad we ended up together. Thank you to the team at Lake Union and Amazon Publishing: Danielle Marshall, Rachael Clark, Jen Bentham, and Gabe Dumpit. Thanks to Chris Werner and Jodi Warshaw.

And thank you to my children, Alex, Andrew, Heather, Madeleine, Thomas. My daughter-in-law, Sarah, and my granddaughter, Lily, for bringing me happiness.